THE DEVIL AND PIERRE GERNET

The Devil and Pierre Gernet

• •

STORIES

David Bentley Hart

WILLIAM B. EERDMANS PUBLISHING COMPANY

GRAND RAPIDS, MICHIGAN / CAMBRIDGE, U.K.

Bl. Eerd. 4/12   25.00

Published 2012 by
Wm. B. Eerdmans Publishing Co.
2140 Oak Industrial Drive N.E., Grand Rapids, Michigan 49505 /
P.O. Box 163, Cambridge CB3 9PU U.K.

Printed in the United States of America

18 17 16 15 14 13 12   7 6 5 4 3 2 1

Library of Congress Cataloging-in-Publication Data

Hart, David Bentley.
The Devil and Pierre Gernet: stories / David Bentley Hart.
p.   cm.
ISBN 978-0-8028-1768-6 (pbk.: alk. paper)
I. Title.

PS3608.A7844D48   2012
813'.6 — dc23

2011039490

www.eerdmans.com

For Patrick

Contents

Author's Apologia

A soft but insistent voice within me tells me I should offer some apology for visiting these stories on the world. It is an irrational impulse, I know, since the world is not likely to be inconvenienced by them in the least, or even to take any notice of them. I suppose, though, that I am afraid of trying the patience of readers of my previous books, because those books all dealt with matters of theology and philosophy and cultural criticism, and their literary pretensions were for the most part decently hidden behind veils of argument and exposition. Here those pretensions are wantonly on display. In my defense, though, fiction is a much more natural idiom for me. I have written stories and poems all my life, or at least since fairly early childhood, whereas I conceived an interest in philosophical theology only when, as a young man, I went searching for God; and then, as things turned out, I came to conclude that God is no more likely (and probably a good deal less likely) to be found in theology than in poetry or fiction. I am also conscious of the oddity of the particular pieces I have brought together here. I had originally intended to make the subtitle of this volume *Elaborately Artificial Stories,* since I have chosen five tales that are willfully extravagant in form and content rather than any of the drier, more "realistic" stories I have also written. After all, one likes this sort of thing if it is the sort of thing one likes, but otherwise it can easily prove a little too much of a muchness. These tales seem to me to constitute a natural set, however, if for no other reason than that they all fall into the dismaying category of "fiction of ideas" rather than into the much more respectable category of "ripping yarns." And, for what it is worth, purely at the level of ideas I have never written a more serious book. That, though, is not an aesthetic criterion, and thus cannot be adduced as evidence for how these stories ought to be judged *as* stories. So I shall simply say that this is the only book I have written with which I am truly satisfied.

The most clearly "artificial" of these tales is almost certainly the first, the novella "The Devil and Pierre Gernet": its premise is utterly fantastic, obviously, and it is written in a fairly parodic nineteenth-century style. In form it imitates the conceits of a kind of old-fashioned storytelling to which I have always been especially partial: the tale told at one remove, in which a primary narrator recounts a somewhat incredible story told him by a secondary narrator ("On a night in June, I met Naseby at the club and, at a loss for anything better to do, engaged him in conversation. A peculiar sort of man, Naseby . . ."), with the voice of the latter then rendered in full, flowing periods, with every metaphor exquisitely crafted and every subordinate clause exactly in place. Of course, the form is somewhat subverted by the content; in a story by Kipling or Stevenson, that secondary narrator would go on to serve up a far more picaresque adventure than my tale provides. I notice, moreover, that I seem to have lifted an idea from Dostoevsky, for which perhaps some contrition is in order. I had not consciously recalled, when writing the story, that the devil who appears to the feverish Ivan Karamazov admits at one point to being a materialist in philosophy; but my devil also claims to be a materialist, which may just be an obvious sort of joke, but which may also be a joke I inadvertently "borrowed." If so, I would prefer to think of it not as a "theft," but as a "tribute." The only other borrowing of which I am conscious is from myself: I took the idea of writing a story in that fashion — right down to giving the secondary narrator no name other than "my friend" — from a story I wrote twenty years earlier, when I was a tender undergraduate. That story, "The Ivory Gate," is included here as well, and I have a great affection for it, largely because it is so unrestrained in its shape and tone, but also because it comes from a happy moment in my life.

As for the other stories — "The House of Apollo" came to me while I was preparing the manuscript for this volume. It is probably worth noting that all the major episodes concerning Julian did actually happen, or at least were reported to have happened (even the apparition of Rome's genius in Julian's tent in Persia), though I have embellished them considerably in some cases. Everything concerning the old priest, however, apart from his meeting with the emperor, is my own invention. "A Voice from the Emerald World" arose from a number of experiences and fragmentary thoughts, which for a while existed as little more than a collection of images in my mind. I think the tale finally assumed a definite shape one day when I was teaching an undergraduate seminar on the ancient Gnostics, in the course of which my students professed varying degrees of amazement that the Gnostic vision of reality could ever have seemed convincing to anyone. At first, I assumed they simply meant that they found Gnostic mythologies a bit absurd (which would be fair enough), but it turned out that what really seemed inexplicable to them was the Gnostics' capacity for cosmic despair. This struck my students as simply depressing and incredible. Of course, my students were all very young and had been raised in a society that had protected them since birth from most of the more terrible aspects of life, so I really should not have been surprised. Regarding the last tale, "The Other," I should note that the restaurant it describes is not in fact on Myslikova Street in Prague, but that the Hotel Élite really is on Ostrovni Street. I needed the two to be within walking distance of one another and of the Vltava River. Of the story's protagonist, I will say only that I think I understand his problem, as best I can, and that he has what I consider to be good taste in wine and spirits.

Beyond that, I shall leave the stories to speak for themselves and hope that they are up to the task of doing so.

The Devil and Pierre Gernet

1

My friend — who was a fallen angel who had walked the earth for ages, wearing countless guises and called by a multitude of names — was in the habit of inviting me to his club, The Typhon, for postprandial drinks whenever he had a Friday night free. He enjoyed the extraordinary privilege of reserving a sitting room of almost Borgian magnificence for his private use, and it was here that we usually spent our evenings together, hidden amid a forest of pale marble, polished brass, and glistening silver, encircled by remote prospects of mahogany wainscoting, our voices vanishing into the vault of the dark coffered ceiling high above. We would sit to either side of an immense window that looked out over a terraced garden and wooded park and westward towards the skyline of the distant city — set upon the horizon somewhat to our right — I with my cognac or whiskey, he sipping some nameless ruby cordial from a tiny, tulip-shaped glass, which he held lightly by its stem between the tips of his forefinger and thumb and which, though never replenished, was never empty. "It's not a bibulous drink at all," he once told me, in his plush baritone; "It's a sort of tonic, one of my own concoction. In fact, it induces a deeper sobriety in the drinker. It's a depressant, I suppose; it certainly dampens enthusiasm and cools the temper; but it's not an inebriant. Its effect is a kind of sharp, dry lucidity of thought." And then, after a momentary pause: "As for flavor, it's utterly insipid. Tap water has more taste. We don't really approve of the paltrier sensualisms, you know." This did not surprise me. I knew him to be abstemious in his habits: on those rare occasions when he deigned to eat, he would not touch meat, and his detesta-

1

tion of tobacco was, in his own words, fanatical. At the same time, there was clearly nothing ascetical about him: he appeared comfortably but not excessively corpulent, and the subtle lavishness of his attire — suits as glossily black as India ink, ties of mist-gray or crimson silk fastened with platinum pins, gold cufflinks exquisitely inlaid with armigeral devices, the large emerald ring glittering on his left hand — seemed to me to emanate from a world of unfathomable wealth and unimaginable opulence.

I knew, of course, that an association with a devil was good neither for my spiritual sanity nor for my reputation, but I found his company irresistible: his experience was so vast and various, his erudition so comprehensive and arcane, and his special knowledge so much more exotic than any available to mortal men that I usually parted from him only warmed by drink, but intoxicated by his talk. His conversation did, however, require some getting used to. He was, for one thing, given to rather baroque locutions: he invariably called a taxi a "taximeter cabriolet," for instance, and he had once complained to me, after he had spent a day in the city, of the "unseemly fremescence of the *mobile vulgus*." But, while such phrases would certainly have seemed ponderous witticisms or insufferable affectations coming from anyone else, from him they seemed quite unpretentious. He had, after all, been a courtier of both Xerxes and Shih-Huangdi, an advisor to Antiochus Epiphanes, and an intimate of Valentinus; he had both granted the Cathars the protection of his estates in Toulouse and then joined the French crown's crusade against them, had owned plantations in the Dutch Antilles and Haiti, and had stood an impassive witness in the streets of Paris as many of his fellow aristocrats had been carried by in the tumbrel; he had, in short, been and done so many things that his habits of speech seemed not so much mannered as timeless.

I must confess, though, that certain of his boasts seemed a little too fantastic to credit. "I invented vegetarianism," for example, or (more expansively), "I invented the agricultural revolution . . . and, of course, human sacrifice." On one occasion, he claimed not only to be a champion of the avant-garde but in fact the inventor of all conceptual art and its most generous patron. And his political convictions were somewhat nebulous to me. He confessed, for example, that he was of two minds regarding the end of public executions: the old spectacles, he admitted, had for the most part merely attracted the callous, the brutal, the sadistic, and the deviant, "but then," he added, "who better to enlist upon the side of civilization?" He professed himself an ardent feminist, but when asked to dilate upon this would offer only some coarsely facetious slur, like "Women are probably no less depraved and pitiless than men if left to their own devices, and I can see no reason why their native ebulliences should be suffocated by archaic conventions." He claimed to be both a communist and a devout advocate of the free market. He believed in a strong military and called himself a pacifist. He spoke glowingly of democracy and adored Stalin. Strangely, though, I never had the impression that any of his utterances was frivolous or the expression of a mere transitory mood. I always sensed that I was simply glimpsing facets of what I would have recognized as a single, complex, but internally consistent philosophy if only I could have seen it whole.

We were almost never actually entirely alone, I should mention. My friend was constantly attended (almost haunted, one might say) by a kind of valet, whom he referred to simply as "my man," as if describing a rare curio acquired in a little-frequented shop, and whose narrow frame he draped in a garish antique livery — usually a scarlet coat purfled with gold embroidery and breeches of light blue satin — that had the unfortunate effect of making the poor fellow's desperately unprepossessing features that much more obvious: a distinctly sallow complexion, gaunt cheeks, a sharply prominent nose, fierce small eyes not so much hazel green as sulfurous yellow, and a pronounced widow's peak rising into a low slope of black hair all but lacquered to his scalp by a viscous pomade. I frequently forgot that "my man" was there, however, so unobtrusive was his presence; once he had brought the drinks, he would withdraw to his customary station by the fireplace, alongside the two miniature caryatids supporting the fluted porphyry mantelpiece, where at once he would become so unnaturally immobile that he seemed no more alive than they. Unless called upon to discharge some minor task, there he would remain until, at the end of the evening, my friend would curtly order him to bring the car around; he would then all of a sudden become animate, like a statue brought instantly to life, incline his head somewhat sullenly, hiss a barely audible "Very good, sir," and depart. At first, I found this uncanny self-mastery unsettling, but my unease had dissipated when my friend had confided to me that his servant was also, like himself, "an angel in reduced circumstances."

2

On one of our last evenings together, I had dined early and so — as it was midsummer — had arrived at The Typhon a little before twilight. Our talk was casual and intermittent at first, as we sat and watched the daylight melt away in a succession of splendors: a ruby sun, then a blazing canopy of orange and purple clouds, then a lingering green pallor, and finally a deep crystal blue fading slowly into darkness. But, gradually, something in my friend stirred, and his conversation began to assume its normal grandiosity. When the west had become a great crevasse of glowing violet, and the distant skyscrapers looked like little more than fragile lattices hung with miniature lanterns, he suddenly exclaimed, without any prompting, "You shouldn't pay me much mind. What am I, really, but a desolate remnant, scarred by immemorial wars?" And a little later, when the city had become a swarm of golden tapers floating in a sea of sapphire, he observed, "If men aren't taken in the full flame of their iniquity, they fade like embers in the aftermath of their own wickedness; and there's nothing to be learned from impotence and decrepitude." And then, when the last darkening traces of blue above the horizon had dissolved into a soft, luminous gray, he shook his head sadly and remarked, "Nothing is done with any elegance anymore; society has forgotten all the old ceremonies . . . the deft, fading parry of the cut indirect, the sudden, savage thrust of the cut direct, the balletic grace of the cut celestial, the somber subtlety of the cut infernal. . . . I mean, really, how can anyone be a gentleman until he's learned the proper way to give offense?" And when only the thinnest ghostly glimmer of daylight still clung to the edge of the world, he mused aloud, "The reason the alchemists failed to become real scientists in the proper modern sense is that they tended to eschew sorcery; all they really cared about was spiritual ascent and purification, and so they weren't willing to plunge themselves deep enough into the occult potencies of matter, the way modern sorcerers — or scientists, I suppose you'd call them — are willing to do." And, finally, a few minutes later, he turned his eyes fully towards me and began to utter connected thoughts.

"I'm as egalitarian as it's possible to be. I know you don't believe that, because of how I treat my man" — he waved a finger vaguely in the direction of the fireplace — "but you have to understand, these arrangements are imposed upon us by a certain inflexible and unimaginative set of conventions over which we have no control. When we were hurled down from the heavens into the sublunary atmosphere, and left to struggle with its idiotic turbulences — without trial, I might add — he descended farther than I, and so now he occupies an inferior rank in the Pandemonium. For us, you see, the world here below is a kind of abysmal mirror inversion of our former condition; back in the old days, in the warm light of the spheres above the moon, he actually stood much higher in the angelic hierarchy than I." He glanced briefly at his valet. "He was at first so resentful of his diminished estate that it was all I could do to bend him to service. I had to thrash him almost hourly. His will finally proved amenable to this, luckily; subjugation based purely on power seemed to conform to his moral expectations. In fact, he began to luxuriate in his degradation, to the point that I had to halt the beatings. A wise master denies his servant too many luxuries." He took a pensive sip from his glass. "Of course, this inversion of rank doesn't hold in the special case of our great leader. He was overthrown like the rest of us, but he remains terrible in his ruin. He's still the mightiest among us. . . ." He paused and looked again to the western sky. "At least, I think he is. It's hard to know, really . . . one sees so little of him. He usually dwells at the bottom of a deep, frigid pool whose surface is so shadowy and still and overhung with dead vines that no light can penetrate it. We hear his voice, of course — it issues from the waters in a kind of quiet, mesmerizing, metallic moan. . . . I don't know" — he frowned slightly — "perhaps I could crush him like an insect. But I dare not test his strength: it could be very painful. We're impervious to physical shock, of course, but the stronger among us can inflict real psychical wounds upon the weaker — deep lacerations of despair or anxiety, so to speak — and these are quite horrible to bear. Well, just ask my man if you like."

Night had completely fallen; the lights of the city cast a dim rufous curtain across the darkness in the west; the trees below us were now an indistinguishable mass of shadows.

"Are you much at each other's throats?" I asked.

He looked directly into my eyes and smiled indulgently. "We demons, you mean? We fiends? No, of course not. For one thing, our several strengths are fixed, at least for this age, and we know better now than to try to match ourselves against one another. More importantly, though, we're not naturally aggressive, no matter what you've heard. Our little contretemps with the celestial wardens — what they like to call our rebellion, with a fine contempt for historical accuracy — was simply a dispute between differing philosophies regarding time and eternity. I mean, to be really very simple, one side, *their* side, believed that time should be drawn into and . . . oh, *saturated* by eternity; they believed that time is just a moving mirror of the eternal, so to speak, a surface in which the eternal glories and verities and forms should shine forth, like sunlight on the surface of a calm lake. Well, we simply took the opposite view, that's all: we thought eternity should be dispersed into time . . . time dissipated into it-self. Their vision of things just seemed so unspeakably stultifying to us. We had new ideas, revolutionary ideas — that's all — and certain persons simply found those ideas troubling. But all we wanted was to set time and space free from the ancient forms. We wanted to shatter the mirror, so to speak. We were just an idealistic fraternity of . . . well, of eisoptroclasts — if you don't mind me coining a word."

I feigned an appreciative laugh.

"Honestly," he continued, his tone becoming more emphatic as he spoke, "that's all we were ever about: energy, dynamism, creative ferment. We saw possibilities. We recognized that there was an exciting and unex-ploited potential in chaos, a special kind of fecundity that needed nothing more than to be set loose. And so, of course, this meant that we had to mount a struggle against the heavenly order — against order as such. But it was nothing subversive, our activities weren't clandestine, and what we did we did forthrightly and with firm conviction. Listen" — he pointed a solemn finger at me — "everything's a matter of semantics where ideol-ogy's concerned. They talk of 'war in heaven' and of the 'fall of the angels,' and of course it all sounds monstrous and tragic when you put it that way. But why not speak instead of 'exuberance,' or 'will to power,' or 'the logic of material dialectic,' or 'gales of creative destruction,' or simply 'historical consciousness'? That puts a different complexion on things, doesn't it? But, of course, we don't have a propaganda office to match theirs. So, well . . . there you have it." He paused long enough to take three measured sips from his glass. "Anyway, that's all in the past. Our struggles are over. We're all good Europeans now — quite pacified, quite . . . without ambition."

"Really?" I asked. I shifted in my chair, changed my glass from one hand to the other, and considered my words with care. "Isn't there — I mean, I've always heard there was a kind of continuous spiritual warfare still going on . . . in history and nature . . . in individual souls and in cul-ture and. . . . Isn't that the whole point . . . ?"

"Nonsense." He shook his head and sighed. "Propaganda, as I've said. Of course, I'm only a private citizen of the infernal polity. I'm not on close terms with any of the agents in our secret services, so I don't know what security operations might be going on from time to time. But whatever one hears in that line is certainly exaggerated. At most, we're engaged in gathering information, keeping an eye out for signs of celestial imperial-ism — that sort of thing."

"Imperialism?"

"Well, I'd like to know what you'd call that harrowing of hell incident. And what of this menacing police presence constantly roving the ethereal border — what's that if not plain intimidation, plain irredentist swaggering? I assure you, the gates of hell never posed any threat to the celestial regime; but you should see them now: a great calamitous heap of shattered adamant and broken hinges and twisted bolts. And what can we do? We haven't the resources to repair them, and there's been no whisper of indemnification. The Germans at Versailles enjoyed more generous terms than we've been given. It's all a travesty, frankly. Anyway" — he nodded at my glass, his voice at once softening — "drink up. You're an American, a child of this blessed land of dewy innocence; I can't imagine you're much interested in the intrigues and squabbles of the primordial powers."

The conversation lapsed for several moments. My friend stared out into the night, looking at once wistful and quietly amused. When at last he resumed speaking, he kept his eyes fixed on the darkness beyond the window.

"As I say, energy. The dynamo, not the Virgin. Hard for you to understand, perhaps, with your conservative temperament." He did not look at me, but silenced me with a raised hand before I could reply. "I know, I know: these terms are all relative and plastic. But, even so, I think you'll grant that — well, let's call it 'the progressive view' — that the progressive view has to triumph in the end, because it has emotion on its side; it has *passion*. When I speak of conservatism I simply mean a special kind of philosophical impotence, pervaded by a pathetic, nameless melancholy. But it's progressive thought to which the future belongs, in part because it's *not* heroic. Because, when that squamous brute Demos is set loose, it has only its appetites and most bestial impulses to guide it; and all it really wants is to achieve the right cultural balance between sentimentality and authoritarianism — between license and the leash. Emotion always vanquishes reflection; appetite always conquers nostalgia. You don't really mind me calling you conservative, anyway, do you?" He turned his gaze back to me.

"If you must; it's just that — as you say — the word is so imprecise. Politically, I'm not particularly . . ."

"Yes, but don't bore me. You know what I'm saying. In regard to you, it just means the desire to conserve, whether we're talking about ecology or culture, which to my mind merely makes a fetish of fragility. Tradition, family, shrines, native environments . . . the local, the subsidiary, the vul-

nerable . . . all that curious Shintoism of yours. It's all very silly and enervating, you know. You've made a whole creed out of mere *conservatio in
esse*, the lowest level of plain brute existence. But, you see, you can't have
life without death, or being without nothingness. You just can't. It doesn't
work that way. Now I, by contrast, have no prejudices whatsoever against
the state, or capital, or centralization, or globalization, or corporatism, or
even localism, or anything at all, really — so long as it's a vehicle of progress, of destruction and renewal, of *life* in all its gorgeous, monstrous
wastefulness. I value cleansing rapacity, the strength to break and bind,
the . . . the harsh *hygiene* of progress. So I don't care whether communities
or souls or *genii locorum* or meadows or customs are consumed by the
state or by a corporation or by something else — just so long as a space is
opened up for chaos. Chaos is the womb of innovation, of power, and
that's what's important at the end of the day. No one wants stagnation."

I shifted in my chair again and cleared my throat. "I think I might,
actually."

My words appeared, as very rarely happened, to have caught him un-
prepared; he stared at me for a moment with an expression hovering un-
pleasantly between the bemused and the contemptuous, before regaining
his composure, laughing, and putting on his most avuncular manner.
"Well, yes, maybe you do. All right, that's entirely your affair. But, I warn
you, cleave to that path and you'll end up sinking in a mire of your own
regrets. You'll end up no better than my old friend Pierre Gernet — weak,
bewildered, a storehouse of abortive impulses . . . retreating constantly to
the opiate of fantasy or the ache of romance, to poetry, or sterile scholarship, or . . ." — his eyes became narrow, his voice mordant — *"religion."*

I cleared my throat uneasily. "Forgive my ignorance; I don't think I
know who Pierre Gernet is."

"Who he *was*, rather," my friend replied. "There's no reason why you
should. I've done my best to see that practically no one remembers him,
since I regard him as an especially unwholesome specimen. Still, well . . .
actually, he would have interested you, now that I think about it."

"Why?"

"Well, it's not very . . ." He paused again. "Well, actually, I suppose I
could tell you about him. It might make a point. . . . Would you like me to?"

"If you wish."

He stared into the space above my head for several seconds, lightly
tapping the arm of his chair with his left ring finger, obviously considering his course. "All right, then . . . yes, I will," he said at last. He drank

again from his glass, rested slightly more languidly in his chair, stretched out his legs, half closed his eyes, and began to speak as if reciting an old legend from memory.

3

"Pierre died just short of his thirtieth birthday in Paris in 1898. He was a classicist of extraordinary range, whose work was original and remarkable, and a poet of limited scope, whose work was derivative and precious. He was born near Bordeaux, the bastard son of an abbé and a young, somewhat excessively sentimental village girl. His mother, Marie Gernet — who loved him with great tenderness and who sang very sweetly to him at night, with a very pretty voice — died of pneumonia when he was four. He grew up in a church orphanage, where he distinguished himself from a very early age by his serene amiability, his piety, his innocent gentleness, his *anima naturaliter Christiana,* so to speak, and his striking intelligence and bookishness. He was a handsome lad, with limpid brown eyes, dark, glossy wavelets of hair, and a fair complexion. He was never a particularly robust boy: his torso was slender, his gait was less than fluid, and he was not really very good at games. He applied himself, however, to both prayer and study with effortless cheer and unforced grace, and certainly without any air of superiority that might provoke the hostility of the little savages among whom he was raised. Thus, despite the environs within which his early life was so severely and unpromisingly circumscribed, he acquired neither rivals nor enemies, and his obvious gifts seemed to rouse little if any envy among his peers. He loved poetry from very early on, especially Augustan-age Latin verse and the great works of France's golden age; he formed a special attachment to Ronsard, especially the *Amours de Marie.* Naturally, he would have had no prospects to speak of if his precocity had not been recognized early by the superintendent of the orphanage; he was given good schooling as a result, and his astonishing facility with languages and the literature of antiquity moved the church and city elders to procure a scholarship for him, largely by subscription of the local gentry, which allowed him to study in Paris. First he was enrolled near the city, in a very good lycée, and then later he took the entrance examinations for the École Normale Supérieure, which he passed so brilliantly that he left his examiners astonished — no mean feat, needless to say. In his university studies he excelled, but

9

at the end of his formal tuition he was unable to secure an academic position that would allow him to remain in the city, which he keenly desired to do. He even turned down a perfectly good offer of a post as a teacher in a rural school. He was constantly impoverished, and fed himself by publishing reviews, borrowing from friends, and acting as an occasional private secretary to . . . well, to me.

"When I took him up, he had become something of a Byzantinist, but the grand project he was planning, and for which he was forever furiously compiling notes, was a great systematic tome on classical myth, religion, and metaphysics, all framed around a single passage from Macrobius suggesting a secret identity between Apollo and Dionysus. Its working title, *Paean and Dithyramb,* was taken from some remarks of Plutarch's on the liturgical calendar of Delphi. He was an able and happy secretary for me. He delighted in my incunabula and scrolls and cuneiform tablets, though he often implored me to donate them to a museum rather than keep them in the cabinets and bookcases of my study. In my employ — which I insisted must be irregular — he had a little time for his essays and poems and researches, but not as much as he wanted. My interest in him was uncomplicated: I recognized in him a certain purity of will, but saw also that a certain strength was absent from his nature. I thought that if some sort of purging energy could be fostered in him — something really salubriously destructive — his potential might prove incalculable.

"The Paris of those days, of course, provided an ideal atmosphere for the cultivation of spiritual derangement. In France, as nowhere else in the late nineteenth century, the essential diabolism of modern man's most nihilistic impulses had become perfectly explicit and perfectly refined. Just think of the Satanism of Baudelaire — and he had died the year before Pierre was born. I know, I know: it's conventional now to regard all that as a kind of charade and Baudelaire as some sort of 'backdoor Catholic.' Well, I don't weigh souls in the balance — and that's an office that often seems to be exercised with a certain perverse capriciousness, anyway. But, whatever the case, *fin de siècle* Paris was practically a paradise of mystical materialism: the very empire of negation, the very throne of antichrist. Why France, I'm not quite sure. Perhaps the subterranean persistence of the old Provençal heresy, somewhat curiously inverted over time, though I'm not sure. . . . Or perhaps simply because of the unbroken spiritual continuity of French culture. You know what I mean. One can't really say that Romanticism ever overthrew Classicism in France, can one? Not the way it seemed to do in Germany and England, anyway. Blake's Gnosticism, Byron's demonism, Hölderlin's Christian paganism — all that convulsive, evanescent, anti-Enlightenment anguish. In France there was only organic development, with a sudden late ornamental infusion of Romanticism at best — or of post-Romantic decadence. The eighteenth century's 'sensibility' slowly mellowing into the cold, cruel tenderness of Proust; Classicism ripening into its full decadence from within, passing from the Horatian directly to the Petronian without significant interruption. You know, it's really quite wonderful. Enlightenment, if left unclouded by pathetic fancy, leads to a very special and bracing sort of nihilism — positivist, rationalist . . . merciless. The Cartesian mind seeks to penetrate ever more deeply into first principles, to master truth like an object in its grasp, till it succumbs to the sway of the goetic and reaches that place where reason and unreason, rationalism and occultism, are indistinguishable. It's so clear and so pure. The ego awakens to itself, that grand little rebellious Lucifer within, and resolves to make itself the source of worldly order. . . . There's a genuine magnificence there, a quiet sublimity. . . . I'm being obscure, I know. Excuse an ancient spirit's digressions. All I mean to say is that all of that — Gérard de Nerval's blasphemies, and his lobster, and Baudelaire's and Mallarmé's and Rimbaud's dissociations and diabolisms and diseases . . . goodness, even old Anatole France's *La Révolte des Anges* (what an exquisite little humoresque that is, and yet so wise) . . . and of course everything that followed . . . Artaud, Klosowski, Deleuze — all of it represents not the disintegration of the Enlightenment, but its fruition. The Marquis de Sade turning out to have been the truest *philosophe* of all. . . . And just at the end of the nineteenth century, the age of the most perfectly remorseless aestheticism, it was perfect: a nocturnal world where demons frolicked . . . where men fell silent before the cold majesty of Satan in the starlight. . . . Lovely, really, and quite incomparably French.

"But I'm losing the thread of my story. And, in truth, none of that really mattered very much. Pierre was so removed from most earthly longings that he was immersed for years in that element without being touched by it. As far as he was ever aware, he lived in the France of Girard de Rousillon and Bernard de Clairvaux. Do you know, comical as it seems, when he climbed Montmartre once the unfinished basilica was opened for services, he actually went to pray? Honestly. He would just sink down in the darkness of Sacré-Coeur, wait for the massive stone angels looming over him on the great pendentives gradually to emerge from the shadows as his eyes adjusted to the shadows, and would then drift off into a quiet rapture of supplication. He could remain like that for an hour or more. And the same was true of his frequent visits to Sainte Chapelle: he went to marvel at the stained glass, like everyone else, but he also went to offer thanks to his God and his God's lieutenants, and in a moment would lose himself utterly in the subaquatic depths of all that prismatic light. I never accompanied him, obviously, but I can summon up the image of him in my mind without any effort; I see him floating in those polychromatic gulfs, suspended like a mote of dust before those fabulous, kaleidoscopic walls of radiant glass. And, for him, that really was the true surface of the world, as he saw it at all moments: a glorious, opalescent effusion of form and color and lovely brilliancies through which the light of another world ceaselessly poured. That was his 'real' world — an abyss of color in which the clear light of the eternal displayed itself as multiplicity and complexity and shape. That was Pierre's truth — that was Pierre. Sadly. But what could one do? I never despaired of my charge, of course. Never. I knew from long experience how small an interval actually separates the ascetic from the voluptuary, or the saint from the decadent, and I hoped if nothing else that some flicker of resentment at his pitiable earnings might at least be roused in his breast.

"I was inadvertently aided in my designs by Pierre's closest friend from his university days, Robert. I withhold the surname, as the family is still quite prominent, and I'm a friend to some of them. Suffice it to say that Robert was heir to a country seat in — well, let's say somewhere to the south, in *la France profonde* — and was in consequence quite well provided for. He kept apartments in the city, being too much of a cosmopolitan and boulevardier to endure life on the family estates. He was a bit profligate, but he had the means to be. He would on occasion bring Pierre good wine and food, and never hesitated to provide what money Pierre would accept. Whenever he prevailed upon Pierre to visit him, he considerately made sure neither of his mistresses was about, so as not to scandalize his very dear friend, whose piety he loved, if not as a virtue, at least as something charming and rustical and quaint and 'true to the land,' whose special qualities he could appreciate with a kind of sympathetic *terroir*. He would not have spoiled that innocence for anything.

"It was through Robert that Pierre's soul suffered its great crisis — not (as I had initially hoped) on account of Robert's wealth, of which Pierre was not sufficiently envious, but on account of Robert's sister, Eugénie, who early in February 1897 gained her father's permission to stay with her brother in Paris right through the spring and summer, so long as the latter would undertake to act as her chaperone. Robert adored his sister, and happily consented. Eugénie was nineteen, extremely lovely, witty, overly fond of novels, but with occasional pretensions to being something of a bluestocking — in a purely patrician key, of course. Not that she had excessive ambitions in that direction. For a girl of that class, to be accomplished, in the eighteenth-century sense, was still considered admirable; to be fully educated, however, would have been considered rather vulgar. And accomplished she was. Her father was of a harshly conservative temper in most things, but he had not been illiberal in the education of his daughter: to the age of sixteen she had received much the same instruction as her brother, and superior tutelage in music and the arts. She possessed, if nothing else, considerable virtuosity as a conversationalist, especially if one liked one's conversation nimble, a bit frothy, and pleasantly *light.*

"At the time of her arrival in Paris, Pierre was enjoying some small critical — if not financial — success on account of a monograph he had published on later Byzantine and Florentine Platonism, from Michael Psellus to Pico della Mirandola. When he accepted an invitation to Robert's rooms for a celebratory luncheon and met Eugénie, he was enchanted at once by her beauty, her youth, her gaiety, her social graces, her obvious intelligence . . . and by a free-spokenness to which women in his class (at least, those he knew) were not given. I would be omitting something of more than passing consequence, also, if I failed to mention her figure, to which even Pierre could scarcely be insensible. She was not, I must say, one of those androgynously gracile Beardsleyan sylphs that throng the more sexually ambiguous decorative motifs of the period; she was, I suppose you'd say, shapely — voluptuous, really — and she undoubtedly was the first woman upon whom Pierre ever found himself reflecting as an object of truly sensuous beauty. For myself, of course, I find female bodies rather absurd — tremulous, mollescent things, inefficient, ravaged by obscene irruences and chronic perturbations, and subject to a positively bizarre elasticity — and the more generously proportioned and protuberant they are, in the normal fashion, fore and aft, port and starboard, the more grotesque I find them. There's such an air of pure organism, of gross animality about them that it repels me. I'm not drawn to any kind of female type, needless to say, but I much prefer women built on a more rectilinear model, with clear angularities; they appall me slightly less. Anyway, that's neither here nor there, really; and Pierre, being a beast of flesh and fancy, was entirely susceptible to the sheer brute luxu-

13

riance of all her rounded . . . well, let's just say her 'loveliness.' And as, in subsequent days, the acquaintance deepened — with Robert's somewhat surprised but delighted encouragement — Pierre was entirely overcome. He wasn't some oafish peon, admittedly, but his experience had nevertheless been limited by his circumstances. He couldn't imagine from what empyrean so exquisite a creature could have descended. And, before long, that austerely pure nature was for the first time invaded by a host of inexpressible yearnings. I wonder even — his journals, unfortunately, give no clue — if his mind perhaps occasionally drifted forward upon the tides of reverie to thoughts of an enchanted hymeneal night: the trembling fingers upon her buttons, the loosening of her ribbons, the bodice slipping away, all those sweet, terrifying raptures of the *zonam solvere,* the fervid sighs, the tender, hesitant intimacies of the newly wedded, the ravishing thrill of receiving the surrender of that once-forbidden, sacrosanct, unimaginably smooth and yielding flesh . . . the lilac-scented darkness of a room in the countryside, the soft breezes of the night entering at a slightly opened window. . . . I do wonder. He must have had such thoughts, of course, but Pierre was so chaste of mind that he hesitated to share such confidences even with himself; and, while I can read much of a man's motives from his acts and can even make out the reflections that pass upon the surface of his mind — I'm quite acute in that regard, like all my kind — I can't peer into his deepest thoughts and desires without some sort of documentary assistance. But I really do have to wonder.

"In any event, for her part, Eugénie was almost as taken with him. He was handsome; as I say, he was never rude of health, but she interpreted his frailty as a sign of spiritual refinement; his social awkwardness and curious dignity touched her. And she too had never known anyone like him: that combination of intensity, brilliance, innocence, and gentleness had for her a sort of pale, feverish glamour about it. When he showed her some of his verse, its fluent prettiness seemed like Petrarchan eloquence to her. And when he presented her with a sonnet written especially for her, her infatuation turned to ardor — of a kind, at least.

"Anyway, the story of their romance — its tender birth, its brief idyllic flowering, its demise — would no doubt make for quite a diverting *nouvelle.* All that bores me, however. I'll only tell you that, though they saw each other almost every day, they constantly exchanged letters. Their warmly palpitating missives were like eager little linnets flitting back and forth along the avenues of Paris. His were full of sincerity and fervent lyricism; hers were at first light and flirtatious, then more florid and serious, and then — how should one say it? — passionate, but in a rather theatrical way. She was, after all, very young. You can imagine all the rest: conversations growing ever more earnest and candid, vespertine strolls along the Seine, dinners sans chaperone, girlish solemnities and manly credulities, the daring exchange of devoted gazes and then of kisses, and finally overt talk of marriage. More letters, more poems, trembling professions of affection, delirious happiness . . . all the trite ceremonies and silly emotions one associates with love among the higher primates. Naturally, of course, Pierre was frequently distracted in his work during those days, and I was forced to reduce his wages.

"The whole thing was quite hopeless. Somehow, Robert convinced himself that if he and Eugénie were to take Pierre down to the country to meet their father, the old man would take a liking to Pierre and might even in time consent to the union. How Robert could have so thoroughly forgotten his father's character — and how Eugénie could have deluded herself as to the plausibility of their scheme — I can't begin to imagine. Perhaps they believed no one could remain entirely untouched by Pierre's unfailingly attractive personality. But the old man, you see, was of a wholly insensible and unimaginative cast of mind; he had buried his wife fourteen years before, and since then, with the absence of any feminine influence to soften his naturally fibrous nature, he had steadily hardened into viduous morbidity, devoting all his energies to his dogs, his genealogies, and the patient labor of perfecting his prejudices. Still, Robert was absurdly confident of his designs; he lent his friend money for new clothing, and he and his sister took the hapless fellow home with them for a week in late June.

"As far as Pierre was concerned, the week was delightful. Eugénie's proximity by itself would have been enough to keep him in a state of bliss, but the beauty of the deep French countryside also worked upon him, reviving the happier memories of his boyhood. I can't really tell you what it was about the setting that captivated him so, since I detest organic nature and can scarcely be bothered to tell a hawk from a housefly. Let's say it was the trilling of birds — whatever birds they were — in trees of some sort or another; and the melodious booming of frogs in ditches — if there were any frogs and if that's what frogs do. Perhaps the gentle, sweetly creaking stridulations of crickets in the night, assuming there were crickets about, doing cricketish things. He made copious observations in his diary, anyway, about fragrant breezes from the woods adjoining the estate, meadows glistening with dew in the morning sun, a shimmer of blue wildflowers amid green grasses, undulations of silver passing over fields stirred by the wind, gleaming gossamer clouds of insects swarming over sunlit fields — that sort of thing. And there was the ruin of an old abbey, inside the boundaries of the original manorial demesne, whose entire history Pierre happened of course to know and which, early one evening, amid long blue shadows cast by shattered walls, he recited to Eugénie in a transport of happy antiquarian distraction, feeling an ineffable thrill of joy every time he turned to her and saw the loveliness of her face, rendered almost dreamlike in its flawlessness by the twilight, never once noticing — on account not of the fading light, but of his own emotional simplicity — the look of deepening despair filling her eyes.

"He was so happy, in fact, that he entirely failed to notice how much Eugénie's father despised him — for his poverty, for his suspect constitution, for being a scholar . . . above all for his manifestly plebeian provenance. Pierre was obviously and (to the old man) contemptibly astonished by the somber baronial grandeurs all about him. At one point, Eugénie and her father observed Pierre standing transfixed in the slanting golden light of an oriel window, simply gazing up at the glass as if it were something miraculous. In her, the sight roused an ache of tenderness; in her father, a surge of repugnance. 'The fellow's like a trout from a village pond,' the old man remarked to Robert later in the day, 'who's suddenly found himself floating in the South Seas' (which really must be accounted something of a triumph, given the old man's almost total incapacity for similes). One, moreover, could scarcely fail to observe Pierre's provincial discomfort around servants, his indecorous tendency to thank them for their assistance, his shy, almost deferential reluctance to request anything of them, and his unseemly habit of noticing their existence when there was no need to do so. And the sight of Pierre at his dinner — visibly reserved, rigid, not daring to touch a spoon until he had seen someone else do so, his few ungainly attempts at light persiflage quickly dissolving into incoherent murmurs — excited only the old man's loathing. Naturally, Pierre was quite unable to dissemble the depth of his feelings for Eugénie, while she — for all her pretense of nonchalance — deceived her father no more than she'd have done had she been as guileless as her lover. Thus, by the time Pierre departed again for Paris — Eugénie and Robert remaining behind at their father's behest, to discuss matters of 'family concern' — the shadow had already fallen.

"The old man had no difficulty in discovering the details of Pierre's shameful paternity and even more shameful poverty. The greater liberality of cosmopolitan French culture had still not spread to much of the landed gentry of France in those days, incredible as that may seem, and at the center of the old man's moral philosophy was his devotion to the pedigree of his dogs, the principles of which he tended to apply by analogy to such lesser matters as his daughter's suitors. This is not to say that a considerable fortune would not have palliated any objections he might have had to any particular young swain who might have appeared below his daughter's windowsill; but a penurious bastard from the provinces was much farther down the scale of nature than he could possibly allow any fruit of his loins to descend. He forbade his daughter any further association with Pierre, rebuked his son ferociously, even briefly suspended Robert's allowance, and — when Eugénie's disobedience looked as though it might persist for a while — threatened disinheritance. I know, it all sounds like idiotic Victorian melodrama now, but it did happen. It was a different age.

"At first — to her credit, I suppose — Eugénie was defiant and histrionic. Her attachment to Pierre was, after all, quite real and, to a nineteen-year-old girl, indistinguishable from genuine adoration; and it was easy for her to fancy herself a kind of romantic heroine persecuted by unreasoning prejudice. She resisted her father's will for more than two weeks, in fact. But, though she was young, she was not imprudent, and she was well aware that her father's resolve — in this as in all things — was unbending. And, well, she had seen Pierre's garret one afternoon, you see, and she had enough of the emotional subtlety of her class to be able to weigh a girlish infatuation against the prospect of real poverty; and, as she could not doubt her father's longevity — the sheer obduracy of his nature made his death unimaginable to her — she could scarcely hope to be rescued by her brother while she was still young and life was worth living. Of course, the sentimental formation of the patrician caste has many and much richer nuances than does that of the lower bipeds; if nothing else, with her addiction to novels, she had read enough to know that the memory and legend of a first love from whom she had been tragically torn might come in time to constitute a particularly precious ornament in the galleries of her sensibility, and might even lend a certain attractive flush of lugubrious purple to her private atmosphere. For a coarser temperament, you know, romance is usually just a boringly stark set of alternatives — either love or love lost, either happiness or misery — but she was of a more intricate design. She was able to console herself with a presentiment of how deeply moving she might come to seem, to herself and others, once the thread had been severed and she could ever thereafter recall that first enchantment with a tender, throbbing regret. The sheer poetry of the notion had worked its way into her reflections well before she had made any conscious decision to capitulate.

"In truth, Robert was ultimately more obstinate than she was: he loved both his sister and his friend and argued with his father daily on their behalf; but, when he realized that his own devotion to the cause was greater than Eugénie's, and that his sister was after all still little more than a child, he relented and — not wanting to face Pierre in the months ahead — made arrangements for a sojourn in Italy and Greece of indeterminate duration. For Eugénie, by that point, Pierre had already substantially become a *dramatis persona* in the larger fiction of her life, one who had already discharged his part. Hence, at the last — as could scarcely have been otherwise — she proved docile to her father's wishes. His wealth was simply too sweet a captivity to flee, especially to the embrace of so impoverished a liberator. So, with a few emptily theatrical professions of anguish and pledges of undying affection in a lyric diminuendo of rose-scented letters, she brought an end to the affair.

"Pierre was, as you might imagine, stunned, and at first reacted with bewilderment and with a desperate incredulity. Three times he sent letters to Eugénie, seeking to sway her from her decision, reminding her of all that had passed between them, renewing his avowals of eternal devotion, and so on; and each time her response was more removed from any reality he recognized, all too obviously a work of willful imagination rather than of deep feeling. He, of course, was more romantic than she at the end of the day, not simply because he was something of a naïf, but because he was singularly lacking in the sort of callousness that only a monstrously brutal or excessively cultured upbringing produces in a soul; but he was intelligent enough to grasp that the love he had thought more real than life itself had already become for her something essentially fabulous. It was Robert — who had sent Pierre an address in Italy where he might be reached, and to whom Pierre frantically wrote — who finally provided Pierre with a clear and candid account of the situation, along with a few pained condolences and sincere expressions of disappointment with his sister and of shame at his own ineptitude and folly.

"When, at last, Pierre accepted — or rather surrendered to — what had happened, he sank for a time into an almost deranged melancholy; he became even more withdrawn from the world around him: morose, nocturnal, capable of only fitful sleep. That was to be expected — the scholar, the lunatic, the saint, the artist all suffer from the same disorder, a sort of neurological agitation whose chief symptoms are fanatical singleness of mind and chronic insomnia. He had always been of a — how to say it? — a *wakeful* temper. For a long time, also, he neglected everything: his journal, the notes for his grand project, his poetry. He could have sent to Robert for money at any time and been plenteously rewarded, obviously, but wouldn't do so; and on the two or three occasions when Robert wrote, offering to provide some money, Pierre replied by assuring his friend that he was quite solvent. In fact, I was his sole support during the last eight months or so of his life. His work for me had become even more unsatisfactory, and I had no choice but to reduce his wages yet further; but to this he offered no protest. And I got into the habit of visiting him in his garret, to commiserate with him and to bring him wine and absinthe — along with lozenges of sugar to go with the latter, of course: I doubt he could have afforded even those without feeling the cost. To the absinthe he became immediately and profoundly devoted — to its curious flavor, and to its exquisite green or glaucous hue, but chiefly to its hallucinogenic effects (though those might really have been attributable to the tincture of laudanum with which I also provided him, as a soporific).

"He continued to pray, I fear. I couldn't dissuade him from this; I could at best distract him. But after a few months the absinthe — consumed as it was in altogether immoderate quantities and in a distracted temper — had begun to work a transformation in his personality, and its special magic probably provided him far profounder solace than the sterile mysteries of religion ever had. And there were the other opiates, which I procured for him in ever-greater quantities. That was no more than simple mercy. He resumed his scholarship and his poetry late in September. The former, though, had become something wilder, more speculative, more impressionistic, more daring than it had formerly been; and the latter had become stranger, more dreamlike, symbolic, even a bit blasphemous. Intellectually he had drifted back towards his work on the Florentine Academy, but only to its more Gnostic and occult elements — the Chaldean Oracles or the *Corpus Hermeticum,* and so on. In his last days, he enjoyed strange, lovely, and terrifying visions and auditions: half-formed glimpses of devils or angels, strange spectral gleams at the margins of his sight, the quick, flickering glitter of a dragonfly, jewel-blue, darting across his room to vanish in the shadows of his drapes, the distant sound of children singing or of flowing waters, sudden ripples of shadow and light coursing through his room, like the sun shining through the swaying boughs of apple trees, chimes from a hidden garden, and a girl's delighted laughter. . . .

"I was greatly pleased, to be honest, especially as January reached its close. At last, in this slow disintegration of the conventional, pious, trusting, superficial personality to which he had been confined all his life, I saw another, more primordial, more chaotic energy breaking forth. He was becoming free, I thought. Rather, I knew. As the winter had come and now was passing, his health had begun rapidly to fail: he suffered a series of bronchial infections that he thought might be the beginnings of consumption but that he didn't bother to treat; he was so poor and so indifferent to his well-being that he did nothing to fend off the chill and dampness of his room; malnutrition and absinthe were quickly weakening him; he became paler, leaner, more disheveled; he gnawed his fingernails. You might think it ridiculous that the failure of a brief, sentimental, silly romance could precipitate such ruin in a man, but Pierre wasn't durably molded. Below the smooth surface of all that vapid, abstracted, untried gentleness there had always been an essential fragility — a brittleness, even. He was never vigorous, of course, as I've repeatedly said; I doubt he was very long for this world, anyway, whatever fate may have brought his way. The Eugénie affair merely prompted a somewhat more rapid decline in his health than might otherwise have been the case. But at least his death came without illusion, and so one has to say that that fickle little gamine had in fact done something for him that no one else could have done. When I think of him in the final weeks of his life, I still see in my mind a more or less perfect *tableau* of the self-destructive power of despair yielded to — which is, as far as I'm concerned, a creative power as well. The more dissolute and delicate he became, the more I saw a flame of . . . well, let's say 'heroic defiance' in him. A Promethean rebellion against the absurdity of his life and so — surely — against the heavens. It was so clear. His end showed all the signs of a wanton embrace of emptiness, a final feat of self-liberation.

"I was even present when he expired. Visiting him one afternoon with a bottle of absinthe, after having spent six days away from Paris, I received no answer to my knocking, and since his door was never locked, I let myself in and found him supine and scarcely conscious upon his bed. He had kicked his bedclothes to the floor, and he was still in his shabby trousers and shirtsleeves, collarless, and extremely pallid and damp with sweat, breathing hoarsely, though quietly. He opened his eyes to look at me once only, for no more than a few seconds, and I doubt he was really aware who I was. Other than that, he merely shifted and writhed a bit and murmured a few words, mostly too softly for even my preternaturally sensitive ears to make out. I did definitely hear Eugénie's name twice, though, and what may have been a phrase or two of invocation of some saint, but that was interrupted by a sudden fit of coughing that, despite its violence, did not wake him. Within two hours he had died of what a physician later called — rather quaintly — exacerbated inanition: hunger, fatigue, and more than a touch of pneumonia. It was the end of the third week of February, not quite one year since he'd met Eugénie. But I'll tell you, in the second or so that passed after he exhaled his last breath, I saw him whole. To me his entire life had become, finally, a thing perfectly wrought, superbly and finely detailed and thoroughly polished. There in the wreckage of his flesh was an ideal monument to the futility of all those transcendental ecstasies that had tormented him throughout the years, and to the devastation that such things inflict upon the health of the mind and body, and — more importantly — to that final act of rejection that had set him free. It was perfect, really. When I had first known him, my every attempt to penetrate that serene moral and imaginative simplicity of his was like tapping my fingernail on a bright porcelain glaze: always the same high, pure note rang out, and always the surface was left unmarred. But now the little saint's statuette had fallen from its niche and shattered. He had become something new, something altogether different. I knew, you see — *I knew* — he had taken our side at the last. I mean, after all, the way he'd neglected his health, and had soaked his mind in hallucinogens, and had done nothing to secure better employment, and had all but ceased eating by the end — surely, I thought, *surely* this must count as a suicide, and an act of *eternal* abjuration. I may lack the ability to gaze deeply into men's souls, but I can certainly read the signs of a man's life — or of his death.

"Imagine my indignation, then, when all at once I found myself crushingly, searingly assailed by the sudden arrival in that small garret of a kind of . . . enormous *light* with which I was all too familiar. I can't really describe what I mean to you, since your animal senses are so happily insulated against that particular kind of radiation. It's a sort of burning immensity of sheer presence, a sort of overwhelming surfeit of being. It crowds in on one intolerably. Another angel was in the room, you see, a celestial angel, and that's how they announce themselves. I couldn't actually see him as a distinct object or anything like that, you understand. One just doesn't in those circumstances. Instead, his presence simply flooded into all my faculties; it poured over the walls of my psyche; it swallowed me up in a fathomless sea of pure . . . pure . . . exposure. I know, that's very vague. Imagine, if you can, suddenly standing naked before millions, and being plunged into the middle of the ocean, and being wrapped in scorching flames, and freezing and gasping for air atop some desolate Himalayan peak — imagine all that at once and you might form some faint analogy in your mind of what I was being subjected to as I stood there innocently, only as a sympathetic comrade . . . only . . . only . . .

"It's all just idiotic ostentation, of course, a crass stage effect, nothing but empty, vulgar, pasteboard spectacle. But, if you've the resources for that sort of thing, you might as well flaunt them, I suppose. I was furious, though. There was no question what this entirely unwarranted and despicable invasion meant; and of course I was incapable of preventing what was about to happen, since we were entirely stripped of discretion in these matters ages ago, as a condition of the armistice. So, as I watched, predictably, Pierre's soul, like a white, transparent, crystalline vapor of light rose up from the bed where his body lay; it was bright and flawless, and already endowed with a shape and a special luminosity to which my powers of perception were no longer quite adequate. I couldn't actually see it fully, in itself; I saw only its phenomenal sheathe, so to speak, its ethereal chrysalis, and so my only impression of it was of something shining and mostly indistinct. This limitation of vision is just another one of the humiliations our persecutors are pleased that we should suffer, you understand; it's not a natural limitation, but a kind of fetter we're not allowed to slip off. Anyway, Pierre's soul continued to rise, to the ceiling and through, and then was gone, beyond my reach, and at once the angelic presence vanished as well, without any sign that any notice had been taken of me at all. As if they would deign to do us the courtesy. This was not the first time I'd been despoiled of an ally I thought I'd fairly gained — by precisely this same ridiculous device of a sudden *deus ex machina* just as the curtain was about to drop — but that made it no easier to bear. This gross liberality of interpretation, as I've said, is absolutely typical of the way in which these assessments are conducted. I remain firm in my opinion that when all the evidence points towards the due dereliction of a soul, but the agents of the celestial regime come to collect their treasure all the same, it's nothing but caprice and whimsy, done principally to taunt us with the weakness of our state. I mean, again, to think of all that Pierre had done and failed to do in those last weeks — but of course all of that always gets rewritten as a kind of 'dark night of the soul' or as a purgatorial passage through the desert of despair or something else of that sort. Why not embrace absurdity completely, I say, and call it a 'speculative Good Friday'? It's dreadful. I would have protested there and then, while that cretinous factotum of the powers on high was still in the room, but . . . well, the sheer boorishness of his manner, the sheer obtrusiveness of his . . . his energy, or light, or presence, or whatever you'd call it . . . well, it had obliged me briefly to shrink to the size of a microbe; so my voice would have been inaudible. And then of course it was all over, in the flickering of an eyelash. Frankly, it's terrorism, the way they behave, simple terrorism.

"Anyway, there it is: they took him — plundered him, if you will — frozen forever in the impotence of his infirmity and delirium and exhausted hopes. That's how heaven wants them, of course: broken, thwarted, passive, servile to what they call grace . . . drained of dignity, emptied of energy, helpless . . . endlessly grateful. . . . Yes."

4

My friend ceased talking for several moments, gazing once again towards the window. Apparently his valet had discreetly switched on several of the lamps standing immediately about us as the night had worn on, though I had not noticed him doing so, and as a result — apart from our own reflections, lambently pressed against the backdrop of the night's darkness — nothing was visible between us and the distant glitter of the city's lights. He drank more of his cordial, his mind obviously drifting away towards some unspoken memory or thought.

I straightened my back, cleared my throat, and said, with a certain tentativeness, "You always make heaven sound like an eternal convalescents' ward."

He turned his eyes back to me with a pitying look. "You imagine, no doubt, that you'll take the Kingdom by violence, your dignity intact, passing through the gates like a young god striding across a world he's lately formed with his own hands. No, that's not how it works. You have to abase yourself, lad, and grovel and simper silly litanies of obsequious gratitude — forever. You know, I do have some knowledge of these things."

"Yes, of course, but . . . well . . ." I filled my glass again. After a few seconds, with as insouciant an air as I could affect, I said, "And — forgive me — exactly how does this story apply to me?"

"Rather obviously, I would have thought." He sighed, took a sip from his glass, drew in his legs, and sat perfectly upright. "I don't mean to suggest you're anything like Pierre. You've none of his saccharine piety, for one thing. All I mean to say is that what ultimately destroyed him was his own pathetic devotion to a largely mythical past, to 'timeless truth' rather than to the truth of time — the truth of becoming, that is to say. Simple enough, really: it's just a cautionary tale. There was so much intellect there, you know, and so much real potential, if only it could have been nourished and set loose from confining fideisms and nostalgias. He might even have become a significant poet if he could have learned to doubt and to hate, if he'd learned how to derange his faculties so that something more primitive and formless could break through all those conventions of thought and habit and perception and poetic formality that imprisoned him. But instead he dreamed away the days, and grew ever frailer and more defenseless and more vulnerable, and at the first cold blast of winter wind, he withered away. A little girl was able to kill him with a smile and a laugh and a few kisses. Ridiculous. But I'm not really finished telling the story."

"Oh, I'm sorry. I thought you were done."

"Not quite. You see, there's the matter of his literary remains. He left behind a virtual archive of his inner world; it was a startlingly voluminous witness to everything curtailed and stifled and aborted in his nature — everything unfinished, everything half-formed and futile. I know, because I saw all of it. As soon as Pierre's soul had passed beyond my ken and that great blundering oaf of an angel had departed again, I resumed my customary anthropine dimensions and stood for a time on the side of the room opposite the cadaver until the better part of my fury had subsided and I was able to regain my composure. My disappointment on having my friend spirited away at the last moment by the rapacity of some officious little cosmic excise man was mitigated by the realization that, as I stood there in the stillness of that dismal, tiny room, I enjoyed effective possession of almost the whole of Gernet's life's work, saving only those few brief reviews and that small monograph he'd published. On the wretched table where he wrote, and on the shelves by the door, and in stacks in the corners and by the foot of his miserable bed, and in fact all about me, lay the pages of all the larger projects he had never completed, all his notes, all those fragments of ideas, all those ephemeral inspirations, all those intimate observations and poems and . . . everything. Very well, I thought, heaven take his ghost, but I'll have his earthly substance to myself. For an angelic intellect, it was the work of moments to read and commit to memory everything he'd left behind, while his corpse lay there unprotesting on its sordid linens. You can't imagine how much there was, too: literally thousands of pages, written in a minute and — for human eyes — barely legible hand. I had not known how very industrious — though diffusely industrious — he'd really been. There was, first of all, his great *opus imperfectum* on the secret identity of Dionysus and Apollo: whole chapters, long involved passages, scrawled jottings and variant pages, and hundreds upon hundreds of research notes, full of citations and transcriptions from classical sources; there were also thirty-six short essays on historical, philological, and religious topics, only four of which seemed to be in something like final form; there were his journals, containing every banal recollection, ecstatic intuition, or morose reflection that had happened to occur to him on a given day — the final pages of which were quite dark and despondent and confused; and there were seventy-eight poems, sixteen of which appeared in more than one version, and five of which were in Latin and were obviously school exercises he had thought worth saving. When five minutes or so had elapsed, and I had absorbed Pierre's entire posthumous corpus — to put it in a rather grisly way — I descended the stairs, found the landlady at home, and told her that I had just discovered Pierre's body. She expressed no very great alarm, apart from a few ceremonious exclamations of impersonal pity, but asked if I knew of anyone who would take responsibility for his two months' delinquency in paying his rent. I answered for the debt there and then, in cash, and gave her a handsome gratuity as well, telling her that once the body had been removed, I would be grateful if his books could be sent to me, whereupon I would indemnify her for any expenses thrice over. His other personal effects, such as they were, I told her she could sell or give away, and said that his private papers, being worthless, she should burn, which she assured me she would do."

I was on the verge of taking a sip from my glass, but I at once lowered it from my lips. "What? What do you mean?" I felt a slight, queer shiver of revulsion pass over the surface of my skin. "You had all his work destroyed?"

He stared at me for a moment — impassively, it seemed, except for a faint flicker of what looked like malice in his eyes. "Of course, naturally. What do you expect?"

"But that's monstrous." My voice was weak and extremely quiet; I found it something of an effort to speak.

He laughed, almost indulgently. "Monstrous, is it? My, my, my, is that supposed to be a reproach? Dear me. I'm a devil, after all. Don't you expect me to be monstrous?"

"Yes, I suppose . . ." For perhaps the first time since I had met him, I felt something like fear in his presence, or at least a foretaste of fear. Somehow it seemed that he was telling me something more terrible than he ever had before, though I was sure this could not really be so. "I don't know what to say."

He shook his head gently. "Look, calm yourself. It's not as wicked as all that. Mine was the action of a moralist. We all have to obey the principles in which we believe, you'd surely grant. And I've told you where my values lie: in energy, in the strength of those who are willing to destroy in order to make room for the new and the vital and the unprecedented. I'm an ally of the strong poet, the man willing to forge himself, even if he must set the world ablaze to do it. Pierre, for most of his life, was the very epitome of the weak poet, the derivative soul, the diffident, studious curator. He was a collector, an embalmer . . . a necrophiliac. Everything about him was unwholesome, except for that one last act of defiance, that one victorious gesture of rejection that — no matter what the heavenly hosts might claim — constituted the final weeks of his life. *That's* what merited preserving, not the miserable scraps of prettiness and longing and vain curiosity he left behind, not that congealed congeries of sentimental souvenirs and backward glances and nostalgic dreaming. What was all of that but so much afterbirth that needed to be scoured away so that the wonderful, terrible infant prodigy he had finally become could be seen full and splendid, free from the obfuscations of all those obsolete fixations of his? There he was, at last, lying upon his bed, newborn, pure . . ."

"And dead."

"Yes, well, the path of liberation is parlous indeed. You can't really count the cost if you're to get on. And, you know, really, you need an eye for symmetries, for the finer things, quite to understand — the damp pallor of a corpse amid a tangle of squalid bedclothes can be as poignant as the gleam of an alabaster king upon a marble catafalque if you know what to look for, or what the story is. And anyway, as I say, it doesn't really matter, since they caught him in their nets after all, in the end, before he could quite spring free. But I know it should have been otherwise, and I also know . . ."

"Congealed." I murmured suddenly, scarcely intending to do so, but desperate for a moment's respite from the flow of his expatiations.

"What? I'm sorry, I didn't catch that." I had evidently surprised him.

"You should say 'congealed,' not 'congelated.' I don't think that works even as a whimsical archaism."

He was silent for a few moments, gazing at me with no discernible expression whatsoever; then the slightest of smiles appeared on his lips (though not in his eyes). "Ah, so, I seem to have touched a nerve. Curious. You've never been so . . . unamiable before that I recall. So, I see, you don't mind me being callous, but this — what? — this you think positively cruel? Harsh, fanatical, spiteful . . . what, exactly?"

"I don't know. It seems . . . extraordinary to rob a man of his posterity, when he had nothing else."

"To rob him of his posterity, but not his soul? That seems well within bounds to you, does it?"

I hesitated to answer, swallowed some of my whiskey, breathed deeply, and said, in a somewhat less aggressive tone, "Are you speaking about yourself or the angel who arrived when Gernet died?"

My friend's smile broadened, and with a slight shrug he said, "I suppose there are at least two ways of looking at everything. I take it you know where I stand. As I've told you, we're not engaged in secret stratagems or conducting some clandestine war. I was acting as a private citizen and, as it happens, a philanthropist. I wanted to help him and, yes, to enlist him on the side of our philosophy, as much for his own good as anything else. I was inviting him — subtly, I admit — to join us on our side of the great cosmic dividing line, to find faith in the future, to learn how to live honestly and to be truly, truly free. I sought to take nothing by force. Nothing. Anyway," — he took a sip from his glass and waved his free hand before his face with a limp elegance, as if to chase our last exchange away — "since you've decided to be bothered by archaisms, you've little right to rebuke me. Pierre was nothing if not a treasury — an engine — of archaisms. If you'd only seen some of his poems! The later ones showed some promise, perhaps, but even then the last thing he produced in that line — if I follow his journals right — was his sequence of sonnets on seven figures from Byzantine history — if you can imagine a poetic topic so grippingly thrilling." He shook his head and laughed in a way he clearly meant to sound fond. "In a sense, they said it all."

"Said all of what?"

"All that needs be said about empty doting on the distant past, and pathetic devotion to what's faded away, and vain fascination with the so-called eternal verities. The sonnets aren't marked by any explicit symptoms of the travails of his final days, admittedly. And who knows? Maybe he wrote them much earlier and had merely put them in final order at the end. Whatever the case, the thing that's so enchanting about them, despite all the tiresome sweetness and backwardness of the prosody and diction, is the tone of sublime resignation that pervades them. It's as if some deeper intelligence in him were working through all his silly conceits to shake him from his idiot delight in the dust of ages past. Their stiltedness and preciosity would simply be damning, taken by themselves, and very, very dull; but what makes the poems interesting is that they constitute a kind of inadvertent confession on Pierre's part." My friend stared at me pensively for several seconds, with something of an amused expression, and then — for once setting his glass aside — placed the fingertips of his two hands together before him and inclined his head forward until his lips nearly touched them. "They definitely say it all." He peered at me from under his brow and, in a casual tone, said, "Listen, I'll recite them to you, if you like. All right? As a diversion, at least?"

This somewhat surprised me, but as I was intent upon regaining a proper semblance of calm, I merely furrowed my brow and answered, "Oh, of course. I wouldn't mind at all. I'm rather curious, actually."

"Good." He leaned his head back again and closed his eyes. "Just a moment, then. Let's see. Yes." He opened his eyes again. "Right, well then, the first thing to tell you is that the poems follow the rise and fall of the Eastern Roman Empire. He called them the *Byzantine Sonnets*, which I think you'll agree is a pretty ghastly way to begin, and then subtitled them simply *A Palindrome*. That part, at least, has the virtue of being descriptive, because the sequence is built around a certain structural conceit: its design is that of an arc — or, better, a bow, an archer's bow, aimed upward towards the sky. It really is palindromic, because it rises from the first sonnet to the fourth in a kind of climactic ascent, and then descends again from the fourth to the seventh. The middle poem is symmetrically flanked: the first and seventh poems are about emperors — the first and last Constantine, in fact, the beginning and end of the Byzantine empire; the second and sixth concern notorious pagan apostates from the imperial cult; the third and fifth mirror each other somewhat more imperfectly, I suppose, since the former concerns an emperor and the latter a philosopher and historian, but I expect Pierre meant the one to represent the rising greatness of a Christian empire and the latter to represent the beginnings of its slow decline; and at the very center of the cycle is a poem about — depressingly and predictably enough — a mystic. Oh, and I should note that the arc of the palindrome should also be imagined as the arc of an arrow in flight, though, of course, arrows don't really fly in arcs; the shaft is fired in the first lines of the first sonnet and falls to earth in the last lines of the last sonnet. Anyway, I'm sorry for so elaborate a preface. I'm sure you'd catch all this on the fly, so to speak, but I thought it would be best to make sure you see the shape of the thing first."

"I don't mind," I said.

"Fine. And since the simian brain, dependent as it is upon its material substrate and its phantasmic processes, is not nearly as retentive as the angelic, I'll have my man transcribe the verses as I recite them, so you'll have a record." He turned his head towards the fireplace and raised a forefinger, saying nothing, and as I too turned to look I saw that his valet had somehow already produced a plain black writing palette, which he held braced against his ribcage with his left hand, as well as a long, lustrous raven's quill, which he held in his right hand, poised above the paper; and upon the mantelpiece to his right he had already placed a small bottle of ink, the glass of which was a murky algoid green. "You see," said my friend, turning back to me, "I know you'll want to reflect on them later, and you'll never be able to remember them otherwise. Look how I cosset your infirmities."

I returned my gaze to him. "Thank you."

"Of course. Now, I'll just have to translate them *ex tempore,* but you needn't worry . . ."

"Excuse me," I interrupted, "but don't bother, please. I can follow them in French perfectly well."

"Ah, no, you've not quite understood me. I couldn't possibly just give them to you as he wrote them. I vowed long ago to keep everything of his I took in on the day he died locked away forever, deep in the vaults of memory."

"Forever?"

"Well, at least till the seas yield up their dead and all that, I suppose."

"But why?"

He sighed, and a hint of impatience entered his voice. "Look, I've told you: because it's all deadly, poisonous nonsense. It's diseased, not to put too fine a point on it. And, anyway," — he shrugged and ventured a jocular frown — "let's say it's my little revenge for the way in which I was cheated all those years ago."

"I really can't see what harm . . ."

"Listen," — he was now quite obviously becoming annoyed — "that's the best I can do. If it's not good enough, we can forgo the whole ceremony. I'm not exactly desperate to declaim the odious things to you, you know."

I hesitated to answer for a moment. I felt a slight impulse to tell him that my interest had passed; the sheer pettiness (it seemed to me) of denying Gernet even so much posterity as a posthumous recitation of a few unpublished sonnets struck me as absurdly cruel; but curiosity proved the stronger impulse, so I relented. "All right, as you wish."

"Good man. And, really, you needn't worry overly much. The powers of an angelic intellect are quite adequate to the task. I'll have no trouble transcribing his images and tone and sensibility into English verse — I'll even keep the varying rhyme scheme intact, which is important because they aren't classically Petrarchan or Spenserian . . . or Shakespearean, for that matter, except by accident in one case: in each of them the octave has four sets of two rhymed lines, rather than two sets of four, and the sestet has three sets of two, and the order of rhyme changes from poem to poem. The last sonnet is really just seven couplets, though not heroics. Anyway, you'll know I've been faithful to his silly little inflated bagatelles if the effect is like, say, one of those suave, shiny, brightly enameled, insipid, rhymed translations of Gérard de Nerval or Baudelaire or Apollinaire one so often sees — only in this case the doggerel will be a proper reflection of the original."

"I'll have to take your word on that."

"Yes, you will. But my word's always good. Now," he said, leaning his head back and clearing his throat, "each sonnet's title is the name and dates of the particular historical figure it concerns. The first is called 'Constantine the Great (c. 285-337)', and it goes this way . . ." — and, in a grave and gradual voice, though without any excess of drama, he began to recite:

Empire is born of mind — that taut bent bow
    That flings its arrow at the deathless sun,
That sea whose surface makes suns blaze below,
    That world desire's pure force must first have won:
There colonnades and domes of gold arise,
    Beyond the battlefields of fire and blood,
Pavilioned by opulent Eastern skies,
    Beside Marmara's silver, shining flood.

It happened as I said: the sign, the dream,
  The oracle. I slept, Rome's light declined,
But now I saw a brighter radiance stream
  From another city's heart, in my mind —
    My mind the bow, desire the bowstring drawn.
    From twilight I had seized the gold of dawn.

When he had finished, my friend stared intently at me for several moments. Then, when I offered no comment, he said simply, "Well?"

"Yes, well. I'm not entirely sure what to say. It's rather hard to judge, just hearing it for the first time. It seems smooth and . . . and . . ."

"Precious?"

"I suppose."

"In any event," said my friend, continuing to inspect my expression with more than his customary attentiveness, "that's how it starts. Pierre believed the story of Constantine's vision, incidentally: the entire *in hoc signo* story, though he seems to have inclined more towards Lactantius's version — the dream story — than towards Eusebius's. Either way, I give him credit for at least recognizing the ambition in the man as well. But this notion that every battle is won in the mind before it's fought in the flesh, that everything flows from the aspiration of the mind . . . it's a constant tendency in his work. It's a sort of instinctive and incorrigible Platonism, I suppose. And his belief that there's a point where the mind is open to flashes of divine purpose, moments of revelation, and . . . yes, well, no need to go into that. But that's how it begins, a little pornographically, if I can put it that way, with Constantinople's conception in the womb of Constantine's dreaming mind."

"Right." I nodded. "Who comes next?"

"The next poem is 'Julian the Apostate (c. 331-363).' Perhaps the one I like second least, as it happens. I knew Julian quite well, you know — indeed, it was my privilege to serve in his household before and during his brief, golden reign — and the poem does him no justice. Admittedly, I think the religion he adopted as ridiculous as the one he abandoned, but I object to the way in which Pierre's picture of him makes him sound like a feeble lunatic, which he certainly wasn't. Pierre simply lacked the necessary imagination. I mean, I understand that Pierre couldn't think well of anyone who'd turned his back on the Nazarene religion, but the poem really comes close to simple calumny."

"I'm sorry, you say you knew Julian? You never told me." My curiosity had all at once been spurred in a different direction. "I wonder, then, can you tell me . . . ?"

"Ah," he said, wagging a quick, metronomically minatory finger at me, "no, of course not. But don't allow yourself to be diverted. All that can wait till some other time. The sonnet first, all right?"

"Yes. Sorry."

He smiled, cleared his throat again, and resumed:

He dreams the Cumaean sibyl's leaves, which lay
   Outside her cave's dark mouth, before he read,
By cold and sudden wind were caught away;
   He wakes, a fever beating in his head —
As when, through plangent woods, a wild god's drums
   Had throbbed, and horns had wailed, while bull's blood flowed,
In darkness, down on him, and fragrant gums
   Had burned in braziers where red embers glowed.

He says, The sun-drenched flower on the vine
Still turns to drink the day like golden wine;
   So spirit bends against its carnal root:
   The body is the ancient, restive brute
     That must be slain in fires of sacrifice —
     This is empire, and treasure beyond price.

His voice died away, lingering momentarily on the final syllable, and again he stared at me with that inquisitive and uncertain look. "Anything?"

"It's, well, as far as I can tell it's rather nice in a pleasantly florid way. Very *fin de siècle*. Again, though, hearing it for the first time, and through a translation also, it's hard to say much. But it doesn't seem bad, or particularly slanderous. I mean, Julian's religion was rather anti-corporeal, wasn't it?"

"Well, yes, of course, but that's not what annoys me. My problem, I suppose, is how weak it makes Julian sound. That pathetic image of the sibyl's leaves blowing away before he can read them, I mean, as if to say he has no vision of the future. He's made to seem bewildered and deranged and helpless in the poem, it seems to me, and that's simply off the mark. I assure you, Julian was anything but destiny's slave, or some spiritual stripling tormented by nostalgia. He was decisive, a bold warrior, and he had a very firm vision of the future, even if it was not particularly profound.

Actually it was little more than a pagan version of Christianity, if you ask me. But, as a man . . . well. Anyway, I suppose that doesn't matter very much. You do understand what's going on in the poem, I take it. The bits about the bull's blood and the burning incense and all of that?"

"He's recalling his initiation into one of the mysteries. Mithras . . . or Cybele, I suppose: the *taurobolium,* the baptism in bull's blood — that's from the mysteries of Cybele, right? Was it used also in the mysteries of Mithras? I know that the bull sacrifice was part of Mithraic lore, going back to ancient Persia. He's surely not describing the Dionysian or Eleusinian mysteries, I'm certain of that. Or the Orphic, of course."

"Yes, well, you're getting too involved in your thinking; it would have to be Cybele, if one wants to take it very literally, but it's all quite impressionistic the way Pierre presents it, really; I think it's just a general picture of all the mysteries, though it's a poor picture, I assure you. The tauroctony was Mithraic — really little more than a roast beef banquet, to be honest — but the baptism in bull's blood was for consecration in the mysteries of the Great Mother, principally priestly consecration. Pierre, though, probably has Mithras and Cybele both vaguely and indiscriminately in mind. Confidentially, the latter occupied a far more significant place in Julian's private piety than the former, as well as in his sense of what constituted a proper imperial cult. He was sure it was the *Magna Mater* who would restore Rome's native vigor, if invoked and worshiped with sufficient devotion. But don't go looking for precision in the poem. Who's this 'wild god,' for instance? Dionysus? Sabazius? I doubt it matters, really. Anyway, it's not the inaccuracy of the imagery in the poem that bothers me. I'm more concerned about the subtle sarcasm of it all. I suppose there's some rhetorical profit to be reaped from stressing Julian's link with the mysteries, of course, but, really, no one who was ever witness to those grand, solemn, darkly gorgeous rites ever found it possible to hold them in contempt. And the haunting stories behind them. . . . They left me unmoved, of course, because I find the whole transcendence obsession incomprehensible, like any infantile fixation. But, really, people are so parochial about such things." He took up his cordial again and sipped it meditatively.

"I suppose it's inevitable," I said after a moment, just to keep the conversation moving; "what one hears about the mystery religions, after all, sounds a bit silly. And Iamblichan theurgy, obviously — you know, invoking Hecate and summoning demons into statues and children, and all that. And all that business about the seven ranks of Mithraic initiates — it sounds like the Free Masons."

"Perhaps, but then the mystery religion to which Pierre himself belonged sounds rather silly to many ears as well. What's that but purblindness on your part, really? An arbitrary preference for one acquired taste over another? So what if someone prefers his sacraments and ceremonies, his myth of creation and salvation, his rites of confession and rebirth, his baptism and theophagy and tales of redeeming sacrifice? I mean, some like Wagner and some like Verdi, but it's all nonsense seen from one vantage or another."

"Yes, yes . . . ." I cleared my throat. "I suppose that's true." I too drank, and after another moment asked, "And the next sonnet?"

"'Justinian I (482-565),'" said my friend, apparently happy to change the subject, "and a more plausible beast there never was. The scene, one gathers right away, is the emperor's first entry into Hagia Sophia, just after its completion, though his giddy cry of 'Solomon, I have surpassed thee!' doesn't appear anywhere in the poem. You'll like it, probably." This time he took a deep breath and growled quietly before commencing his (rather stiff) declamation:

> The vast dome floats upon a ring of light,
>   A gulf of gold; mosaics' lazulite blue,
>   And porphyry, and gems that shine like dew,
> And silver lamps, ethereal, cool, and bright,
> And the broad gleaming marble floors daze him:
>   It is as if, he thinks, the sun were turned
>   As cold and hard as stone, and here there burned
> Its frozen dawn, pearl heart, and sapphire rim.
>
> This Great Church, Holy Wisdom, is the whole
>   Of empire gathered, its deep-dreaming mind,
>   While I walk where only Uriel once trod:
> The fiery axletree, the blazing soul
>   Of earth and heaven, and am not struck blind —
>   One Caesar, of one empire and one God.

My friend waited a moment and then sighed quietly. "Uriel," he murmured with a slight, derisive laugh. "Well, of course; who else? There you have all the images, really, of Pierre's fascination with changelessness, eternity, unity, stagnation: the empire, the church, the sun. . . . Yes, the sun — now that's interesting, isn't it? I sometimes wonder if it's not all really just another solar cult after all. Constantine's *Sol Invictus* might have changed names, but . . ." He waved the back of his hand emptily towards the ceiling and drank again from his glass. "Then comes the sonnet I like least, a clammily, daintily, moistly pious little trifle, cloyingly, sweetly aromatic with Greek incense. It's called 'Symeon the New Theologian (949-1022).'"

"Oh," I said, sitting forward almost involuntarily, "all right. Please, go on."

"Yes, I knew that would interest you. He was a very unwholesome specimen, you know, when all's said and done — Symeon, I mean — and more than a bit demented. I suppose that's what made him a saint. Anyway . . ." And he commenced, his voice now slightly harsher and unmistakably suffused by a quality of dry disdain:

> He lifts his glass to see the day stream through
> > The ruby wine, and says, This agile light
> > Is sweeter than the liquors that excite
> The tongue with floral musks and honeydew;
> Earth's tremulous beauties the Spirit fills
> > With light more ravishing than endless suns
> > Pour on the earth, the leaf, the juice that runs,
> The ecstasy that from the winepress spills.
>
> And all his Kingdom's ecstasies I've known,
> Raised up above all realms and every throne,
> > Ablaze, as lightning cleaves the star-bright deep:
> > > Light calls to light, love to love, bliss to bliss,
> > The soul's sharp bolt takes flight, wild, swift, and steep,
> > > Into his beauty's infinite abyss.

My friend did not look at me at all this time, but rather stared pensively at his own hands for several moments in silence.

After a while, I became slightly uncomfortable at the inexplicably lingering caesura in our conversation and so coughed and said, "That's rather flowery — the way you render it, at any rate — but it has a nice lushness to it, I think. The imagery's the typical . . ."

"Yes, lush," he said, interrupting me but still not turning his eyes towards me: "lush and sumptuous and syrupy. It almost makes my lips stick together to recite it. Honey, sugar-water, toffee — sweets of every variety." A faint note of despondency had insinuated itself into his voice.

"Who knows? It almost makes me think heaven was within its rights after all, spiriting the boy away. Anyway" — now he did look at me — "the imagery is familiar, as you say. The French original is every bit as pretty and pink. And Symeon did love to gush about wine and his fluttering heart and his effeminate ecstasies and enthusiasms."

"Effeminate?"

"Not worth talking about," said my friend with a peremptory finality and a melancholy smile. "The next one's called 'Michael Psellus (1018– c. 1078).' Psellus was a sort of ideal for Pierre, as you might imagine. Of course, he would have been drawn to anyone of such high and pure Byzantinism, but he also saw Psellus as simultaneously the great grandfather of the Renaissance and the late-born child of Greek antiquity, come to rescue antique metaphysics from scholastic aridity. And of course the combination of interests was right in Pierre's line: metaphysics, religions, theology, poetry, history, occult lore. Psellus's revival of Platonism especially enchanted and fascinated Pierre, and the university curriculum he devised, and his years in the Constantinopolitan court. I think Pierre genuinely took the *Chronographia* as a model of sound historical writing, quaintly enough. Incredibly enough, Psellus the scholar and poet and historian and polymath was a kind of hero to Pierre."

"Which, I suppose, depresses you."

"But of course." He smiled again and shook his head slightly. "Not really. Anyway, the poem."

"Yes, the poem." I straightened my back and waited attentively.

"Yes, so . . ." — and again he began to recite, though his voice now was somewhat quieter, almost thoughtful in its intonation, and it was more deliberate and less clipped than before:

Here in his hand a stolen starlight lies;
    A paler beauty, though, dwells in his mind:
A light spilled down time's empty azure skies
    On matter's cold abyss, sterile and blind.
He writes of bellowing brass, battles won,
    The radiance and triumphs of deathless empires,
But gazes where a still, mysterious Sun
    Surmounts the turning spheres, their ancient fires.

Now close the book; the everlasting dance
    Ignores our mighty ages, nor bends down:

The changeless guards its measures against chance.
　　The years are prisms, the light in which we stand
　We must gather up again (lest light drown)
　In mind's pale beauty — starlight in the hand.

After another several moments of silence, I said, "I think I like that one best of all. It's rather . . . hushed."

"I expect that's what he intended. An atmosphere of stillness . . . a last moment of refined grandeur before the slow decline of a civilization . . . quiet anticipation, and memory . . . all things drawing to a pause . . . gathering up the scattered remnants of the past to preserve them from the night. The wistful pure note of Platonism — something that aspires to timelessness, perhaps. I don't know — I'm not a poet. Your drink needs refreshing."

I looked down at my glass, which was indeed empty, but then set it aside. "No, I've had enough, I think. Excellent, as always."

"All right." He drank from his own glass again. "I hope you note that one of the lines is aurally elongated by the use of two y-glides, which — not to revel too much in my own ingenuity — rather elegantly reproduces the effect of the French original."

"Oh yes? How does that go?"

My friend smiled at me as though at a mischievous child. "Wouldn't you like to know. You won't catch me out like that, lad."

I raised my palms in mock surrender. "No, all right. What's next, then?"

"Why, the other apostate, of course: 'George Gemistus Plethon (c. 1355–c. 1452).' The last of the true Hellenes, you know. The true father of the Renaissance, if you think about it; and the precious link to the Florentine Academy that Pierre so adored. Not that Pierre could ever understand why a man of such great culture would retreat to the old gods and the old Platonism — though one might just as well ask how someone of Pierre's learning and intellectual refinements could retreat to the equally obsolete god of pre-Enlightenment Europe. Anyway, my own opinion of George was always mixed; no one could deny his brilliance, or his pathos, but really, from my point of view, Platonism . . . well, what's there to say? The same poison in a different bottle, as far as I'm concerned — a degenerate, enervating 'eternalism,' though without some of the more degrading dogmas of Christian Platonism, I suppose."

"How does the poem go?" I asked, sensing the imminence of another long digression.

"I'm getting to it." He was obviously mildly annoyed. "Don't rush me."

"I'm sorry."

He stared at me for a moment with a look of patent disapprobation; then, raising his eyebrows, he said, "All right, all right. Like this . . ." — and, without turning his gaze from me, declaimed:

> He says, Mine is bright heaven's mind, and I
>   Can see all things; the soul's a mirror, bright,
>   A surface that, turned upward to the light,
> Conceives within itself the depths of sky;
> To know the One, one must stare on the glass,
>   Grow still, look where all vanishes, there find,
>   Reflected in the unmoved height of mind,
> The changeless source, whose splendors never pass.
>
> I'll turn no more the mirror of my soul
>   To time's horizon or history's waste —
>   No empire, Caesar, God upon his throne —
> From such cruel fires no titan ever stole
>   The brand of truth: Law's honey one must taste
>   In raptures, seized alone to the alone.

For the first time, I noticed the faint scratching of the quill far off to my right. I turned and saw my friend's servant, gaunt and stark in the distant yellow light of our lamps, his head bent over his quill, the expression on his hideous face sullen to the point of malevolence.

"Your . . . your man is getting weary, I think."

My friend narrowed his eyes and cast a plainly contemptuous glance towards his valet, whose face remained angrily inclined above the palette, though he had ceased writing. "I can scarcely imagine," said my friend, "a contingency to which I could possibly be more profoundly indifferent. Anyway, he's immune to fatigue, as am I; it would be better to say he's becoming petulant, as he often does. But I could charge him to stand there a millennium, transcribing every accidental noise he hears, and he would never feel a moment's weariness in his limbs. He chafes at the ignominy of his servitude, but he can't be overtaxed."

I looked again at my friend's valet, who had altered neither his pose nor his expression. "Yes," I said. "I imagine that's true."

"In any event, he'll be delivered from his boredom shortly. There's only one sonnet left, and I think I'll be going soon. The night calls me to other tasks."

"But, wait, just out of curiosity, was Pierre an admirer of Plethon's? It sounds as if he had some sympathy for the man — seeing the end of the empire, turning towards the eternal above and within, and so on."

"Oh, who knows?" said my friend with a faint smile. "I suppose he did, really, to a point. But apostasy he could love in no man, though at the end . . . Well, let's not rehearse all that again. Anyway, the cycle ends as I told you: 'Constantine XI Palaeologos (1404-1453), the last emperor of the Byzantine Empire. The poem, clearly, is set in the last days or hours of his life, as the Turks are about to breach the walls of Constantinople, just before his death fighting alongside his 'gallant' friends, preferring death in battle to the torments that Mechmet would have visited upon him . . . knowing the Great Church — the dream and delirious longing of all the barbarians — will soon pass into the hands of an alien creed. . . . I remember it all quite vividly. Well, of course I do: I'm incapable of forgetting anything, since my intellect isn't confined to viscid gray coils of ganglia, as yours is. Pierre's poem is almost evocative of the scene, though it's obviously written by someone who never visited Byzantium. It was all fantastic and vague to him. The Sea of Marmara a stone's throw from every city wall, and the city itself a perfect wilderness of gold and porphyry. It's not even Robert Byron's dragon-green, gong-tormented haunt of serpents. Pierre's was another city, a Constantinople of the mind, a fairy kingdom by the shore of a magical sea, where saints and scholars and emperors floated in clouds of electrum and lapis lazuli."

"Well, how does the poem go, then?"

My friend sighed yet again. "I generally think impatience is a virtue; but it does tend to ruin a good conversation, you know."

I nodded. "Yes, of course. I'm sorry. But how does it go?"

He laughed curtly, shrugged, and said, "Oh, very well . . . yet again. It goes like this . . .":

A dying man, a sinking empire, a flood
Of fire, wind bitterly fruited with blood —
    The twilight melts the streets, shadows enfold
    The tenuous towers and the domes of gold;
The cannons' thunder and the trumpets' blare
Have stilled; he gazes through the smoke-dim air

And sees an ember's glow, now day has died,
Burn where Marmara's pale bright billows glide.

He thinks, Great Holy Wisdom nears eclipse —
I taste God's fiery flesh pressed to my lips —
A thousand years fall short of the desire
And force that through an age's arc aspire
As from the bended bow the arrow flies:
But bowstring breaks . . . arrow falls . . . empire dies.

The distant scratching of the quill halted abruptly, scarcely a second after the last syllable had faded; neither of us spoke for several moments, and for a short while all was still and silent around our small island of light.

5

It was an oddly, almost hypnotically peaceful scene: the milky luculence of white marble, the sallow gleam of brass, the cold shimmer of silver, the hovering, somehow audible hush of the vaulted space overhead . . . the coffering of the ceiling now little more than a pattern of regularly variegated shadows converging upon a slightly lighter area of dully lustrous varnish directly above us . . . high above us . . . and then the brief, sudden flare of a firefly outside the window . . . and there the moist sheen of my friend's gray tie, the dense, heavy gold and green glitter of his ring . . . the stern but vacant expression on his face. I began to feel almost drowsy; at least, my thoughts seemed to be floating away from our conversation in no direction in particular. But at last my friend stirred, raising his glass to his lips, pausing a moment before taking a sip, and remarking, in a quiet voice, "Perhaps I shouldn't have shared the poems with you. I suspect you like that sort of thing too much to see the essential point."

"Oh, I don't know," I said, sitting up a bit more erectly, becoming alert again; "it rather depends on what your point is."

"My point," said my friend, in a tone of mild exasperation, "is *rather* the point of that arrow, precisely where it struck the ground. I don't really care what Pierre's intention was in those sonnets, or even if — as I say — they really are his last statement on things. But I know what breaks through their pretty sugar-glass surface. At least, it's clear to me that at the end, in the ruin of his life — in the ruin he was actively visiting upon *himself* — he caught a glimpse of something irreducibly true. He saw all those shining towers of his imagination and desire and ideals falling to earth, brought to nothing, laid waste. The sadness or wistfulness or whatever it is that pollutes his poems doesn't mean a thing to me; but the knowledge the poems themselves betray does. To know time for what it is — that's the first step towards affirmation . . . real affirmation, of what really *is*, free from reaction or anxiety or melancholy or regret. So perhaps his first step was his last, but . . ."

I could see that a line of conversation that had become intolerably tedious to me was threatening to resume; so — desperate that it not — I interrupted him: "Well, I suppose the final judgment on the meaning of his life — or on his poems — was out of your hands."

My friend scarcely reacted at all — certainly he showed none of the annoyance I had expected at my comment — but merely continued, in a somewhat bored voice. "It matters very little in the end. But there he was, longing to be ravished by transcendental ecstasies and unworldly elations while his poems, relentlessly, were telling another story: the futility, the ultimate emptiness of the great religious, cultural, political, spiritual, aesthetic venture that was the constant mythic backdrop to the little aimless drama of his days — the atmosphere of vanished hopes and absurd expectations on which he nourished his dreams and self-deceptions. Of course I know where his sympathies were concentrated — at the height of the arrow's arc, in the meridian splendor of Byzantium's last great flourishing, with Symeon; but that's not where the truth would allow him to linger, was it? So, there it is. All long ago and exhausted and unavailing now. That's all I mean — those silly poems represent nothing more to me than a momentary awakening before the end, intimations of true vision fitfully descried through his habitual haze of mirages . . ."

"He's at peace now, isn't he?" I said, strangely emboldened to persist in interrupting my friend. "I imagine that's what matters in the end. I mean, *that's* the story you've told me, after all, at least as far as I can tell."

He gazed at me for a few seconds, with a smile so faint and mournful and eyes so indifferent that I thought he would rise any moment to depart. Then, with a slight shake of his head, he swallowed his cordial and set his glass — now all at once empty — on the small table to the right of his chair. "Yes, I know," he said, his voice calm, almost gentle, in fact, "that's what you would think. Men always hear what they choose to hear — it's one of their special gifts. So, then, that's where I suppose we must leave Pierre: afloat in his Elysian daze, suckled on the frothy cream of witless bliss, adrift forever in a universe of joy without strife, wrapped in pearly vapors of sickly, shadowless glory. *Animula, vagula, blandula . . . pallidula . . . nudula . . .* extracted from the morass of blood and fire here below. But, ask yourself, what remains of him then? Everything he was, or just a portion — a pitiful remnant of his life, expurgated and rendered down to an insipid, sticky residue? He was pious and weak and sensitive, that's true, but he wasn't wholly impregnable to dark desires and despair and *sins*," — my friend pronounced this last word with obvious, even laborious irony — "so what was saved in the end, really? Pierre or Pierre's shadow? Him or a thin trace of who he was? The things that were left here below, like an evacuated cocoon — the egoism, the despairs, the slow, self-destructive rage simmering in him in those final days, the addictions, the febrile visions, the rebellions and rejections and negations — were those really only transitory aberrations in his nature, stages through which he was passing, extrinsic conditions? And was the real Pierre just that abstract, featureless quintessence that was carried off to endless serenity?"

"Oh, I don't believe that," I said, now entirely unconcerned about the reaction I might provoke; "I can't believe in a heaven that's some kind of pink, sugary vacuum, or that the soul is just some small fragment broken off of one's life. You're trying to frighten me with Hollywood and Sunday-school kitsch — harps and gold lamé wings and linen robes; you're just trying to scare me with images of such . . . horrid banality that hell looks glamorous by comparison." I was beginning to enjoy the sensation of speaking back to my friend with such unaccustomed vigor. "Existence would have no purpose otherwise. You're simply trying to convince me of something absurd."

My friend merely shrugged and lifted his hands in limp resignation. "So now you think it's a devil's task to make you believe in heaven? Very well. Existence would have no meaning. That's a pathetic argument, you know; and, you know, perhaps we can make the meaningless to have meaning — if we have the will. Anyway," — he turned to his valet and beckoned him with two quick, imperious waves of his left hand — "I'll leave you with your souvenirs and take my leave." As my friend's servant approached, almost gliding across the floor, glowering with that expression of barely concealed indignation that never left his features, my friend directed him towards me with a curt shake of his finger. Without condescending to meet my eyes, "my man" turned slightly in my direction, contemptuously tossed seven leaves of pale yellow parchment into my lap, and then turned again fully to his master. "Go down," my friend said to him after a moment, in a harsh, impatient tone, "and bring the car around. Wait for me; I'll descend presently."

"Very good, sir" was the inevitable reply, sharp, soft, somewhere between a whisper and a growl; then, inclining his head forward a fraction and turning about, he left the room with an unnatural suddenness and an even more unnatural silence.

My friend said nothing for a moment; then, without turning his eyes from the door through which his valet had departed, he remarked, "I think I'll dress him in fustian hereafter. Lately — the last century or so — I've taken a fancy to livery of more pavonine hues; but, when one is dressed like a peacock, one is tempted to behave like a peacock. I suspect that too much color has excited an unfortunate dignity in him, which it would be well to extinguish before it takes flame. Anyway," he sighed, now looking at me, "I absolutely refuse to start beating him again: the psychic exertion wouldn't be particularly great, given our current relative strengths, but to my mind everything that's already been done is a cliché. Which is, I suppose, the most serious reproach I would bring against Pierre. Or against you, I think."

"What reproach is that?"

"What I find myself wondering, when I think back on that young, brilliant, delicate lad, is just this: When was his *now?* When did he ever enjoy that perfectly private moment in which he was simply himself — that moment without which none of us ever really knows himself? When was there a real instant for him, if you follow me, free from past or future, pregnant with possibilities not heaped upon his back by all the generations that came before? That one moment of ecstatic self-forgetting and terrible self-knowledge when he was allowed his transgressive adventure and time of experiment, his time for the art of violation, his days of blasphemous liberty — his season in hell, as Rimbaud put it? His freedom to experience the extremes of things, to descend into a purifying derangement of the senses. . . . Well, if it ever came for him, it was there at the very end, wasn't it? For just that once he *wasn't* a cliché."

"I don't know about that," I said. "I mean, isn't transgression something of a cliché also? Or drunkenness or addiction? Or the death of a failed poet in a Parisian garret? Or death by broken heart? Actually, I'm beginning to wonder whether you've made the whole story up, it has so many operatic elements."

My friend's face at last seemed to betray the first signs of real displeasure; it would have required only a slightly more pronounced narrowing of his eyes for his features to take on an expression of genuine wrath. "Devils do not write poems," he said in a frigid voice, "even if we do translate them. The translation of poetry is a properly diabolical art; its composition, however, is beneath us."

I looked, for the first time, at the thin, stiff, softly golden pages his valet had left with me; I lifted them from my lap and glanced at them long enough to take note of the perfect penmanship with which each poem had been transcribed, and of how oddly, depressingly stark and grim the italic shapes of the letters seemed. I resolved immediately to copy the sonnets out in my own hand when I reached home that night and to destroy the originals. "No," I said, looking up at my friend again, "that I believe. All right, I'll take these as proof. So it's a true story."

"I only tell it to you, after all," my friend continued, somewhat mollified, "as a cautionary epitome. What need would I have to fabricate anything so elaborate in order to make so simple a point? It happened to rise to the surface of my thoughts as we were talking — a tale about where too much dwelling on the past can lead . . . the lethal effects nostalgia can have on otherwise healthy organisms." He smiled now. "We got onto this topic only because I described you as a kind of conservative, as I recall — which, vague though it may be, is an apt description of your general temper. You do believe so very much in the past, don't you? Or, at any rate, in your indistinct — educated, but indistinct — impression of the past. And you can bring yourself to have no greater hope for the future than that it will consent to be a faithful continuation of the past."

"This is all very general," I said; "it's hardly a simple matter . . ."

"Tradition," he said, taking no notice of my protest, "the patrimony of an ancient civilization that could scarcely be deader — the ceaseless, pointless labor of preserving and passing on while all the bulwarks continue to disintegrate and all the dams continue to break apart before the pressure of time. It's quite asinine — stubborn and incorrigibly self-indulgent. The story of Pierre Gernet isn't important — I needn't have brought it up, except to satisfy a whim — because all I'm doing is attempting to communicate a bit of practical philosophy to you, for the sake of your future sanity and happiness and peace of mind. All right? All I hope you'd remember to think upon is the sheer terrific fecundity of the now — *the now* — which it's a crime to allow to slip away unexploited and unenjoyed. The now, I mean, liberated from past and future alike, or from the future understood as a mere mirror of the past; I'm talking about *this* moment, *this* rupture in the fabric and flow of time, *this* instant of the possible, which is something so precious and fleeting and *impossible* to call back. This is the event as such, the only event, eternally repeated and unrepeatable. Its energy is boundless: an absolute end and an absolute beginning, if only you're willing to seize it with a perfect, spontaneous, radical movement of the will, free of all moral, metaphysical, or sentimental preconceptions or loyalties or apprehensions. Try, just try, for even a moment, to see the world that way. Waken from your slumber, if you can. Just to try it on, so to speak. The past as prologue, passé, the future resolved into a pure futurity, an endless sequence of nows, one break with the past after another, always starting anew . . . interminable adventure . . . year zero, as those merry ironists in the Khmer Rouge liked to say . . ."

"I see," I said, realizing for perhaps the first time just how monotonously repetitive my friend could be. "Well, I'll take your counsels to heart and . . ."

But he could not yet be deterred: "Fields, farms, and forests," he said with another of his sighs; "faith, custom, and ceremony; ancient allegiances, momentary fidelities, babes yet unborn and trees still uncut . . . clinging to the transient as though it were eternal, and to eternity as if it were a kind of life. It's all such nonsense in the end. Everything that springs to life succumbs sooner or later to time's fire, to the turning of Fortuna's wheel; thanatos quells the brief, idiot élan of eros. That's the first wisdom worth possessing, and the last. It's only when you're willing to rescue yourself from subservience to the perishable that you're able to embrace the real energy of becoming that underlies this whole empty pageant — the illusory play of forms and figures and actions and souls, the opiate of beauty, the diversions of duty. Underneath it all, where there are no essences or substances to cling to, no enticing phantoms to torment desire and imprison the mind, there endures the only truly permanent thing: becoming, arising and perishing, the infinite speed of a passage from nothing to nothing, where creation and destruction are one and the same . . . a single indivisible flux. Not participation in some higher realm of eternal forms and ideal truths to which time must be made obedient, but infinite and pure rupture, pure apostasy from the nothing and from being alike. It's a realm of absolute possibility, where *only* the will is real. And that, and that alone, is freedom."

"Surely there's no such thing as pure becoming," I said suddenly, rather emphatically, "or a pure now. Or will without memory. It would be nothing at all, surely."

"Yes," he said, his eyes and his smile widening, his voice beginning to acquire a familiar tone, not so much enthusiastic as appetent, "yes, and everything. That's the place where . . ."

I wanted to silence him now more than ever; my vague feeling of general vexation had begun to degenerate into a somewhat more acute sense of revulsion, both at the inexorable circularity of our conversation and at the — suddenly very apparent — smallness of his philosophy. "You know," I said, quite loudly, clearly meaning to curtail his latest disquisition before it took wing again, "what you haven't told me is what became of Eugénie."

"What?" At last he had been brought up short. "Oh, well, I hadn't thought that would matter. Do you really care? Why, what do you want to know about her?"

"Well, how did Pierre's death affect her? She must have heard of it, surely — her brother would have surely found . . ."

"Must you keep saying 'surely' so often? Yes, she heard of it, almost two months after. How do you expect it affected her? She wept, of course; she was desolate. I mean, she'd been very fond of him, and even if he'd shrunk — or, rather, expanded — to the proportions of an ornamental fiction of her inner life, she wasn't inhuman. He'd also been a real person to her, after all, and she'd been almost as attached to him as she was now to the revised memory of him that she'd already learned to treasure with such grateful despondency. She was utterly inconsolable for a very long time, and she grieved for him with a fine, only partly self-conscious abandon that everyone who knew her admired immensely. At her age, of course, and with her education, and coming from her class, I doubt she could have made any clear separation of the genuine from the fictional elements in her feelings, or of the sincere from the theatrical. It would have been unrealistic to expect it of her. She did suffer, though, I assure you, quite earnestly — or, at least, she was earnestly convinced of her complete earnestness; but, of course, she also took pains to suffer with poetic grace: she was, at some level, always conscious of how she appeared, even if only to herself. The tears were certainly copious, though, and the feelings of hopelessness and of something precious and irretrievably lost were all quite authentic; of that I think we need have no doubt. Her diary — which she neglected for a week after hearing the news — came finally to bristle with professions of epic misery and to writhe with long, incoherent concatenations of 'oh, my poor, dear, young . . .' and 'my gentle, kind . . .' and 'my brilliant, young . . .' and 'poor, poor dear . . .' and 'never,

never . . .' and 'how can I ever . . .' and 'I can't . . .' and 'oh, never, never will I . . .' and so on, full of tremolos and in ever more colorful and emphatic — if ever less expressive — combinations. Yes, it was all quite painful for her; and, of course, quite perfect. I mean — and you shouldn't pass judgment on her — Pierre's death did give such a finish to the story of her first love. Now he was forever exquisitely frozen in his frail, perishing beauty and in his ever more mythic youthfulness, passionate and full of promise and so very in love. Well, anyway, love is always equal parts fantasy and biochemistry, and for a pretty girl of twenty . . ." He paused for a moment, evidently reflecting upon something that had just occurred to him. "I suppose, really, that the sequel was rather interesting, now that I think about it. There's a rather . . . touching story attached to it all."

"Touching?"

"Oh, exceedingly touching — if, that is, one is susceptible to being touched. For myself, I must confess to being entirely . . . *intangible* in that regard." He smiled in the general direction of his shoes, evidently pleased with his witticism. "But I can recognize charm when it insists on thrusting itself upon me. You see, neither Robert nor she was aware that Pierre had died till he was well interred, and after Robert had returned home to console her, and after her first, second, and third hysterical convulsions of grief had subsided, and just as her father's impatience with the profligacy of her lamentations had finally overwhelmed his tepidly affected air of solemn pity for his daughter's deceased paramour and he had begun insisting that she pull herself together, the two siblings resolved to go to Paris the following month to visit Pierre's grave. Well, actually, in point of fact, both were engaged to be in Paris then in any event, to attend a ball; Robert was to escort his sister. It was to be quite a splendid affair, and thereafter they were to stay on in Paris for an indefinite period. Robert had taken — or, rather, his father had purchased — a house in the city, a large, well-lit urban mansion with a small enclosed garden, and had had it furnished, and staff had already gone ahead, and two new maids and a cook and a gardener had been hired in Paris. Eugénie, naturally, spoke of the ball now as if it no longer meant anything to her — how could it possibly? — and Robert told her he knew this already; but, even so, she never actually said that she didn't intend to go, nor did Robert suggest she should not. After all, she dolefully mused, it was all arranged, and it gave her an occasion for visiting the graveside of her poor, poor, dear et cetera to which her father could scarcely raise any objection. She would simply have to go and make as good a presentation of herself as she could through her bereavement. Which, in the event, is precisely what she did: both her prodigious charm and her magnificent sorrow were on full display at the ball, in so enchantingly balanced an amalgamation that scarcely anyone who attended could talk of the night afterward without adverting to her sadness and her bravery and her grace and her utterly incandescent beauty. But I shouldn't get ahead of myself, as all that came afterward. In preparation for the journey, Robert made inquiries regarding the whereabouts of Pierre's remains. He had no idea what Pierre's parish had been, and he had never thought to wonder what sort of sepulture was accorded the indigent, but he wrote — I believe — to the office of the coroner, or to some acquaintance he and Pierre had shared; he did not write to me, in any event. Actually, the details of this part of the story are somewhat obscure to me, as I was in Istanbul at the time, and the two subordinates I had left behind to keep an eye on things were of so quarrelsome a nature that they were incapable of conducting the most elementary reconnaissances without arguing furiously over who was to go and who to stay behind; but I know that there was some clerical mishap, or some comical misunderstanding along the way, or some confusion regarding whose death was at issue, and the long and short of it is that Robert was given the name of a graveyard where he could find Pierre's headstone that was entirely wrong. Pierre was a mile and a half away, without any headstone at all, as it happens. This would have been only an inconvenience had the two siblings not waited till the day of the ball itself to attempt their visit to the grave. But they had arrived in Paris only a week before, and what with one thing and another — a necessary last-moment alteration of Eugénie's gown, a number of quite unavoidable calls at the homes of socially important friends and acquaintances of Robert's or of the family's, a night spent at the opera (Eugénie on the arm of one of Robert's dashing and wealthy friends and Robert accompanied by his newest mistress) — they simply had been unable to make time for the tender ceremony on which they'd agreed. Robert, I think, preferred not to see where Pierre was buried in any event, and so failed to urge the trip to the graveyard with any force; he had, as I say, loved his friend, and had known Pierre far longer than Eugénie had, and of course he couldn't fall back upon the sort of consolations that his sister's lovely, dark, romantic fable of lost love provided her. At last, though, on the day itself, in those fallow hours stretching between Eugénie's rising from bed (a little before noon) and her light meal and early evening nap before dressing for the ball (which began at midnight), the two of them betook themselves to the little churchyard where they believed Pierre's grave was to be found. The day was very gray, somewhat chillier than might have been expected, and a strong metallic fragrance of rain was in the air. Eugénie had written out a letter upon two gilded sheets of her loveliest stationery to leave at the graveside, had sealed it in a heliotrope envelope, and had tied it by a small, black silk ribbon to a single red rose; she had accoutered herself in something very like mourning — mostly black with something vaguely approximating a veil, a scarf of black gauze that she draped very prettily from her hat and along one cheek and around her throat — had brought tears to her eyes with little effort, and had composed her thoughts carefully in preparation for the few, broken, whispered confidences she intended to speak over the grave once she had asked her brother to leave her and stand a little distance off. All was in readiness. They summoned their barouche, made their way to the church, and entered the yard with a stately and measured gait, solemn, dignified, saying nothing as they walked; then, when Robert had left Eugénie to rest upon a bench under a tree in one corner of the cemetery, he went to search for the headstone. I expect I needn't describe for you the states of mind through which he passed as he walked again and again among the rows looking for the grave — the growing anxiety or annoyance, the moments of positive exasperation, the small seizures of despair. Most of the graves were plainly too old, in any case, and it was not long before he realized that there were no new headstones anywhere to be seen. Finally, after more than twenty minutes, he did discover what appeared to be two graves recently dug, very near one another at the north end of the churchyard, neither of them marked, and concluded that one of these must be Pierre's. He went to tell Eugénie, who was obviously becoming somewhat agitated as she waited for him to bring her word, anxious as she was to discharge her part in the day's solemnities with grace but also with some expedition. She was more than a little dismayed at Robert's tidings and found herself uncertain what to do; after several minutes of indecision on her part, Robert decided to take one more survey of the grounds and left her again, only to return with the same news a quarter hour later. Now Eugénie's eyes began to fill with tears, which affected her brother — with his deep tenderness for his sister — profoundly, especially given his own misery; he took her hands and spoke to her with rare gentleness and kissed her upon her damp cheek and told her not to fret, and when she was somewhat calmer, he left her again and entered the church. No one was there, so he left again and walked around the premises to see if he could find a rear door or quarters where a priest might live. All he found was an ancient gardener — of small and malnourished build and with a hideous face rather like a dissolute troll's — who was pulling up weeds from around the church foundations by hand. Robert practically had to shout before this withered little homunculus — staring at Robert stupidly out of watery eyes, from below drooping lids, and constantly licking a pendulous lower lip — finally understood what he was being asked; he informed Robert, in a somewhat slurred, sibilant, and expectorant way, that he was himself the church's gravedigger and could assure Robert that no young man lay buried in either of the recently used plots: one contained an elderly bank clerk who had died in his sleep, and the other a middle-aged woman florist who had been killed when a horse-cart had rolled back against her, thrown her down, and caused her to strike her head against a curbstone. At first Robert insisted that the old man must be mistaken, but the odd, crooked little creature was both adamant and obviously lucid (if not particularly agile) of mind, and Robert finally understood that he'd been sent to the wrong place; so — having no wish at that moment to expose Eugénie to the old gardener's repulsive face, or his swampy diction, or its epiphenomenal spittle — he simply gave the warped little goblin some money and returned to the tree where his sister waited. He expected Eugénie to dissolve into a fit of weeping, but in fact she bore the news with considerable equanimity; tears still glittered prettily in her eyes, of course, as much as they could on so cloudy a day, and a few inarticulate moans of unhappiness issued from her lips, but soon she gathered her wits and will together and began to consider what she should do next. Robert said that they could attempt again to find Pierre's true resting place — perhaps he could write someone even today, or visit some official bureau or other while she returned home to eat and sleep — and that on another day — they'd be in Paris, after all, for months — they could at last make their visit to Pierre's grave. At first, she seemed to be considering Robert's suggestion; she gazed away into the distance, saying nothing, merely running one fingertip lightly back and forth along the edge of the heliotrope envelope where it lay in her lap. The truth is that, for some reason — emotional, aesthetic, what have you — she desperately wanted to 'finish the tale,' so to speak, before the night came and brought with it the *brilliant* occasion that had filled her imagination for some time now. Somehow the ball had come to represent in her mind some sort of conclusion — tragic, ironic, lyrical, or something of the sort — to the story of her 'first love.' She could not conceive of leaving things unfinished now, or even imagine what effort of will could prompt her to attempt such an expedition again, at the wrong time, once the narrative had been so awkwardly interrupted. So, after a few moments, dropping her gaze to the rose and letter in her lap, she quietly told Robert that, after all, it had been so painful to come to this place, and that she wasn't sure she could prepare herself again, and that Pierre would understand if . . . ; and then, after a few more moments, she raised her eyes to Robert's and told him that he was wrong to accept the word of a senile gardener so credulously and that Pierre's grave was certainly one of the two recently dug — after all, how many newly dead people could there really be in the city? And then, when Robert said nothing, but merely gazed back at her with an expression of quizzical tenderness, she looked down again and in a soft, almost pouting voice repeated her assertion that Pierre was here, nearby — she could feel it — and claimed that she would know which of the graves was his. Robert again said nothing; so, after several more moments, without looking at her brother, Eugénie rose and resolutely, if slowly, walked to the northern end of the cemetery. Robert watched her as she came to a halt about midway between the two new graves and for several moments held the sort of pose one might perhaps — if one were to see someone strike it in a *tableau* at a salon — associate with a kind of vatic trance, or some sort of mystic communion with a realm of higher sensibility or intuition. As she stood there, though, rain began to fall, lightly but with an ominous persistence; Eugénie raised a hand to her hat after a few seconds, as if startled, and then, her auguries abruptly concluded, she turned hastily to her right and delicately kneeled — or, more accurately, folded her legs beneath her skirt and half-reclined — at the edge of the grave that she had obviously elected as Pierre's as soon as she had become aware of the rain. As her back was still to him, Robert could not tell if she were speaking, though he was sure she was. After a minute or so, the rain began to grow harder; Eugénie glanced up anxiously at the sky and then turned back to the soft, greening mound of soil beneath which the dead woman florist lay peacefully moldering, no doubt whispered a few more fervent words of farewell to her darling Pierre, placed the flower and the letter at what she wrongly imagined was the head of the grave, where soon they would be thoroughly soaked, and rose hurriedly to rejoin her brother, who watched her return with an expression of kindly and slightly melancholy acceptance on his face. He took her arm, fondly patted her hand, and the two of them returned to their carriage; she began crying more volubly as they walked, and again assured him — in a voice almost desperately insistent — that this was indeed the correct graveyard, she was certain of it, and that that had definitely been Pierre's grave, she knew it with an absolute conviction; and he said that, yes, he too was certain of it, he knew it now, he could feel it himself, and she had done precisely the right thing; and, as he helped her in under the unfurled canopy of the barouche and kissed her once more upon her cheek and drew her head to rest on his shoulder while she wept, he thought to himself, once again, that his sister was after all still very young, and somewhat silly, and extremely accomplished, and very sweet at heart; and he thought, also, of how much he loved her and how much he missed his friend and how little it mattered to him where Pierre was buried, since all he cared to know was that he could never speak to his friend again. And when they had returned home and he had seen Eugénie sup on soup and fish and assorted friands, and then ascend the stairs with her maid to undress and sleep, he went out into the garden; the rain had passed, leaving in its wake a soft, moist breeze rinsed of all impurities, a marvelous, cool, fragrant freshness all around, a slight taste of silver in the air, golden sunlight erratically flickering from behind small, swiftly thinning clouds, tiny diamond flashes of iridescence on every side, and the sweet crystal crepitations of dripping eaves. He smoked a cigar, stared at the glistening, tawny gravel of the garden path without really focusing his eyes, and for a while quietly shed tears. Then, after going back into the house and changing his clothes, he went to keep an assignation with his favorite mistress. He too wished to rest before the ball."

After several moments of silence, I breathed deeply and attempted a wry smile. "You certainly have a gift for telling a tale in a sinister way," I remarked.

"Oh, nonsense," said my friend, almost affably; "if I were being malicious, I would scarcely tell you of Robert's tears, or even acknowledge that any element of Eugénie's grief was authentic. If you find my rendering of her behavior sinister, I submit you're the one who's showing little compassion for human frailty. A girl of twenty, sheltered all her short life from the harder edges of reality, who'd suffered a brief, intense infatuation with an eccentric, sickly, otherworldly man and who was scarcely old or wise enough to know how deep her own feelings went . . . well, really, what do you expect?"

I shrugged and then nodded. "Yes," I said, "all right, that's fair."

"After all, in my experience it seems a fairly universal condition of your race that you're often forced to adjust your feelings to accommodate combinations of emotions to which your various individual natures are instrumentally inadequate; it's a sort of psychological *scordatura,* so to speak, a sort of downward re-attunement of your inward parts that lets you — at the very least — approximate the . . . the music of richer hearts, let's say. Otherwise you'd all be entirely defeated by the intractable limitations of your own organs of sentiment any time you were confronted by demands for magnitudes of sympathy or emotional wisdom for which you've no real natural aptitude. And, forgive me for sounding so moralistic, but it seems to me that one should adjust one's expectations of others in accord with their limitations. Isn't that what you'd call . . . charity?"

"Yes, of course. I understand all that. I'm scarcely someone who has a right to be sanctimonious on that score." Then, after a pause of several seconds, I asked, "Did she ever come to . . . think more clearly about the whole affair? Did she — do you know? — did she think of Pierre much in later years?"

"Oh, yes, most emphatically. Yes, indeed. In fact, thinking about Pierre became very much a vital part of her character — her atmosphere, as I like to say."

"In what way?"

"In an *artful* way, of course." He smiled now as if genuinely amused. "She was a minor artist, obviously, and her only production was her own life, and her only materials her body and mind and circumstances; but she worked tirelessly upon the details, and perfected them to the utmost limits of her inspiration and eye for proportion. And in everything she did with herself there was an enchanting quality of naïveté, the innocence of the passionate, unreflective poetess, warbling woodnotes wild, who can't really distinguish between artifice and nature and who, as a result, is never guilty of insincerity — or of sincerity, for that matter. She was her own fiction; her fiction was her true self; by the end, one could no more separate the one from the other than separate lightning from its own flashing. She simply was."

"Ah. Yes. I don't suppose you could be more concrete, perhaps? I'm only curious . . ."

"Yes. I can. And yes, of course you are, I know. Well, to begin with, you should know that, less than two years after Pierre's death, she married a suitable man: a dozen years her senior, the scion of an established banking clan with a deeply rooted and widely ramifying family tree, to one branch of which had even accrued a minor title some generations earlier; he was her inferior in certain aspects of general culture, but of a naturally commanding and confident nature, capable of providing for her as she required and of gently discouraging some of her more impetuous whims, conscious of her social graces and station, and really quite devoted to her. She, it may disappoint you to learn, seemed to find his air of natural confidence and competence rather appealing, and probably formed an attachment to him more earnest than anything produced by her infatuation with Pierre. I doubt she — as you might say — *loved* him, at least not past a certain point of calm affection and occasional glandular agitation; but he did carry himself extremely well, he was handsome, he rode with an excellent seat, and he was able to excite a degree of girlish fascination in her at the right moments. Her father, needless to say, was exceedingly pleased with the union; he tended to think bankers little more than glorified merchants and merchants little more than aggrandized peasants, and of course he suspected anyone involved in banking or finance of having some Jewish blood in his veins; but on satisfying himself as to the young man's purity of pedigree and enormous wealth, he did everything he could, in his maladroit and obvious way, to encourage a speedy engagement and marriage; anyway, to his mind, at twenty-two his daughter was already five years late in coming to the altar. Eugénie's husband was, in fact, a kind if somewhat boring man. Of his young wife he expected nothing more onerous than that she adorn his home and social engagements with the special diaphanous sparkle of her beauty and charm, and that she bear him children. The latter duty she discharged every bit as diligently as the former. She was more than amenable to her husband's caresses — her fantastical habits of thought did nothing to impair her animal vitality — and she discovered she rather liked having children, actually. In fact, she had eleven in all: four boys and seven girls. Her eldest child, Robert, was born in 1902 and so was too young to fight in the Great War; but she lost her daughter Louise — four years old at the time — to the Spanish influenza in 1919; and her youngest son, Jean-Louis, was killed in the Second World War. She was, though, survived by nine of her children when she died in 1965, at the age of eighty-seven, some twenty-seven years after her husband's death, and eighteen after her brother's. I think we can say that she was, apart from her bereavements, quite happy, especially as she had more than sufficient time over the years to work upon the finer details of the fiction of her life. She never knew want; not even during the wars did her husband's fortunes suffer — though he himself certainly did, losing his left arm below the elbow in 1916. Anyway, there was certainly nothing her husband would deny her if she asked winsomely enough. They lived half the time in Paris, the other half in their country home, about sixty miles north of where she'd grown up; and on the grounds of the latter she convinced her husband to build her a sort of small summer house at the far reaches of their extensive gardens. I say small, though many a lower middle-class family would have considered it a perfectly respectable home. Had Eugénie's husband obeyed his own initial impulses, it would have been something far more lavish, on the order of a small replica of the *Petit Trianon,* bedizened with oriental opulences and exorbitances and flourishes, and imbricated with all kinds of shining gauds and baubles; he was a sober man of business, it's true, but where his wife was concerned, he was somewhat given to *le grand geste;* he never really lost his desire to impress her, nor his sense that he wasn't quite her equal in derivation or refinement. Eugénie, however, prevailed upon him to reduce the scale of his generosity; she wanted nothing that suggested vulgar ostentation, as she had a very precise purpose in mind in asking for the house; and so, in the end, he provided her with what one might describe as an uncommonly spacious and well-appointed cottage, to which was adjoined a small greenhouse with a roof of emerald glass. To this little house she would retreat sometimes for the whole day, taking only a maid to tend to her needs; and here, over a period of some years, she gathered to herself a carefully selected circle of female friends who would come in various numbers — as few as two, as many as eight — to sit with her through the afternoons, at the western side of the house, with its large windows, to talk and share confidences and consume English teas, to laugh and gently malign their husbands and tell tales of their children, to delight in the marvelous beauty of countless sunsets, and — above all — to hear Eugénie recount, again and again, the story of her childhood and of her first love. That summer house, to tell the truth, was the crucible in which — patiently, unrelentingly, with infinite care — Eugénie forged her final self and purged away everything impure, imperfect, superfluous, and inconsonant. It was, I think, some time in her middle or late forties that her great work assumed its ultimate and perfect shape; the hesitant, inchoate, dreamy sketches of her nonage, the constant revisions of the design as she ripened into her first fecund womanhood, the new bride's constantly revised waxen models, the gradual dissipation of the delirious haze of youth before the clear outlines of a mother's more exact ideas and more resolute aspirations, then the final choice of medium and materials, and the first experimental moldings and flawed castings — all of that finally had its consummation in that exquisite, darkly shining, airy, but imperishable bronze. Thereafter, her office changed from that of artist to that of curator and critic, and all that was really incumbent upon her was to see that the figure she'd produced kept its fine high gleaming polish, and to shield it from any shock that might mar its surface, and to keep it from the gaze of unappreciative philistines, and faithfully and indefatigably to call attention to its subtler details and bolder lines and cunning complexities and haunting enigmas and clever conceits. To this office her devotion never lapsed, except during those terrible periods that followed upon the death of one of her children; and from those shadows she both times emerged — when she emerged — an even more devout votary in the temple she'd built to shelter her masterpiece. She was, I suppose you'd have to say, a true believer. She'd been patient in her craft, during those years of uncomplaining labor, and had never thought — as far as I can tell — to ask herself what it was she was doing, who she was, or any of those tedious, morose, precious questions that pompous moralists think one should ask oneself; everything had been accomplished with absolute care and absolute conviction. And I don't think I can exaggerate how vital an ingredient Pierre provided in that complicated, mysterious alchemy of twilight and flowers and feminine scrutiny and sentimental confabulation and slowly shifting memories. He occupied for her — in her conversation and, so, in her imagination — the place of the gentle lover lost long ago, the indispensable and unalterable romantic myth — formally unalterable, at least, if not materially; and around him she constantly wove an ever more intricate filigree of fancy and solemn happiness and serene sadness. She acquired the habit, after a few years, of referring to Pierre — when she spoke of him to her little circle of confidantes — as 'that boy,' 'that lad,' 'that *garçon*,' in a voice of wistful, aching sweetness; but she never spoke of him at all until the crepuscular light had risen in the west, and now and then, while she was telling her tale, she would pause upon a fading note and turn her eyes to the dying daylight and stare into the distance, as if suddenly called away by a quiet inner voice to some golden moment in a long-distant past, or perhaps to some cool and timeless sylvan place, far from all their forgotten voices, beside a quiet river, where she might gaze for a while obliviously at its glassy surface and at the dim green shadows cast upon its dark, softly flowing waters by ancient trees, while farther downstream, out of sight, around a bend, a barque of spectral gray and silver glided silently away, bearing its phantom passengers into the perpetual evening of the lands of the dead; and her friends would wait in sympathetic silence for her to resume her narrative, exchanging glances of pained solicitude with one another, or perhaps one would venture, after some moments, to lay a gentle hand upon her wrist to summon her back kindly to the present, and she would stir herself with a distracted and mournfully blissful look in her eyes, and a desolate, sagacious smile, and then an expression of shared but ineffable understanding, and her friends would nod and think her quite touching and profound and strange and unutterably, wisely dolorous, and she would think it herself, quite without dissimulation or guile or any sense of dramatic pretense, while the evening shadows wrapped themselves about her; and, seeing herself reflected thus, in the bright mirrors of their admiration, the visage of that emotional fiction — or semi-fiction, really — became her true face, at least as she saw it in her own mind, and that lovely, wordless grief became the secret, murmurous music of her . . . oh, *unfathomable* heart. So . . . well, so, you see. Pierre enjoyed that much earthly immortality, after all, even if all his works and longings came to naught. And, really, maybe that was a richer posterity than he would have had if all of that ridiculous, stifled, sterile scholarship and laboriously mannered verse had survived, like the dry, flaking cerements of a mummy, to be dithered over by the boring little men of later generations. She kept him ever with her, desperately and fondly, like a corsage kept frozen and unfading by an American girl to commemorate her first formal dance. In Eugénie's later years, when she'd become a graceful and venerable widow with a majestic profile, clad in lace and dowager's sables, aglow with all the lost elegance of another age, she retired more or less permanently to her summer house, where visitors continued to call, and Pierre's ghost or shadow or echo faithfully danced attendance upon her to the very last. His absent presence or present absence — or whatever you'd call it — suffused the air with the purple hue and heavy fragrance of lilacs. And who can say, really, that that wasn't how he'd have wanted it? Perhaps he would have been pleased to know he had afforded her such solace . . . so inexhaustible a wellspring of . . . well, again, of atmosphere."

6

The expression on my friend's face was so oddly serene, and he seemed so perfectly at ease, that I began to doubt he was going to leave after all. This troubled me, since just at that moment I wanted nothing so much as his departure. His story, I was certain, had reached its end, or — if not — would simply meander on in a sort of bleak montage, each successive episode drained yet a little further of any element of human sweetness; and the sound of his voice — its relentless, pitilessly regular, almost incantatory cadence — had all at once become unbearable for me. I was at a loss to divine what his purpose was in telling me his tale, or whether he had succeeded or failed in inducing in me the mood he desired; but I knew that it would be foolish to doubt the subtlety of the diabolic mind, or to imagine that I was immune to whatever spell he meant to weave. But I was uncertain what to say. Of course, I knew I could leave first if I chose, pleading fatigue or another engagement; but it seemed to me that nothing I might say of that sort would sound particularly convincing. So I made a show of looking through the poems in my lap again, shuffling the pages slowly for several moments, while I attempted to think of some way to draw our conversation to a close as quickly and courteously as possible.

"I like the abysses," I said at last, more softly than I intended.

"Excuse me," my friend replied, as if roused from deep reflection; "what's that?"

"The abysses," I repeated; "I like the way the Symeon sonnet ends with the abyss of divine beauty and then the Psellus sonnet immediately turns down to the abyss of matter. It's a clever transition — ecstasy and then despondency — rather like Symeon's descriptions of the mystical life."

"Oh, well, of course. Yes, I see what you mean. Well, that's just what I . . ."

"*Accidie,*" I said suddenly, the thought having occurred to me even as I spoke it.

Again he appeared to be taken somewhat off his guard. "I'm sorry, what?"

"You're trying to induce *accidie* in me."

My friend raised his eyebrows and stared at me with an expression of frank amusement. "Now, how do you arrive at that brilliant little deduction?"

"Well," I said, shrugging slightly, "you're clearly not trying to turn me into an atheist or a materialist; you're not trying to make me deny God or the soul. I suppose you can't, really, given what I know of your history. I mean, who would take a materialist demon seriously? But you do seem intent on making it all seem somehow inconsequential and dreary — heaven, hell, good, evil."

"But surely you must be aware," he said, his smile becoming broader, his voice mockingly smooth, "*accidie* is the office of the noonday devil, and

I — as you well know — am a spirit of the night . . . a companion of the bat and the owl." He shook his head, and a barely audible laugh issued from behind his unparted lips. "Really, I had no idea you thought I was intriguing against you. Actually, I talk to you because I enjoy doing so. I'm rather hurt to discover that you suspect me of some secret design upon your . . . what, your virtue? Your soul? What a morbid imagination you have. I don't care about any of that. I never did, really; in the modern world, that sort of thing . . . And even if I were the sort of vulgar little imp who slips in over monks' window ledges to torment the poor, deranged wretches with salacious apparitions and whispered blasphemies, I wouldn't waste my efforts on you. You're not really a hero of the spirit, now, are you? Do you really believe anything, other than that God is a very appealing idea, and that you'd like to live forever in some shady deer park above the clouds?"

At once I felt abashed — not necessarily because I believed his protestations of innocence, but only because his final rebuke was embarrassingly just. "Yes," I said, very quietly, "well . . . yes, I suppose not."

"Anyway, as it happens, I *am* a materialist; I'm not at all certain I see any sense in the notion of 'pure spirit,' and I tend to think in terms of subtler and grosser forms of materiality — though I'll grant that materialism for me is not really a metaphysical prejudice so much as an ideological commitment. And the existence of higher levels of corporeity is no better evidence of the reality of a transcendent 'God' than is the existence of any other sort of material thing. But, all that aside, you've managed to invert my meaning entirely. At least, you've got the emphasis wrong. I'm not trying to deaden your will, but awaken it. I just mean to say that time hurries on; it soon overtakes you. At the end, you might realize how much time you've squandered, or how many of your deepest vital impulses you allowed to dissipate in dreams and uncertainties and diffuse longings. But then it's over and . . . time devours you and leaves nothing behind, unless you're one of those rare, bold wills who take the chaos of time in their hands and fashion something remarkable — some prodigy of creativity and destructiveness — and make meaning out of meaninglessness. Now, how very cunning do I have to be to tell you that? But it's definitely *will*, not talent, that makes the difference. Pierre's story is tragic because he had an abundance of talent, and perhaps even a touch of genius; what he could never summon up in himself — until the end, at least — was the power of the will to reject or to affirm according to its own forces. He lacked the brutal, noble exuberance that would have vied with time, or nature, or God, or what have you, rather than allow itself to die out unanswered, unconquering. . . . He could have been another Rimbaud, or Nietzsche, or Byron, perhaps. . . . Anyway, I think you're tired of hearing me repeat myself, aren't you?"

I smiled what I hoped looked like a genial smile and nodded. "Yes, that's probably true. It's getting late. And, anyway, I don't think I can quite be persuaded to see the man you've described as such a waste."

"Really?" My friend leaned forward, as if preparing to rise. "In the end, you know, he was just a shadow that passed along the peripheries of other lives. A pretty ornament that glittered just at the edge of sight — or, really, not even that, but just a fugitive trick of the light. Part of the stage scenery in someone else's silly melodrama. A tale to be told over cognac. He came to nothing."

"Well, if his literary remains had been left intact, perhaps . . ."

"I doubt it. But that's not worth speculating on. It's all locked away up here now," he said, lightly tapping his forehead with his right forefinger, "till the end of days, or whatever the phrase is." A single curt laugh now broke from his lips; he shook his head and looked at me with something approximating a grin. "Now isn't that a curious little habit I've acquired down here among you sophistical apes? I've just made an anthropomorphism of myself. Here I am pointing to my head as if I had discrete organs and kept my intellect stored in something as revolting as an animal brain. I might just as well have pointed at my toe. I may have been forced to exchange an ethereal for an aerial frame all those ages ago, but my degradation goes no farther than that. We're vital in every part, as Milton says. All my life is fixed forever in the simplicity of my substance." He nodded to himself, his expression becoming somewhat soberer. "Fixed forever." He stared at me again, with only the remotest of smiles. Then, after a few seconds, he said, "Well, let's take our leave of one another, then — all right?" And, at once, in a single fluid motion so wholly devoid of any sign of effort, sinew, or gravity that it would have been impossible for any normally corporeal being, he rose to his feet.

Startled, I rather awkwardly gathered together the poems from my lap and rose from my chair. "Yes, right then," I said with a cough. "Thanks for your hospitality, as always."

"You needn't go yet," said my friend affably, "if you'd care to enjoy the solitude for a bit longer. The room is permanently reserved for my use. I'm sorry to leave you here, but I can tell them downstairs to bring you some coffee before you set out. I know you take it especially strong. Would you like that?"

"Yes," I replied. "Thank you. That would be very welcome."

"Good, I'll see to that. Well, then . . ." And he extended his hand to me, though with his arm rigidly straight, more or less at the level of my collar, and with his wrist bent in such a way that his thumb was extended towards me, less than a foot away, while his fingers were pointed almost directly downward. The gesture was intended, I imagine, to have a certain *de haut en bas* quality about it, but it was also a little absurd, given that he was no taller than I. With my elbow pressed against my ribs, I reached up and took his hand — which was, as always, oddly cool and softly glabrous, like a kind of clammily resilient alabaster — and shook it at an angle similar to that at which a small child must shake the hand of an adult. His grip was oddly, almost daintily flaccid, but he gave my fingers a small squeeze before releasing them, as if to reassure me of something (what, I could not guess). "I'll go now," he said. "You'll hear from me again, of course." He turned to leave.

Curiously enough, though, as anxious as I was for him to go, I suddenly found myself wishing to say something more, perhaps so as, for once, to have the final word; or perhaps because the pages I held in my hand seemed to me to amount to some sort of obligation. "It occurs to me . . ." I said, and paused.

My friend turned about again, with no particular expression on his face. "Yes?"

"Well . . . ," I said, hesitating for a second or two, and then glancing again at the leaves of parchment. "Well, it simply occurs to me that these poems don't really seem at all naïve regarding the transience of things."

"Did I say they were?"

"Yes, I think so. You made it sound as if he wasn't even aware of what he . . ."

"No, no," said my friend, quite firmly, "that's not quite what I said. I meant only that the poems may very well be all about time and eternity, and some sort of mysterious liaison between them, but they . . . well, of course, they can be read quite differently. But, certainly, I grant that the tone of the sonnets is consciously melancholy."

"Well, then," I said, rather surprised at my own persistence, "there's no reason not to take them the way he intended. The image of the arrow in flight, fired at the sun, rising to its apex and then falling back . . . it's just a single, ephemeral moment for him too, isn't it? It's just that, for him, there's the moment, at the height of the arc, where a civilization touches the eternal . . . or where a soul touches the eternal . . . and . . ."

"Why, pray tell," said my friend, in a tone of amused impatience, "are you stating the obvious to me?"

I was somewhat disconcerted by this. "I'm sorry. I suppose it is obvious, really."

"And this mystically condensed moment, pregnant with all eternity, what does it really do? What is it, exactly?"

"I don't know how . . . ," I began, and then fell silent. When, though, he said nothing, but merely gazed at me as if content to continue waiting for my response, I resumed: "I suppose it's rather like that image of the prism — I can't remember which sonnet it was in — or like the light you described coming through the windows of Sainte Chapelle. The light of eternity pours through . . ."

"Pours through the prism," my friend interrupted, making a sound somewhere between a sigh and a laugh as he did so: "a single ray of the sun, shattered into brilliant colors, becomes beautiful iridescences here below. Pretty rainbows, great cathedrals, cantatas, noble deeds. And civilizations are born in the radiance, and forms and purposes spring up from the sterile soil of prime matter and flourish, and souls open up to the light like new blossoms, and poems are written, and music is composed, and all nature and history have meaning given to them from above, and deep harmonies and patterns suffuse the whole fabric of time, and eternity lies hidden in each instant and each thing. And, oh, of course, one knows it in fleeting moments of bliss or insight — gazing at rabbits and daisies and children at play, hearing a flute in the night or a cello sonata or a Slavic choir . . . ravished by mystical union with God . . . sipping calvados under a lime tree as evening falls and cicadas thrum through the crimsoned air . . . books, the Japanese tea ceremony . . . restoring the façades of old churches, or the shingles of old houses . . . strolling along magnolia-shaded avenues, collecting Chinese jades, perfecting the Windsor knot . . . painting a picture, becoming absorbed in the deep mysteries of line and coloration . . . writing poems about the Byzantine Empire. . . . Standards, sentiment, contemplation, vision . . . rapture. Yes, yes, I've heard it all before. A moving mirror of eternity, remember? I said it to you already." He stared at me with a final look of indulgent helplessness. "I wish you could grasp how outmoded all that dreamy nonsense is. Really, what have Athens and Jerusalem to do with the modern world? But . . . yes, well, we're all prisoners of our desires, I suppose. Anyway, we really are talking in circles again."

I smiled again and lowered my eyes. "Yes, I suppose we are."

"Honestly, then," he said, "let's call it a night." His tone was still wholly amiable. "Coffee will arrive soon. Relax for a bit. Good night for now." He turned from me again and departed with such uncanny swiftness and such perfect balance that it was almost as if he had been wafted suddenly away.

I remained for a while where he had left me, staring vaguely in the direction of the door through which he had left. The silence was palpably and soothingly immense; to my left and right, the cool, marmoreal glow of the floor melted softly into the darkness of the room's farther reaches, while a few demure glints of silver and brass shone out gently amid the shadows beyond the circle of lamplight in which I stood. After several moments, I placed the poems in my chair, stretched my arms and legs, walked over to the near window — switching off the two lamps closest to it as I did so — and gazed out towards the west. Far off, slightly to my right, the lights of the city glittered on the horizon with an exquisitely pure brilliance, like small, incandescent diamonds, and in the park below the inconstant golden gleams of fireflies floated languidly above the grass. "Only in America," I murmured to myself, and then breathed in deeply. I knew that if I were to raise the window sash — which I had no desire to do — the hot, humid air of the summer night would flood in, bringing with it the sweet, heavy, torpid fragrances of mimosa and honeysuckle (the time of the lilac, and even of the rose, having passed); but, viewed through its veil of glass, the scene looked almost wintry. The darkness of the night had been invaded by an astonishingly intense lunar light of argent blue, and the whole world — the slender, tangled silhouettes of dogwoods, the pale, ghostly bark of sycamores, the smoothly terraced slopes rising from the park's southwest border, the woods beyond those, the treeless plain to their north — appeared to be everywhere edged with shimmering frost. There were now no clouds overhead, and the dim red nimbus of the city drowned out the stars in only one small portion of the sky, while high above the earth, shedding her lovely, mild splendor on city, garden, forest, and fields alike, the full and brightly shining moon — chaste and opaline — sailed gracefully and gradually on, tireless in her ancient, unwavering course.

2005

The House of Apollo

Εἴπατε τῷ βασιλεῖ, χαμαὶ πέσε δαίδαλος αὐλά·
Οὐκέτι Φοῖβος ἔχει καλύβαν, οὐ μάντιδα δάφνην,
Οὐ παγάν λαλέουσαν, ἀπέσβετο καὶ λάλον ὕδωρ·

The Delphic Pythia to Oribasius

The Emperor Julian arrived in the "golden" city of Antioch on the Orontes in July of that year (362 by the calendar of the Galilaeans), very nearly in a state of elation. Since having inaugurated his great revival of the old faith the previous autumn, he had suffered more disappointments than he cared to recall, and none bitterer than his recent visit to the shrine of Cybele in Pessinus, where he had discovered only neglect and indifference. But here in Antioch, he had convinced himself, he would find a people eager for his restoration of the ancient ways: a garden of true piety awaiting only the warming winds of imperial favor to flower anew. It had been principally for this reason that he had elected to delay his invasion of Persia until the spring and garrison his army in the city through the winter. And when he caught his first glimpse of the city's walls, still mostly covered by the slowly withdrawing morning shadows descending from Mount Silpius to the east, but brilliantly cusped to the west and north by the gleaming waters of the great river, he trembled slightly in anticipation and turned to confide to his physician Oribasius, almost giddily, that he could well imagine translating the imperial seat from the Bosphorus to the Orontes once he had returned in triumph from Ctesiphon. And then, speaking mostly to himself, he whispered, "I shall make it a city of marble."

Not that Julian was unaware that Antioch had been one of the cradles of the Galilaean superstition, or that its Christians were both numerous and insufferably proud of their church's apostolic pedigrees. Nor was he ignorant of the city's reputation for licentiousness and irreverence: he had heard it remarked often enough by his own retainers that the Galilaeans and Hellenes of Antioch were more devoted to the hippodrome and the theater than to either basilica or temple; and, in a letter that had met him upon the way weeks before, his Uncle Julianus, Prefect of the East, had described the Antiochenes as a vulgar, profane, and frivolous people, wholly inapt for philosophy, with an indigenous aristocracy that was little more refined in its tastes and manners than were the city's immense mercantile and banausic classes. But Julian had vested his faith in Antioch's glorious past, and in the peculiar blessedness of its sacred places, most particularly the Apolloneion and Artemision of the grove of Daphne a few miles to the city's south. He even cherished the hope that the example of his own austere personal piety might serve to chasten the consciences of Hellenes who had drifted from their devotions during the decades of Galilaean ascendancy in the empire, and help to re-awaken the holier impulses of their natures.

So, for a few luminous hours among the colonnades of the city's great high street and before the exquisite fountain in the Temple of the Nymphs at the city's center, as he proceeded with his retinue and personal guard towards the Tetrapylon of the Elephants and from there towards the huge Imperial Palace on the city's northern river island, all the way accompanied by the loud, formal acclamations of the crowds — "A salutary star shines upon the East!" — he allowed himself a rare, vaguely voluptuous surrender to the euphoria of the moment. Many in his party, however, followed with distinct expressions of disquiet on their faces, having been deeply shaken by the first sounds they had heard emanating from the city as they had approached the Bridge Gate: the music of flutes, but of a peculiarly dissonant, disordered, and melancholy kind, and voices raised in song, but in the starkest, most strident tones of lamentation. It had been an uncanny and even slightly frightening noise, with an odd oriental cadence and pitch, moving across strange and bleak intervals, and rising again and again to a shrill, prolonged wail. Julian had himself been somewhat disconcerted until his uncle and the imperial treasurer Felix, who together with a delegation of senators had greeted him just inside the Seleucan Wall, had explained that today was the Adonia, and that those sounds were solemn threnodies being sung over the sacred effigy of Adonis as it was ritually bathed, wrapped in scarlet burial cloths, and strewn with red anemone petals. Julian had smiled at that and gently mocked himself for not having known the date; then, turning his head to take a deeper breath of the sweet, resinous incense wafting his way, he had pronounced himself pleased by this, the music of true reverence — indeed, deeply moved by it — and remarked that he would have gladly joined the mourners had he come prepared. Several of his attendants, however, could not refrain from quietly observing, as the procession moved on, that it was hardly an auspicious sign for their young emperor and lover of the gods to arrive at his final stop on the way to Persian battlefields amid ritual ululations for the young and beautiful paramour of the goddess. "Whose funeral dirges are we really hearing?" one of Julian's secretaries had murmured to another.

It was only a few days, however, before Julian's enchantment with Antioch began to wane a little; after only two weeks, the household slaves were amused to note that he had ceased eating or conducting official business in the broad porches that afforded a prospect of the city, and now generally preferred the western side of the palace, from which he could gaze across the falcated outer branch of the Orontes, over the vast verdant plain that stretched away towards Mount Cassius and the peaks of the Amanus range, and far down to the distant sea. By that point, he had already learned not only of the extent of the city's grain crisis, but of the venal intransigence of the municipal curia in dealing with it. More exasperating still, his exhortations to the wealthy Hellenes to exhibit some degree of godly *philanthropia,* and to alleviate the sufferings of the poor in the city and its annexes by opening their private stores and reducing grain prices, had elicited little more than somber silence to his face and (so he had heard) ridicule behind his back. All of the noble houses had client families, of course, which for the most part were sufficiently supplied by their patrons. But here, as everywhere else, he had discovered that whatever meager provision was made for those most in need, of either faith or of none, came all but entirely from the Galilaeans, and more precisely from a small set of noblewomen who were — typical of their kind — utterly indiscriminate about whom they chose to bless with their largesse; they even made a virtue of taking food to criminals in prison. "It's enough of a disgrace that these uxorious little men allow their wealth to be squandered on wicked wretches, just so their wives can revel in their ostentatious false piety," Julian told Oribasius one evening; "but the greater disgrace is that the Hellenes refuse to care even for those who are *worthy* of their kindness."

66

At this, Oribasius nodded sagely. "The more labile sex," he said pensively, "nature's peasantry. It's a religion of the womb, of course. Women are unfortunately susceptible — hysteric saltations, mensal fluctuations, the periodic ebbing of vital spirits. . . . And, even when not deranged, the balance of a woman's humors tends to make frenzy . . ."

But Julian interrupted him: "Be that as it may, if it weren't for their husbands' laxity, they wouldn't be able to make such a vulgar spectacle of their . . . charity." He bowed his head and stroked his beard with that faint tremor of agitation to which he was often prone. "Too few of these Antiochenes have ever learned to revere the gods with any decent sense of fear," he said after a moment: "they've grown up on such close terms with the Galilaean atheists. I swear, but for the happy circumstance of meeting Libanius here, I'm not sure . . ." He paused and sighed, and then shook his head resignedly. "Well, I suppose I'll have to intervene myself in the end."

Oribasius made some respectful remarks regarding the intolerable onerousness of Julian's responsibilities, and then began to recommend a draft of hot wine infused with garlic and soporific herbs, along with an external application of warm oil and heated linens to the royal bowels; but the emperor brought the conversation to a sudden end and retired for the night.

JULIAN'S TEMPER BECAME somewhat more buoyant again, however, at the approach of the local feast of Apollo a week and a half later. For years he had longed to take part in the solemnities at the grove of Daphne, and months before had sent word to his uncle from Constantinople ordering the restoration of the god's fane, using whatever materials could be procured for the purpose. On the eve of the festival, he sent word to the curia that he would be in attendance for the sacrifices. On the day itself, shortly after dawn, he left the palace with a small entourage and mounted guard and visited the temple of Zeus Cassius, where he prayed and made an offering of incense; then, later in the day, he journeyed south to Daphne, arriving at the grove well into the afternoon. He entered the grounds on foot, attended by his informal advisors Maximus and Priscus, with only two young officers and seven armed soldiers in his train. For the occasion, he had donned robes of pure white, over which he wore a pontifical stole of his own devising, dyed a deep Tyrian purple and adorned with intricate gold and silver embroideries of laurel leaves, stars, and the sun and moon, and in his hair he wore a delicate gold chaplet fashioned like a wreath of laurel leaves. Maximus and Priscus were also in white, and each wore his philosopher's mantle. The party walked among purling lime-stone springs and pines and laurel trees of so dark a green that they looked almost blue under the cool, ubiquitous shade of the massive cy-presses; the air was sweet with the odor of fresh grass and myrtle and co-nifers, as well as the fragrance of some flower that neither Julian nor his companions recognized, but whose scent all agreed was peculiarly lovely. They spoke only in tones of hushed reverence, and then sparingly, though when the temples of Apollo and Artemis came distantly into view, Julian casually asked the two philosophers what allegory either might make of the tale of Daphne.

"That the soul that flees the fire of the divine Eros becomes rooted in the world of carnal generation," ventured Priscus, "perhaps until the next age."

But Julian sighed at that. "I suppose that makes considerable sense," he said, "but I find a certain tenderness in the story that suggests some-thing more. Perhaps something about the humid spirit seeking to rise up out of the chaos of generation, being transformed into something more stable and fruitful by the god's love . . . perhaps the god's ardor is a kind of play, a gracious pretense, meant to goad the soul's transformation into . . . yes, into something that bears fruit from itself, purified by being with-drawn from the flux of animal carnality and mutability, strengthened and made fertile by chastity and contemplation, so that it can now be nour-ished only by the hand of the god."

Maximus delightedly pronounced this much the better allegory, and Priscus quickly concurred, though each suggested a few improvements upon it, and then all three fell silent as they came into the temple pre-cincts. It was evident that the renovations had been completed compe-tently, though obvious also that some columns of diverse shape had been plundered from other structures to shore up the porticoes, and that not all were of solid marble. This did not trouble them, as it was quite in keeping with the emperor's original instructions; there would be time for better rebuilding later. What did perplex them, however, was the quiet of the place, and its emptiness. There were fresh garlands of white flowers laid on the altar in the forecourt and a burning brazier nearby, but no other signs of celebration. They paused and looked about them for some time; then Julian instructed one of his officers to search out the priests while he and his companions entered the shrine. Once inside, the three men allowed themselves several moments to take in the beauty of the place, and to imagine how much more beautiful it once had been. Here, at least, the original marble was quite intact, worn with age but softly lustrous, and the exquisite statues of the muses that ringed the central colossus of Apollo Musagetes had been newly painted in vivid pigments and, to Julian's eye, good taste. And then, of course, there was the colossus itself, the marvel of Daphne, which nearly filled the shrine and reached into the very vault of the high wooden ceiling. The figure of the god had been carved by the great Bryaxis from some darkly golden wood, so cunningly fitted together that it seemed of a single piece; the god's robes, hair, and laurel crown were all of hammered gold, and his eyes were deep purple amethysts; in his left hand he held a gold lyre folded against his breast, and with his right hand a gold patera tipped slightly downward, as though he were pouring out a libation; his lips were parted, in song perhaps, and his expression seemed almost one of grief. Julian was seized for a time with that awe that overcame him whenever he was certain that a god had truly shown himself; he gazed upward for a long time, rapt and silent, and then at last reverently lowered his eyes from the theophany, and still did not move or speak for several moments more. He noticed approvingly, however, that a small figure of Cybele had been installed by the statue's base. At last, he turned back to his companions and remarked that he could not imagine where the votaries were; certainly he could not have mistaken the day. So the three left the shrine in the same state of perplexity in which they had entered it, and were greatly relieved to discover that the officer had at least been able to find a steward and the high priest of the temple. The latter he had brought back with him: an older man with graying, somewhat unruly hair, a heavy beard, and dark, melancholy eyes, in very clean sacerdotal garb, and with a look of dismay on his face. As Julian approached him, the priest fell to his knees and attempted to make his proskynesis; but Julian immediately waved to his officer, who lifted the old man up before his brow could touch the ground. "Please," said Julian gently, "save your worship for the gods — and let even that be dignified, I implore you. Seemly deference is the most any man deserves."

The old priest bowed his head and said, in a surprisingly strong and resonant voice, with a fairly heavy Levantine accent, "Forgive me, Augustus. I have never before . . ."

"I understand entirely," said Julian quickly. "Constantine introduced these oriental manners into court etiquette, but I don't care for them. I'm a Roman, not a Persian despot."

"Yes, Augustus," the old man said. "Please forgive me."

"This is the feast day of the god, is it not?" Julian asked.

"Yes, Augustus."

"Where are the worshipers then? Where are the animals for the slaughter? There's not even any incense on the altar." Julian looked about again, and then returned his gaze to the priest. "Is everyone awaiting some signal from me, as supreme pontiff?"

The old man stared at the emperor in amazement and for a moment could not speak; then he said, "There is no one else here, Augustus — only I. I am just now preparing . . ." He paused as a look of indignant incredulity appeared on the emperor's face. "I have not yet lit the incense," he resumed after a moment, "and, well, I did not know that you would be here, or . . ."

"No one sent word from the curia?" Julian asked, a stern coldness insinuating itself into his voice.

"No, Augustus. I swear, had they done so, I should have been ready to greet you in the name of the god — here before his house. I'm sure you expected as much, but . . ."

"What I expected," said Julian, his voice becoming quieter but also quite furious, "was that the curials would be here themselves, and the people of Daphne and Antioch." His lower lip trembled visibly, and he bit it until it became still. Then, obviously attempting to control his anger, he said, "In fact, I've come expecting exactly what piety demands — a solemn procession with laurel branches . . . youths in white, with laurel crowns and ivy, the singing of paeans . . . lyres and flutes . . . and honey cakes and incense . . . libations . . . *worshipers* . . ." He looked around him yet again, almost as if he were hoping to see it all summoned up before his eyes as he spoke. "And sacrifices," he said, looking back to the old man: "at least a hundred oxen — at least one hecatomb — I should think. I came expecting to join in the offering with my own hands, in fact. I expected these" — he indicated his robes — "to be stained with the blood of sacred offerings."

Maximus began to advance towards them, but Julian stopped him with a raised hand.

"Has the curia made any provisions for the festival at all? Have any of the city's nobles sent any of their cattle for the feast?"

"No, Augustus." The priest's voice had become extremely soft now.

"So there is to be no sacrifice at all?"

"Oh, no, Augustus," the old man protested, "the city has made no preparations, it is true, but I have brought the sacrifice myself from home."

Julian raised his eyebrows. "And what is that?"

The priest said nothing, but only meekly raised a hand and pointed off to his left. Julian turned his head. At first, he saw nothing, but after staring for several seconds he at last made out the figure of a lone gray goose standing among the shadows below a laurel tree at the far boundary of the temple precincts; and, after a few seconds more, he could just discern the thin leather cord bound to one of its ankles and tied to the tree's trunk. Julian simply turned his eyes back to the old priest's and gazed into them forlornly, in astonished silence.

"It's all I have to give, Augustus," the old man said after a time.

At this, Julian's expression became somewhat kinder, and he uttered something like a small, sad laugh. "The widow's mite," he said with a faint smile. Then, receiving no answer, he breathed deeply and asked, with a resigned air, whether the priest could show him the sacred laurel. This, the old man gladly replied, he was quite able to do: the river ran behind the temple, and the tree of Daphne still stood on its near bank. And so Julian, Maximus, Priscus, and one of the officers followed the old man to where the rather grand — though not seemingly very ancient — laurel stood. The emperor was polite, but expressed some slight doubt as to its authenticity. The priest, however, only remarked that this was Daphne, that she had stood there since his childhood, and that he had been told even then that she was ceaselessly renewed, age upon age, by her father the river. Julian considered this for a few moments and then decided that he was satisfied — "Here or at the Peneius or the Ladon, it is the same truth" — and, sending for a patera and wine, he made a libation of water and wine at the tree's roots. Then, as the company returned to the temple's forecourt, he asked the priest how long it had been since the local Hellenes had entirely forsaken the observance of the feast. The old man replied that they had never forsaken it *entirely:* "There are Apolline games today in the Olympic stadium of Daphne. Otherwise there would be many people here in the grove."

"So it's only the games that keep them from worship?" Julian asked acidly.

"Ah, no, Augustus," said the priest with a look of embarrassment. "I don't mean that. They would not come to worship in any event. I mean there would be people in the grove taking their leisure by the springs. It is a very beautiful and popular park."

The sound that Julian emitted was very near to a groan. "They remember the games, but not the sacrifices. So" — he lifted his hands in a gesture of helplessness — "so — such, it seems, are the men of Antioch."

At the altar, the priest lit the incense, led the festal liturgy and paeans, and made the offering. The goose's entrails and liver were flawless, and the old man pronounced the haruspication favorable; Julian, though, gave no sign of caring. In all, the ceremony took little more than two hours, and concluded as twilight had begun to rise in the west. When the priest asked whether the emperor would stay to taste the sacrifice, Julian said there seemed little point, and that at any rate it was his practice to abstain from all meats, but that he would leave one of his men behind with a salver to bring some of the goose to the palace for those who might want to taste of the offering. Then, as he was leaving the temple with the priest beside him, he looked indulgently at the old man and said, "I suppose you have not yet been able to persuade any of your neighbors to come to revere the god in his shrine."

The priest looked somewhat abashed at this. "I cannot say I have ever attempted to do so, Augustus."

Julian halted. All at once, the geniality faded from his eyes. "Never? Never at all? And why is that?"

"Well" — the old man looked downward, away from the emperor's frown — "I have never thought it would do much good, I suppose. And it has been only during this past year that the temple has been made suitable again — by your gracious command, Augustus."

But Julian was not mollified. "The god craves love, not just splendid ornaments. And a holy example from his servants. Why are you a priest, after all?"

The old man raised his eyes again. "My father was priest here . . . and I was appointed to it . . . and" — his voice became somewhat more eager — "your munificence has made it possible again to . . ."

"Do *not* speak of money." Julian's voice had become fierce. Not only did his lips tremble now; his hands shook. "Is that all this is to you, your benefice? Is there no more devotion in you than that?" His tone had become contemptuous.

The old priest was so startled by the sudden change in the emperor's demeanor that it took him several seconds to respond; then, in a scarcely audible voice, he was just able to say, "No, Augustus, I swear — I have never failed to love my god."

Julian, though, seemed not to have heard him. "And what do you do with your wages? Do you visit the taverns? Or perhaps you pay for women?"

"No, Augustus, never," the priest replied, more emphatically; "I swear I keep myself pure from everything profane. As my father before me did."

This made Julian pause. He stared at the old man gravely, as if trying to decide what to believe, and then simply asked if the money in the temple coffers was properly distributed to those who came seeking aid.

"Our coffers are often empty, Augustus," the old man said, "at least for now; but there is a poor man who occasionally comes to eat when I make a sacrifice, and what money we have we are willing to give."

Julian took yet another deep breath; he seemed to be trying to calm himself. After a moment, as he had said he would do, he gave instructions for a man to be left behind. Then, withdrawing a purse of coins from his robes, he gave it to the priest from his own hand and turned to leave without saying anything more. Maximus and Priscus followed, each lingering only long enough to give the old man a brief, scornful stare; then the guard fell in behind them, now bearing lit torches (though there was not yet any great need for them), and the remaining soldier immediately repaired to the northern end of the temple precincts. The old priest stood all but motionless for some time, watching the small company gradually disappearing into the deepening shadows beneath the cypresses and laurels, until he could see nothing of them but distant golden gleams sinking away into the darkening depths of green, and then nothing at all. He returned to the altar to gather up the goose and give it to the temple steward to prepare and roast.

WHEN THE MEAT had been cooked, the priest removed a portion large enough to feed both the steward and any indigent who might come to the temple the next day. Then he removed a larger and choicer portion to send to the imperial palace, only insisting that the soldier eat some of the goose himself before departing. What remained he wrapped in clean linen, placed in a leather satchel, and took home with him. As he made his familiar way through the darkness with the aid of only a small lantern, a light rain began to patter among the leaves overhead. His house, such as it was, lay just beyond the eastern boundary of the grove, apart from any of the other houses of Daphne, in a shallow vale between two gently rising hillocks, under the low pavilion of two large fig trees and surrounded by vine-bearing lattices, with pens for goats and fowl a little way off. When he had lit his lamps, he ate a generous quantity of the meat, accompanied by bread, fresh cheeses, olives, and a pungent wine of his own making, and listened serenely to the rain among the fig leaves and on his thatching. His encounter with the emperor had already faded to a matter of utter inconsequence in his mind. If anything, it merely amused him to think that this strange, compelling, but somehow antic and irrelevant young man could openly doubt the depth of his piety, or suspect him of dissipations and carnal congress — he than whom, he was fairly certain, there was no one more devout in the whole valley — but then, of course, neither the emperor nor anyone else could know the secret that he had kept silently within himself for almost forty years now. And it did not matter, really. Since that day long ago, he had acquired a gift — obviously a special blessing bestowed by the god of prophecy — for sensing certain truths about many of those he encountered. Within his first few moments in Julian's presence, he had inwardly concluded that this reputedly fervent young emperor who aspired to be a philosopher and a true lover of the gods was neither particularly wise nor particularly loved by the gods in return, even to the small degree that they were still capable of love for men; and he had sensed also that there was a sad ephemerality about the man, an air of imminent doom, and that nothing Julian had begun to build would ever be finished. So, as he ate, the old man thought chiefly of other things.

He had been born in this small house, one of the only three of his parents' children to survive infancy, though his mother gave birth more than a dozen times between her fourteenth year and the drying up of the springs of her fertility; and, as the other two children were girls, his father — who was one of seven priests at the temples of Artemis and Apollo in the grove — raised him as an apprentice in the cults. Fortunately, he always exhibited an uncommon aptitude for religion. From his early days, he loved the temple of Apollo, and the majestic beauty with which the god condescended to show himself in the statue of Bryaxis, and there were many times when, standing in its presence, he wished — sometimes almost in a state of excited, even terrified anticipation — that the great figure might turn its eyes down towards him and grant him a brief glimpse of the living face of the god. He was still only five when the priests and stewards of the temples began to speak of the precocious attitude of reverence he displayed in the god's house. And then, when he was eleven, he had a vision that the priests deemed prophetic. It happened in Antioch, during the Adonia, before any of the lamentations for Adonis had been sung, just after the pale, waxen figure of the supine god had

been borne out from the shrine of Aphrodite upon its funeral bier. He
had come with his father from Daphne to hear the women sing their la-
chrymals, expecting perhaps to stay throughout the entire day, but he
had also been feeling somewhat ill, and the heat now overwhelmed him,
and he swooned away in the dust of the street. His father carried him
quickly into the shade below the Wall of Justinian, and poured a little water between his lips, and attempted to revive him; but for nearly half an
hour he did not move. As he lay there, however, anxiously watched by his
father and kindly attended by a woman who brought wet rags with which
to bathe his brow, he had a kind of dream, though far more vivid than any
dream he had ever known. He found himself lying upon soft and fragrant
grass in a meadow, under the shadow of a lone pine tree, gazing upward
into a sky of dazzlingly pure blue — somehow deeper and vaster than any
sky he had ever seen — and after a time he looked down at his own body,
which he saw to be clad in a white tunic that was stained scarlet at his
right side and all down his hip and loins, and he knew in an instant that
he was himself Adonis, wounded by the wild boar and pouring out his
life. He felt no pain, but only a profound languor throughout his body — a
pleasant numbness, a sensation of floating — and he turned his eyes back
upward to the sky and gazed into it peacefully, waiting for sleep. But then
there was a woman kneeling at his side and bending over him, laying a
cool hand upon his forehead — an inexpressibly beautiful woman, far
more beautiful than any woman he had ever seen or could ever have
imagined, with eyes the same brilliant blue as the sky above her and lips
as red as the blood on his tunic, her glistening dark hair crowned with a
diadem of dark blue gems, her tresses spilling down over her shoulders
and breasts, and over a dark green dress that shimmered like flowing water — and she looked down at him, into his eyes, with an expression of
such tenderness and yet such inscrutability, both sorrowful and sweetly
happy, that he could do nothing but gaze up at her silently, in entranced
delight; this was the face of the goddess, he was utterly certain, and he
loved her, and knew she loved him, and he was content to die into that
love. But then the scene changed — and afterwards he could never recall
whether it had done so suddenly or gradually, drastically or meltingly —
and he was standing in the forecourt of the Apolloneion of Daphne, at
night but under a clear sky and a refulgent full moon, and he could see
the stones of the yard and the columns of the temple and the bare altar
with perfect clarity; and after many moments he noticed another figure
standing not far away, in the shadow of one of the columns near the doors

of the shrine, which were open wide, though nothing was visible beyond them. Whether it was a man or a woman he could not tell, as it was covered from head to foot in a long, gray, hooded mantle from whose folds only a single hand protruded, resting upon the column — probably an old woman's hand, given how frail and slender it looked in the darkness. He approached the figure but, as he came within ten or so paces, it raised its hand to stop him. Then it spoke to him in a voice whose particular quality he could not remember later, and told him that the house of the beautiful god would not stand much longer, and that those who did not love the gods would pull down their fair dwelling places among men. Then — how long after he could not tell — he regained his senses, and his father and the strange woman — who was neither young nor old, neither lovely nor plain — helped him sit up against the wall; and then the woman took her leave, and his father went to buy him some figs and bread and to gather cold water from a city well not far from where he sat. He ate and drank slowly, and listened to the lamentations for Adonis rising from the next street under a heavy hovering pall of incense smoke, and only when he was sufficiently refreshed, and the sun had passed overhead so that he was no longer shaded by the wall, did he rise and tell his father that he felt able to return home. And only that evening did he relate his vision to his father, who was troubled by the words the veiled figure had spoken. In the morning his father took him to see the other priests of the grove, and he was obliged to repeat the tale several times, in as much detail as he could recall, until the high priest finally remarked that it was significant of something, and something to ponder. Beyond that, the priests had little to say, except to note that he had lain beneath a pine tree in his vision, which suggested that it might also have been a vision of Attis and Cybele. But when word reached Antioch in early winter that a new Augustus who favored the Christians had arisen in the Western Empire, it was generally concluded among the priests in Daphne that this was what the figure in his vision had foretold.

In the spring of his fifteenth year, after he had been admitted to the lowest rank of the priesthood, he accompanied his father on pilgrimage to Pessinus, to the mountain shrine of Cybele. In those days, there were still many devotees of the Great Mother to be found there, and her rites were still celebrated by galli (though not all of these were eunuchs, as they would have been in earlier times, some having preferred to make only an offering of bull's testicles at their initiations, in the Roman fashion), and he was impressed by the raucous holy revelry by day, and moved by the hauntingly rhythmic hymns in the evening. On his second night in the pilgrims' hostel, he dreamed that he was again lying in that meadow, bleeding to death under that pine, now perhaps as Attis, and again he saw the face of the goddess — not nearly as vividly as on the day of the Adonia four years earlier, but still with more immediacy and clarity than was common in dreams — but on this occasion her head was crowned not with jewels but with wildflowers of many colors, and she wore necklaces of gold, and her garment was a dark red, almost purple, of a heavier and richer fabric than before, with a high collar embroidered with images of golden birds; and again, he felt his love for her and her love for him, though in a remoter, more dreamlike way. When he told his father of this the next morning, they together agreed that the pilgrimage had been a fortunate one; but he was glad to begin the return journey to Daphne the next day, as the house of Apollo there was still the only place where he could feel the divine presence as something truly near at hand, and something truly welcoming even in its majesty. Then, three years later, when his father was killed by one of those fevers that the winds carry about the earth during the pestiferous autumn months, he conceived a desire to go on another and much longer pilgrimage, in order to visit places especially sacred to Apollo. He had come to believe, especially since the last war between the Augusti of the West and the East two years earlier, that what the veiled figure in his vision had prophesied would come to pass in his own lifetime. It was nearly two more years, however, before he left on his journey, provided with some silver by the temple and from the funds his father had prudently hoarded over the years. He entrusted the care of his mother to two slaves — one male and one female — donated by a patron in Antioch.

At that time, there were only three other priests who served in the grove of Daphne, and they would much rather he stayed to perform his duties at the altar, but he simply could not. As he had grown to full manhood, he had also grown more devoted not only to the temple there, but to the mystery that dwelled within it. The figure of Apollo now often filled his thoughts, and woke nameless yearnings in him; everything inexplicable and lovely about the god — about the stories and the hymns and the sacred sites — fascinated him. Now even the statue of Bryaxis seemed to him to be only the faintest adumbration of the overpowering glory of a god at once so beautiful and so terrible: a god of purity and brightness and the clarity of perfect form, the most radiant and visible of all that is divine, but also a god always more distant, more hidden, whose arrows fly from farther and ever farther away; the shining one, the lord of poetry and song and prophecy, but also the god of wrathful countenance, who slays with the gentle bolt of instantaneous death; the lord of cleansing sunlight and of the clear, sweet water of living springs, the purifier and the healer, but also the death-dealing god of plague and spiritual contagion; wise, invincible, the god of consummate human and divine splendor, but also the god who can draw near only as the ever-withdrawing, and who can dwell among men only in the radiant majesty of that which is most exalted and unapproachable, in the cold beauty of a distance that can never be crossed; the god whose voice is as thunder, before whom one knows only one's own transience, but the god also of delight and kindly music and earthly joy; the slayer of the dragon and the one who speaks from the mouth of the dragon; baneful, beneficent; all beauty, all light and darkness; perfect revelation as perfect mystery. Surely, the priest had come to believe, this god was the image of everything highest and everything most incomprehensible in the divine. And he had come to believe as well that indeed this god would soon depart, not only as in the winter months, to sojourn in Lycia or among the Hyperboreans or in his hidden garden, but forever, going away finally into some region utterly beyond this world; and he longed with a kind of constant desperation to see whatever vestiges he could — whatever still-burning sparks of that passing glory remained — before the darkness fell. So he went from Antioch by sea and for more than a year sought out as many of Apollo's most celebrated shrines as he could with the resources at his disposal, staying nowhere more than four days. He was assisted on his way by the treasuries of various temples and by occasional donations from men or women who wished him to remember them in the god's holy places; he saw Erythrae, Clarus, Bassae, Abae, and Tenea, and went even as far as Cumae; he sought passage to Delos only once, but was told by a sailor and a Greek priest that the temples there were no longer in use or even intact, and that the sea lanes were not safe from pirates. Then, only as he was beginning his return journey, he made his visit to Delphi. He arrived in the spring, in time for the *Theophaneia,* and joined in the celebrations welcoming the god's yearly return to his temple and to the undying flame of its hearth, and enjoyed the rare privilege of seeing the divine images of the inner sanctuary briefly unveiled; it was the only time in his life that he experienced a moment of reverent amazement similar to what he had often felt before the great statue in Daphne, and he never spoke of it afterwards. Then he waited for another two weeks, merely wandering about the precincts of the temple and all the lesser shrines that stood upon the

terraced slopes of Parnassus, unwilling to leave before he himself had received an oracle from the Pythia. He had been quite aware before coming
that Delphi had known seasons of greatness and seasons of decline, and
had suffered many spoliations over the centuries — by Caesars principally, but also by barbarians — followed by only partial restorations; but
he had not known before his arrival that the Augustus Constantine had
recently begun removing many of the city's treasures and monuments
again, with a rapacity to rival Nero's. Even so, there were still countless
votive statues to see, as well as the Stoa of the Athenians, and the rock of
the Sibyl, and the black marble Altar of the Chians; the Castalian Spring
still flowed through the ravine between the Phaedriades and flooded the
great fountains' basins; and each day he entered the temple of Apollo itself and felt the deep, silent, shadowy uncanniness of the place, and the
nameless elation and fear it roused in him. He could quite contentedly
have waited in Delphi another year or more. But, at the end of those two
weeks, he was granted his audience, one warm, clear evening when all
other votaries had been sent away. He had expected that the priests
would bring him the message in hexameters, having first crafted it themselves from the ecstatic utterances of the Pythia in her mantic trance; this
was, he had always been told, the way in which the god spoke in this
place. Instead, however, the Pythia herself emerged from the interior of
the temple to speak to him among the columns of its eastern porch. He
could not tell from the austerely emotionless faces of the two priests who
supported her on either side whether this was the extraordinary event he
thought it to be; and of her face he could see nothing but her chin and
lower lip, as she was shrouded from head to foot in a mantle that appeared black to him at first, but that he soon saw to be a deep midnight
blue. The resemblance to the veiled figure in his vision years before, in so
similar a setting, struck him immediately, and he felt a small agitation of
unease as he watched her approach. When she spoke, her voice was obviously that of an old woman, though it was still quite strong and clear. She
stood before him for only a few moments and then, without any prelude,
simply pronounced the oracle: "Say to him:

'The waters of prophecy will cease to flow, the singing lyre be
    silenced;
The sacred laurels will no longer flower; the golden roof will fall;
Phoebus will have no house among men; now you shall be his
    house.'"

Then, saying nothing else, but only nodding to her attendants, she went again into the shrine and left him there. For a long time he lingered among the columns, watching the darkness descend and deepen, scarcely able to conceive a coherent thought. Then he made his way slowly along the roads of the terraces, down the side of the mountain to the pilgrims' hostel where he stayed at night, and where he was at present the sole tenant. He took his pallet outside so that he could sleep in the temperate air, under the stars. And that night he had a dream, or something much more than a dream, just as vivid as his vision had been during the Adonia long ago, simpler in form, perhaps, but far more powerful and troubling. He found himself again in Daphne, walking across the forecourt of the temple of Apollo towards the shrine, seemingly on a late autumn day. Though it was obviously not much later than noon, he was quite alone. As he passed the altar, he saw that there were garlands of flowers upon it, but that they were entirely withered; and plainly the courtyard had not been swept in some time, as dust and dead leaves were everywhere about him. On entering the shrine, he found that the wind had scattered more leaves through the open doors and across the floor, and that the dust here had been allowed to gather so thickly that it glimmered like pale silver on the heads and shoulders of the statues of the muses. Somehow, though, none of this seemed odd to him; he merely took it in for a few moments and then turned his eyes upward to the great statue of Apollo. This, he knew, was why he was here. He stared at the massive head and shoulders and felt the familiar thrill of elation and fear, but far more acutely than ever before, because somehow he already knew what was to come; and, as he looked, the great figure did indeed begin to move, slowly, with almost terrifying casualness, turning its jeweled, impersonal gaze down towards him. His entire body shook uncontrollably, he felt his breath grow heavy in his lungs, his limbs felt hopelessly weak, but he did not try to move away. And then, all at once, it was not the statue of Bryaxis that looked down on him, but the face of the living god, unutterably beautiful, unutterably glorious; everything else faded away on every side, and nothing was visible to him apart from the unbearable and overwhelming splendor of that countenance; and in an instant he was lost to himself, in rapture, annihilated in that beauty, falling away from everything. Then he lost any sense of anything at all. When he awoke, he had been unconscious for nearly two days. The old man and woman who kept the hostel had already summoned a physician, who had tried to wake him with a variety of pungent herbs and wine and myrrh and so forth, and they would have shortly had him carried to the small Asclepieion near the temple of Apollo had he not revived when he did. When he had sufficiently recovered, he thanked them and told them to keep the three silver coins they had extracted from his purse for (they said) a votive offering to the god of healing. Then, two days later, in a state of distraction that would linger on for another week or so, he left Delphi and made his desultory way back to Antioch and to the priestly duties that awaited him in Daphne, visiting Hierapolis Bambyce, Didyma, and Patara along the way.

And so he served for the next four decades, as the empire was united under a single Augustus and the old cults were, to one degree or another, abandoned or suppressed. He retained his priestly office even in those bleak periods when the sacrifices were officially proscribed (though they never entirely ceased), and he labored on even as the sanctuary's frequent neglect by the city senate began to become all too visible. Two years after his return from his pilgrimage, he took a wife — the daughter of a dyer in Daphne — but she died in childbirth fourteen months later, and the baby girl was stillborn. He never married again, and yielded to sexual temptation on only four occasions during the next five years; thereafter he was entirely celibate. Sixteen years after his pilgrimage, his mother announced that she had become a Christian, and a year and a half after that she received baptism. This did not perturb him greatly; he had never felt any great dislike for the Christians of Antioch, who by that time seemed clearly to outnumber the indigenous pagans, and he was often impressed — if a bit bemused — by the diligence with which certain Christians, and especially certain Christian women, devoted themselves to the care of the poor and the sick. He understood perfectly well, as far as he was concerned, what it was his mother desired when she spoke to him of God coming to dwell among men, showing his face to those who sought it. And he believed (though he could not have said why precisely) that the woman who had bathed his brow all those years ago as he lay unconscious during the Adonia had been a Christian. But he had no desire for any closer commerce with their creed. In deference to his mother's new piety, he removed all his sacred images from the house and kept them stored in the temple while she lived. She frequently exhorted him with a mother's tenderness to abandon the worship of demons and be baptized; and he always refused as gently as he possibly could. When she lay dying eight years later, however, once he was quite certain there was no hope of recovery and that she had little time left, he lied to her, telling her that he would indeed become a Christian, and this allowed her to pass away with a peaceful spirit. The day after her burial, he restored his household gods to their proper places. By then, he was the most senior of only three priests in the grove. Three years later, there were only two. In the year that Julian came to Antioch, the number had grown to four again as a result of the new imperial patronage, but the old priest was confident that before long he would be quite on his own.

He never again experienced anything comparable to the ecstasy that had ravished his senses away that night in Delphi, nor did he ever expect to do so; there were only occasional moments of quiet transport in the years following, during which he was briefly, tremulously aware of a distant echo of that feeling of mingled bliss and terror: when, say, he happened to see the sunlight passing in gleaming fans through the filtering needles of pine trees, or the morning light descending over Mt. Silpius and just barely touching the waves of the Orontes, or the departing day trailing its purple skirts over the ridges of the Amanus range and melting into a last empty golden lambency hovering over the distant sea. Even so, he knew with absolute certainty that the god now dwelled within him in some mysterious and glorious way, and that he had been entrusted with a secret that he could not have expressed had he wished to do so, and that he had been given an honor he could have done nothing to merit. Now the great colossus of Bryaxis seemed like little more than a shadow to him, only a poor outward symbol of the hidden riches of the divine mystery that lived deep inside of him. He rarely if ever prayed to any image, in fact. Neither, though, did he like to pray to the god within. Any words he spoke always seemed only to violate the ineffability of that divine intimacy, and to dilute it with something alien to it. Even in utmost nearness, it seemed, Apollo necessarily had to remain ever more distant, ever more exalted; that was always how the god dwelled on earth, after all, and it was not the priest's place to presume upon the privilege he had been granted by addressing the divine with familiarity. All he could do was look out on the world, somehow at the god's side, reverently saying nothing, simply allowing the world to show itself to him as the home from which the god was going away. In a sense, he took his deepest comfort precisely from that coldly radiant distance within, which seemed to him a kind of proof that that god who ever withdraws was really there, withdrawing himself gradually from all visibility, out of the shining world and into the silence of an inner realm. Perhaps — he did not understand this, but believed it nonetheless — this withdrawal was a final, beautiful gesture of gracious and unapproachable divinity, the blessing of farewell, and he was content and humbled to be the last witness of that splendor as it passed beyond the world.

When he had eaten enough and drained his cup four times, the old priest gathered up the remaining morsels of his meal and carefully stored them, and then prepared to sleep. The day had been long, and the appearance of the young emperor in the grove had been a singularly unwelcome surprise. But he was quite at peace when at last he lay down, pleased that the rain was continuing to fall, soaking the earth about his vine lattices and making a lovely whispering noise among the fig trees and upon his roof.

FROM THAT POINT ON, Julian's sojourn in Antioch became ever bitterer. The city was more intransigently Galilaean than he could ever have suspected before his arrival, and the indigenous Hellenes, who seemed to regard their faith as a matter only of feasts and games, clearly regarded his personal asceticism and devotion to sacrifice as excellent objects of mirth, but certainly not of emulation. Shortly after his disappointment in the grove, he had fiercely berated the curia for its indifference towards the gods, and for the willingness of its members to squander fortunes on private amusements while spending not even a pittance on the demands of religion; but within a few days he learned that all that his words had inspired was a brief, ebullient season of public mockery. As a whole, the citizens of the city resented him more the longer he lived among them with his large and voracious army. His attempts to ameliorate the food crisis were decisive but inept. He reduced taxes, but the poor paid few to begin with; he re-allotted municipal lands for cheap purchase and cultivation, but wealthy landowners merely bought the acreage for themselves and thereby enclosed commons they had long coveted; he imported grain from Chalcis and Hierapolis and imposed price controls within the city, but he did not think to institute a regime of rationing, so the wealthy merchants simply purchased all the imported grain and sold it outside the city at an even more exorbitant rate than before. Naturally this caused the poor of the valley to flood into the city each day in search of bread, the one item in the market that could not be stored and so had to sell at the price Julian had dictated. But the emperor was too distracted by other matters to pay close attention to the havoc his policies had created.

In the autumn, Julian returned to the grove in Daphne to visit the sacred spring there, hoping to obtain an oracle, but the god would not speak to him. When Julian asked why this was, the priest of the spring told him that the oracle had been silenced by the presence of the dead nearby, and that no prophecies would be possible until the pollution had been removed and the site purified. On then learning that in the days of Gallus the body of St. Babylas had been brought from its martyrium in the city and placed in the grove in order to sanctify it, Julian ordered that the "corpse" be returned to Antioch. On the day the bones were moved, a great crowd of Galilaeans lined the road, and formed a funeral cortege to accompany the cart, and all along the way defiantly sang psalms condemning idolatry. In the days that followed, Julian's detractors became ever bolder in their taunts. The noblewoman Publia, the mother of one of Antioch's most prominent Galilaean priests, liked to stand at her window just as Julian's retinue was passing and to sing psalms reviling idolaters and proclaiming the victory of the true God over his enemies. The third time this happened, Julian's equanimity faltered, and he commanded his guard to box her ears, but this only made her sing more loudly. Then he instructed Salutius, his loyal praetorian prefect, to find out who had instigated the protests on the day of Babylas's translation; some of the region's more notorious Galilaean agitators were arrested and tortured with scourges and metal claws, but nothing was learned. Then, one autumn evening, not long after the purification of the grove, the temple of Apollo caught fire and quickly burned down; the great statue of Bryaxis was entirely consumed. The guardians and custodians of the grove all reported that the temple's roof had been struck by lightning, but Julian did not believe them and had them flogged; several peasants who lived near the grove, however, corroborated the story. Still unsatisfied, Julian convened a tribunal of inquisition, which questioned every possible witness at length, including the temple's high priest; when the old man failed to provide any incriminating evidence, the interrogators went so far as to have him stripped and beaten with rods, but even then he refused to accuse any of the local Galilaeans. In the end, the inquiry came to nothing. Julian did, however, use the affair as an excuse for closing the great octagonal Golden Church near the imperial palace; he presided over the removal of its ornaments and precious vessels personally, accompanied by Felix and Julianus. Felix was jubilant, enthusiastically deriding the Galilaeans for the extravagance with which they adorned the temple of their peasant god, while Julianus took it upon himself to defile the altar by urinating upon it (or so it was rumored); but when both men died the next month — Felix continuously vomiting blood, Julianus struck down by a wasting disease that caused his flesh to putrefy even as he lay writhing upon his deathbed — the citizens of Antioch, Hellene no less than Galilaean, naturally saw it as divine retribution.

That same month brought on the celebration of the Saturnalia, just as winter was arriving. It was a feast that in his heart Julian despised, but one consecrated by tradition, and so for three days he feigned tolerant amusement at the city's brief descent into misrule and social inversion; he did not join in the revels, of course, but he did allow the palace slaves relief from all but their most indispensable tasks. As he expected would happen, a great many of the satires and masques performed at the theater and amphitheater and in the streets were directed, either explicitly or implicitly, at him and his beard, but he was resolved to bear every ignominy with a philosopher's composure. Two weeks afterwards, however, his patience was finally conquered. In the hope of inspiring more of the local gentry to offer themselves for the curia, he had decided to have himself and Salutius appointed as consuls for the city. On the day of their inauguration (the first day of the Roman January), the two men processed through the city side by side, garbed in imperial purple (Julian's robes adorned with gems, Salutius's with images of the Caesars of old and golden figures from the zodiac). The crowds put on a seemly display of civic adoration, and Libanius delivered himself of a rhetorically exquisite oration that could scarcely have been courtlier in its sycophancy. All was as it should have been. But when Julian repaired to the circus for the rest of the day's festivities, the assembled spectators began to mock him — gently at first, in keeping with Antioch's traditions of genial irreverence, but more sharply as the hours passed, until whimsical prodding had given way to open ridicule. When he could endure no more, Julian abruptly rose and returned to the palace. A few weeks later, he made his last attempt to reach into the cynical hearts of his fellow Hellenes by publishing a satire of his own at the Tetrapylon of the Elephants; entitled "The Beard Hater," it began in a tone of amiable self-effacement, but soon degenerated into rather petulant recriminations against those who had abused his love for them. His own court regarded the episode as dismayingly undignified, Antioch's wits delighted in a new occasion for mockery, and Julian resolved at last to break forever with this wretched people. His last official act before departing the city at the end of the winter was to appoint Alexander of Phoenicia — a man notorious for his humorlessness and officious brutality — as the new Prefect.

It scarcely mattered. Had he returned in victory from Persia, Julian would have had time to deal with the city at his leisure; but he did not return. His campaign seemed promising at first, but after a few early victories his forces began to fall apart, and he himself began to grow more erratic. At the end of April, he even revived a disused military custom and ordered the decimation of three cavalry squadrons whose only crime was that they had been defeated by a Persian ambush. In May his army won the field outside of Ctesiphon, but could not hope to besiege the city, especially with Persian reinforcements on the way. Rather than retreat then, however, he burned his ships and pushed on eastward into the interior. The Persians, seeing that the Tigris now cut the Romans off from their supply lines and all avenues of quick retreat, simply destroyed all crops and cattle before the Roman advance. As summer arrived with its unbearably savage heat, and with food rations all but exhausted, the whole Roman army knew that the war was lost, and Julian had to consent to a slow withdrawal north, with the Persians continually attacking the Roman lines all along the march. Then one night late in June, at the end of a three-day armistice, Julian awoke from troubling dreams just after midnight and, unable to sleep again, sat up in his bed and began to write out certain stray reflections on philosophical subjects. After several minutes, though, something caused him to raise his head, and he saw the spectral figure of the genius of the empire standing before him. He had been visited thus once before, in Gaul, and on that occasion the genius had exhorted him to seize his destiny as emperor; but now the same figure appeared in robes of mourning, a shadowy gray veil draped over its head and over the cornucopia it bore in its arms, saying nothing for several moments, and then merely turning away and slowly departing through the curtains of the tent. For some time, Julian could not move; then, prayerfully commending his fate to the gods, he rose and followed, and just as he emerged from his tent, he saw a falling star flash brilliantly across the sky and melt away upon the darkness. As the east was just beginning to turn to violet before the first blush of dawn, he had his Etruscan soothsayers brought to his tent to interpret the night's portents for him. They became anxious and declared the signs unpropitious, and then advised against any new undertakings, and especially against venturing onto the battlefield in person, and Julian — as was always his wont with auguries he disliked — ignored their warnings. Later that day he suffered the spear wound to his side that would end his life; he lived two days more, attended by Oribasius, but then died of a violent hemorrhage in the night. Soon thereafter the expeditionary forces resumed their retreat.

THE OLD PRIEST of Apollo, however, lived on and on, more than thirty years longer, past his ninth decade; he even lived to hear of the final closing of all the pagan temples under the Emperor Theodosius. By that time, he was frail, forgetful, and mostly blind, and well past caring about such matters. He had resigned himself long before to the disappearance of the old religion and the withdrawal of the gods, and the only temple to which he had ever belonged had disappeared decades ago. He simply went on tending the secret flame that burned within him, never understanding its mystery, but never wavering in his faith. As the years had passed, he had been sustained by the patronage of one of the few obdurately pagan landed families in the valley, and had occasionally performed small ritual services at their household altar outside Antioch; but, as the laws had become more restrictive and he had grown older, his few remaining responsibilities had simply ceased. For the last dozen years of his life, he rarely left his house, and all his needs were seen to by the two slaves with which his patrons made sure always to provide him; the family kept him as a client partly out of reverence for things that had been, partly out of affection for the quiet old man who had once served at a now-fabled altar. In his last few years, he subsisted almost entirely upon bread, boiled grains, figs from his own trees, cheeses made from the milk of his own goats, and wine made from his own grapes.

When at last he lay dying on his bed, on a warm summer afternoon full of the songs of innumerable birds, he was graced by one last fatidic dream or vision (he could not have said which, as the boundary between sleep and waking — between dreams and visions, between visions and normal consciousness — had by that time been all but erased for him). He found himself again inside the shrine of the temple of Apollo as it had been in the year before its destruction. It was late in the day, and he was quite alone, facing the doors, which lay open to the forecourt; beyond them the light was golden with the first glow of evening, and the chorus of the birds poured through them in a lovely ceaseless clamor. His back was turned to the place where the great statue had always stood, but he did not turn to look up at it, because he was immediately aware of a feeling that he had known often enough in his youth, but that he had not felt for decades — the familiar combination of elation and trepidation, of joyous expectation and sincere dread — but more intense than it had ever been except for that night in Delphi. He knew at once that the temple was full of the god's presence — it surrounded and overwhelmed him — but, as much as he longed for another glimpse of the god's face, he was certain he could not bear that violent ecstasy again; and he knew, he knew — he had spoken the words often enough in years past: *the golden one has come forth, the great one is in house* — what he would see if he should turn to look. So instead he lowered his eyes and moved to his right, past the brightly painted figure of Terpsichore, and slowly made his way to the back of the shrine, not looking up until he had come to a corner that the light rarely reached; only then — slowly, cautiously — did he turn and raise his head. As he had somehow known would be so, it was not the colossus of Bryaxis whose back he saw, but the immense and terrifyingly beautiful form of the living god himself, filling the house from the floor to its roof beams, standing there in a haze of glory, his face turned away towards the open doors, his whole body softly radiant, his hands now hanging empty at his sides; but still he was clad in gold raiment, shod in gold sandals, and the heavy, glistening black locks of his head were crowned by gold laurels. The old man felt his breath growing faint and his limbs trembling. He tried to control his fear or joy — whichever it was, as he could no longer tell the difference — and continued to gaze upward, for how long he did not know. He had never felt so very weak before — so very insubstantial. Finally the great figure began to move forward, with a strange, massive, unearthly stateliness, not looking back, taking no note whatsoever of the priest; the god seemed almost to float across the space, as weightless as the daylight, and yet the floor seemed to shake with his every step, as if it might crack under the burden, and a sound like the sustained echo of distant thunder seemed to emanate from the walls, mingling its deep tones with the music of the birds. It was more than the old man could bear; he felt indescribably weak, as if he were fading away from this place. Everything was beginning to become indistinct around the edges of his vision, and he realized that his eyes were beginning to fill with tears, but he could not even raise his hand to wipe the tears away. Now the darkness was closing in on all sides, the interior of the shrine was vanishing in shadows, the day was melting away into an everdarkening gold; and in the last moments of his life — as the immense figure passed between the enormous doorposts, framed for a moment against a sky the color of honey, and then disappeared into the dying light beyond — the old priest saw the beautiful god depart.

2010

A Voice from the Emerald World

The path into the garden, which leads to the narrow eastern opening in the low, dry stone wall, is bordered and overhung by sprawling clusters of sweet alyssum blossoms, scattered amid the uncut bluegrass and dark English ivy like stars in the night sky. Its slender ribbon of worn flagstones is all but invisible below this miniature Milky Way spreading itself along the green chaos of the yard.

I almost never trim the walk these days, in part because I find a certain degree of wildness pleasing, but mostly because I no longer see any point; and I have let all the fields beyond the upper slopes at the western and northern ends of the property, which were leased for pasturage in the days before I owned the land, go entirely to seed.

Inside the wall, however, my wife still keeps everything quite in order. From the early spring through the late fall, she labors nearly every day in the garden, for many hours at a time, tending the plants, weeding the beds, gathering up the windfall below the apple trees, minding the verges, nurturing her flowers; even in the winter, when weather permits, she is generally to be found there, clearing occasional debris, adjusting the little lattices of twigs and twine she keeps as windbreaks around her more delicate charges during the colder months, or simply staring idly at the bare, thorny branches of her rosebushes.

You, of course, probably already know all of this, looking down as you do from your unassailably elevated vantage; but I prefer to think you pay us no attention.

It is late morning, and I plan to visit Christopher slightly after noon. First, though, I must stop in briefly at the college to leave a letter of recommendation with the secretary in the English department, who has

89

agreed to take care of certain technical details of its submission for me. It merely expresses my support for a friend's elevation to full professorship, but apparently the college must have a signed physical copy, with some departmental form attached, all according to some recondite protocol regarding confidentiality. Kind of her to go to such trouble, really, since we have met only twice; she was hired the year after I left my post. At the moment, I cannot even recall her name.

In any event, I am visiting the garden only to let my wife know that I am going out. She is kneeling at the far end, facing away from me and bent forward over her Ivory Prince hellebore, most of which is now in full, cream-white flower, but of which a few powdery purple buds have yet to open. As it is a plant that generally prefers to be left unmolested, I suspect she is really talking to one of those exquisite coal-black and malachite-green garter snakes of which she is so fond. An old story, of course. Women are forever talking to snakes, blithely indifferent to whatever mischief it might cause. It is their most ancient and irrepressible perversity. She would deny that she does any such thing, of course, but women also tend to take a somewhat oblique approach to the truth.

Not that I have any wish to reproach her. I am very much on the side of the snakes. One might even say I am of their party.

THE DAY PROMISES to be fair. The sky is already a luminously pure blue; the clouds are few and of a picturesquely opaque white; the air is dry and just pleasantly warm; there is a constant breeze, too soft to be especially chilly, but washing everything in a fragrant freshness. Everything glows in the limpid brightness, even the shadows. Every color is alive, and every living thing is stirring.

From here, over the western wall of the garden, across the gently descending gradient of our butterfly meadow — aster, verbena, mallows, mistflower — I see the gauzy crowns of my emerald world swaying, fluttering, flickering. Green and rippling silver. A great wave slowly, continuously cresting and dissolving into spindrift and then surging again. I can even faintly hear the sweet, sharp susurrus of all those tenuous leaves.

I DO NOT RECALL precisely when it became customary for us to call my cultured grove of mixed running bamboos the emerald world, though I know it was sometime in Christopher's early years. Perhaps he was four when he fastened upon the phrase, after I had used it in his hearing two or three times. He was too young to take it as a whimsical circumlocution; to him it was simply a somewhat enchanting proper name.

I had planted most of it half a decade before he was born — or, rather, I had hired landscapers for the task. It is a laborious thing, controlling such an aggressively invasive flora, but making a bamboo forest for myself had been a private desire since boyhood, when I had first lost my way in the ornamental orient of my father's volumes of Lafcadio Hearn, Arthur Waley, Lin Yutang, and Witter Bynner. And I love the plant's graceful simplicity. I purchased this property in large part because I saw at once that it afforded me sufficient space in which to realize my design. The western end of the field next to the house already provided a natural barrier against too ungovernable a proliferation of the bamboo rhizomes: a low but sheer embankment, into which a rough stone wall had been built to help prevent erosion, and atop which a large copse of deciduous trees held the soil firmly in the tangled nets of its roots. From there I needed only to have two fairly deep, curving trenches dug and filled with coarse white dolomite gravel, sweeping convexly to either side of a large, irregularly oval area about sixty yards wide, and nearly converging at the serpentine path of blue slate I had had laid lengthwise across the enclosure. Then it required only moderate vigilance to prevent the grove from swelling beyond its appointed bounds.

It is composed almost entirely of Moso bamboo, with great dark culms and fine feathery leaves, rising perhaps seventy feet from the soil. To either side of the entrance to the grove, however, are broad, contained beds of a more delicate golden bamboo, no more than twenty feet high. And, on its northern side, in another contained bed on the opposite bank of the trench, there is a large stand of black bamboo, particularly lovely, with culms like polished ebony and leaves like dark green tourmaline.

And it was all fully grown when Christopher arrived. It soon became our special retreat, our hidden place — just he and I. We squandered many a clement afternoon and many a cool, hazy morning there, at its center, where the slate path widens into a circle twelve feet across, surrounding a simple bench of levigated granite, and where no one — perhaps not even you — could see us. When he was very small, I often carried his box of wooden blocks along for him, so that he could build and destroy and build again, patiently, lazily, tirelessly. Joyously, without malice. At first, when he was very small indeed, he built only odd, tottering towers or irregularly machicolated walls, which soon fell of their own accord; but as he grew older, his designs grew more elaborate and more redoubtable, and we had to buy better, smaller, more numerous blocks, so that he could erect his astonishing castles and fortified cities with a freer, more gallant hand.

It was there, also, that he acquired his love of tales of chivalry, the more fantastic the better. I read to him and I told him stories of the knights of King Arthur and the paladins of Charlemagne; he became especially fond for a time of the tales that I extracted (quite chastely expurgated, of course) from the Italian Orlando romances. When he was eight, he could keep that strange, grave, curious quiet of his for hours, asking only the very occasional and very precise question — showing me only the dark brown hair of his head, his dark blue eyes always turned downward towards his blocks — as the episodes unfolded: the pursuit of Angelica, Merlin's Font and the Stream of Love, the siege of Albraca or Paris, Orlando harrowing Morgana's fairy kingdom beneath the lake and releasing the captives held in charmed durance below the shimmering dome of crystalline waters, Ruggiero's rescue of Angelica from the sea orc ("Just like Perseus rescuing Andromeda," he remarked, in a tone of delighted discovery, though still without lifting his eyes), Dragontina's garden, Orlando's madness, Rinaldo battling Ruggiero, Ruggiero slaying Rodomonte (just like Aeneas slaying Turnus, he might have remarked, had he known) . . . and I would look down, having till then paid little attention, to see Albraca or Atlante's magic castle at my feet, marvelously conjured up among the pools of violet shadow in a resplendent, faceted polychrome of brightly painted wood.

His Durandal, or Durindana — call it what you like — his shining, unconquerable, infrangible blade — was a slender green (though now pale, ochreous yellow) bamboo rod, two inches in diameter, only about two-and-a-half feet in length, to which we one day affixed a circle of balsa rescued from the ruin of some other toy as a hilt. Its sheath was a long cardboard tube left over from one year's Christmas wrappings.

He loved tales concerning Astolfo best of all, because they were always the most ridiculous: Astolfo carried off by Alcina's whale, transformed into a weeping myrtle bush, catching the giant in Vulcan's net, dashing off with Orrilo's head, ascending to the earthly paradise on the hippogriff, descending to Hades, riding to the moon in Elijah's chariot with the Apostle John to retrieve Orlando's wits . . . He loved Astolfo.

I MUST ADMIT that the sight of my wife crouched over the flower bed still stirs my animal appetites, despite those light-blue twill slacks she has adopted — the sort typically worn by suburban crones once they have reached their calm harbors, far beyond the storms of menopause. It is as if she is determined to grow old before her time. I understand, of course; she was all of thirty-six when she first entered that desolate land where she has wandered for more than nine years now; it is natural for her to want to hasten the story to its end; but her figure resolutely refuses to abandon her.

Bending over her, I lay a hand affectionately on her hip (or thereabouts). "Everything all right, my little callipygean pigeon?" I say, as cheerfully as I can.

She merely glances at me over her shoulder with a wry smirk, gently pats my hand, moves it away, and turns her attention back to the hellebore. "Weeds," she says simply.

"Ah," I reply, as if genuinely deceived, and straighten myself again. "Well, I have to go into the department to drop something off."

"What about Christopher?" she asks, still not looking at me.

"After the department. Before lunch."

"All right."

And that is all. I depart, and she does not look back to see me leave, and I do not linger in the expectation that she will. It is all quite hopeless, really. All the old witticisms are now just souvenirs from another time, a vanished and irretrievable world of sentiment, and all attempts at that playful satyriasis that nourished our love for so many years are now entirely unavailing: labored, vaguely uncomfortable ceremonies honoring an ancient hymeneal covenant, without any of the old savor. Even on those occasions when we temporarily relent from our twin, inseparable solitudes, the act of love has a desperate and pathetic quality to it — though it is certainly not devoid of tenderness. Principally the discharge of a need, three-quarters physical (degradingly enough) and one-quarter emotional (and that emotion mostly anguish). There is always, admittedly, that brief, deliquescent moment of consolation, that instant when each of us succeeds in yielding to the other, but even that is necessarily ephemeral and incomplete. In the end, brute nature is served — as it always must be — but little else.

It is not her fault — or mine, for that matter. And it is not as if the love between us were no longer there; it simply seems to have no purpose any longer. It is so very strange to live on and on when all one's days are aftermath. Ember evenings, ash-blue mornings. Empty hours in the intervals, or hours of oblivion.

And, of course, on those late fall nights when the wind grows mournfully canorous around the house's eaves . . .

But let me not wax too self-indulgent in my melancholy.

THE NEWLY RESTORED, bone-white pavement leading from the lower lot to my erstwhile department is almost incandescent in the late morning sunlight. The breeze is stronger and more persistent here on the college hill, and the broadly spaced row of old Persian ironwoods, with all their thick, forking, beautifully brindled trunks, transforms large sections of the path into quivering, coursing, turbulent undulations of light and shade. The effect is dazzling, even slightly prismatic: the satiny gray shadows of so many leaves, moving so continuously and in such sharp contrast against the bright cement, seem to send out faint, flashing radiations of color from their edges — illusory pale pinks and transparent greens and melting blues. For a moment, it looks rather like mother of pearl, over which a shallow stream of clear water is rapidly flowing. For a briefer moment, I fantasize that I am hovering over a lake clouded with milky minerals, just below whose surface I can see the iridescent silver scales of some immense, gleaming fish, turning its flank upward as it swims quickly by.

Such lovely fancies glint and glimmer and frolic over the dark, mysterious abyss of the thing in itself — such exquisitely diaphanous veils, such beautifully bright brocades. Trinkets for the amusement of children, to distract them from their fears.

Lovely, but . . . Well. . . .

Oh, my love — my love — how did we ever get ourselves into these dreadful straits?

Fate is not really, I have to say, the subtle ironist she is often reputed to be. It was a favorite theme of mine when I first started publishing my poetry, in the days of what one critic has called my "luxuriant formalism," before I graduated to the "austere lyricism" of my more mature verse: marriages grown chill and lifeless, cold women wandering in empty rooms, taciturn Eves patrolling the herbaceous borders of barren Edens, love reduced to sad futility, wedded souls evacuated of old passions and filled in again by the crystal pseudomorphism of inert habit . . . (that is a dismal metaphor). The third poem I ever published, "Epithalamium," was a picture of a man and wife sitting in their living room before a dying fire (a somewhat obvious symbol, you might note), surrounded by a clumsy farrago of cold mineral imagery (equally obvious), and ended with those pretentious lines that no twenty-four-year-old dilettante had any right to commit to paper:

> He says, "I sometimes wonder whether we
> Have somehow each become the other's ghost."
>
> Below their cupola of clear blue light
> His voice grows soft as wind that dwindles in
> The rocks and in dry streambeds comes to nothing.
>
> Their forms have grown as cold as shadows glimpsed
> Below the surface of the sun-stained sea,
> As still and fixed as the eternal splendors.
>
> And thus forever they are framed within
> The silver sheen of their specular world,
> In each the shining figure of the other —
> Diamond, absolute — the changeless idea
> Whose lifeless image each has now become.

Mannered and false, I would say if you were to ask me now. I had some notion that I was describing my parents, though I realize, in long retrospect, that I actually knew almost nothing about them or their interior world.

After all, anyone seeing the two of us might well imagine — might very well imagine, my love — that our life together is little more now than a necessary, disillusioned accommodation, a resignation to mutual dependence, long drained of true affection. Not so. There is such a deep and ineffable tenderness there. No one but us could possibly know.

I AM NOT SURE how felicitously I can continue to maintain this fiction of the present tense, I should interject here. At the moment, I am in truth sitting on my bench here at the heart of my bamboo grove, writing out the day's reminiscences in the afternoon light, which is already beginning to turn to an amber glow among the emerald stalks and languid leaves. It is exceedingly quiet now; no breeze is stirring. Waiting for nothing: I, my fountain pen with the thin, italic nib, this handsome leather-bound notebook I bought just yesterday, a bottle of mineral water, and an eleven-year-old copy of my collected poems (which I brought along only so that I would get the lines I just quoted right).

The days are growing longer, though, and the evening will be long in coming.

Oh, and Durandal, which I brought from the umbrella stand in my study yesterday, purely on impulse, and seem to have left here overnight. Of course, I should not insist on that name alone; there were extended periods when it was Excalibur.

Whatever name it bore, Christopher generally came girded for battle to this enchanted grove, his charmed blade at his side, even when he intended only to lay it aside and devote himself to his building. And he came often, as the two of us retreated to this place more and more frequently once his "behavioral difficulties" had been diagnosed by that curiously vapid young doctor. Not that I found the diagnosis of any particular value — "on the continuum," was the repellently emollient phrase he used, or "very high functioning" — except as a convenient way of making excuses at awkward moments, or of explaining without bothering to explain.

Otherwise I knew, from early on, that mine was a strange and intelligent child who took the world into himself at a somewhat different angle than did children cast in a more ordinary mold. When he was five or six, it was evident to me that he was unable quite to absorb the social grammar of other children, or of anyone else; he could not quite "read" the emotions of others, or even his own emotions. All his responses seemed either too extreme or too mild. And then there was the delightful — but also slightly uncanny — absence of any impulse towards malice in him, and his consequent inability to anticipate or understand malice in others. He always expected — joyously expected — kindness, and could become easily distraught when he belatedly realized that another child wished to mock or provoke him, and was utterly defenseless against the pain and perplexity it could suddenly wake in him; and yet he remained unable to respond in kind. Of himself, after all, he was so boundlessly prepared to be happy, and so innocently ready for everyone else to be happy along with him.

And, really, why — not that I expect you to tell me, of course — should it be any more complicated than that? Such a little fellow, "socially confused," desperate for friendship, so deeply and ecstatically moved when he found it — those occasional, touching, slightly embarrassing effusions of unguarded affection, even towards children who were not disposed to reciprocate — but generally so lonely, and so bemused.

No need to start down that path again, though. Normality is something of a curse too — so often the property of a limited imagination and

a mediocre mind. And, anyway, we had our world here, our deeply mysterious emerald world, all of our own making, blue and lavender shadows,
gold and glassy green light, and so many gloriously happy hours and days.
It was always especially pleasant for me in those periods when a new enthusiasm had seized the foreground of his slightly obsessive interests —
say, the various periods in the development of medieval armor. Anything
that he could arrange in taxonomies, set in order, classify, effortlessly
memorize and recite, with that perfectly precise diction of his, that ring-
ing, invincibly elated voice.

There were four or five months, when he was eight, when he became
utterly fascinated by the various versions of the story of the quest for the
Holy Grail; and, typical of him, he prevailed on me to assist him in making a list of them all, as far as we could find them out, arranged chrono-
logically, which he illustrated with vivid crayon renderings of the object
itself — sacred chalice, serving dish, platter, heavenly stone — as well as
the occasional magic castle or wounded king. I keep it still on the wall of
my study. We never quite completed it, never being certain we had discovered every telling of the tale.

A FEMALE black swallowtail has sailed into the mazy shade here and set-
tled for a moment beside me on the bench — sable wings with flecks of azure and yellow, glittering sapphire hindwings with russet ocellations —
but she will float away again very soon, no doubt, back to the meadow and
all its sweet, drowsy, seductive nectars. She is only temporarily lost. Her
proper world lies out there, just beyond those gates of golden bamboo.

That blue that shimmers on her hindwings is the same color as those
lovely dragonflies — green darners, I believe — who occasionally visited
us on summer days, borne on those fragile, opalescent wings. There is a
stream where they breed on the other side of the embankment at the
western end of the grove. Christopher used to greet the appearance of
any that found its way to us with an excited "Dragonfly! Dragonfly!" —
not so much as a spontaneous expression of surprise, at least not after a
while, but as something like a liturgical acclamation.

I suppose I should go on — should allow my transtemporal gaze to
sink down again, through the golden transparency of the present, back
down into the abysmal hours of this horrid day, down into a more terrible
present, always too present — but it truly is pleasant to linger here in the
soft, viridescent stillness, hiding from you in the cool of the day . . . not
from shame, I assure you.

Do you like the name Christopher, incidentally? I certainly always have.

LISA IS the secretary's name — of course; and, happily, it comes to me just as I enter the departmental office. Lisa something-or-other. Very pretty, as it happens, and rather young, with a predilection for short skirts, though quite married, I believe. She is cheerful and gracious and assures me again that it is no trouble at all for her to take care of the letter for me, and then we exchange a few pleasantries — she asks after my wife, of whom I give a good report, and I ask her, in a much more general way, how she has been. It emerges that she is indeed married, and that her first child was born eight months ago (a girl named Emily, sweetly enough). I apologize for not having heard and then lavish felicitations and a few sagacious bromides upon her, of the sort that the young expect of the middle-aged, telling her how wonderful the whole experience is; her delight and pride in being a mother obviously still lie very near the surface, and are easily coaxed upward into the light; she laments that she has left her little book of photographs at home, so she has none to show me; I tell her I share her regret (which is a lie).

When fewer than ten minutes have passed in this way, I turn to leave, and almost succeed in doing so, but on entering the corridor am forced to pause. Approaching the office is Thomas Brennan, OP, drifting along the hallway in his drab white cassock like a cloud of glutinous ectoplasm, silent but for the delicate, irregular staccato of that grotesquely hypertrophied rosary he wears looped from the cincture around his waist, reaching all the way down to his left ankle and back. I have to say, this particular, comically kitsch affectation of the Dominicans has always struck me as somehow rather lewd; it is so pornographically exaggerated that it comes across as a kind of nasty carnival fetish, like the huge, tumid leather phalluses pagan revelers supposedly wore during the Bacchanalia; and somehow its air of sickly saccharine piety makes it seem all the more limply obscene. But it certainly suits Brennan, what with his lividly pale complexion and flaccid jowls, and those thin purple lips of his, perpetually pursed in that slightly degenerate frown. Of all those ghastly gray specters floating about the campus in their virginal pinafores, wafted along on the mild tropic winds of unmerited privilege and undeserved deference — the whole chattering gaggle of them, sere and gaunt, sleek and oleaginous, or gelatinously obese — he is by far the most immediately repellant of the lot: the most severe, the most pompous, and the most hideous.

Sadly, however, over the years neither of us has taken the trouble to put our intense dislike for one another into words, and now it is too late, so we are obliged to greet one another with at least a show of cold cordiality. As he draws near and athwart, with a faintly suspicious expression on his face, he nods at me very slightly and calls me by my Christian name.

"Tom," I reply, with an equally minimal movement of my head.

He does not care for this, of course; he believes he should always be addressed as "Father," even by his colleagues — it is, for him, a jealously cherished and inalienable appanage of rank — and any coarse familiarity from the laity invariably fills his gaze with a soft, sulfurous gleam. It seems to me such an oddly unfashionable point of ceremony upon which to insist, especially since he would surely never think to address me as "Doctor," and at least my honorific was something I earned (though, admittedly, not very strenuously); but he attaches enormous importance to such things, probably because he has never actually done anything of significance with his life. He sighs quietly, looks at me balefully with the morose, hooded eyes of a disappointed lizard, and in a voice phlegmily eloquent of incipient emphysema asks me how I have been.

Well, I tell him, and ask the same of him.

"Well," he says solemnly. "I'm in a better mood now that this whole limbo affair has passed without anything stupid being done."

I have no idea what he is talking about, needless to say, and tell him so. Foolish of me. My manner is too polite, evidently, because he mistakes my indifference for curiosity; and so he briefly explains that the Vatican had recently been contemplating some definitive statement on limbo, and had even convoked a kind of consultation on the matter, and the fear among many of Brennan's ilk was that the whole idea might be eliminated altogether from the arsenal of Catholic superstitions (not quite how Brennan puts it, of course) — and not in favor of a doctrine of the eternal perdition of unbaptized infant souls, of the sort embraced by that depraved neurotic Augustine and his disciples (Brennan might have found that a tolerable verdict), but in favor of some sentimental notion that God might simply admit such babes into the eternal bliss of the beatific vision without their having been first certified for salvation by a man in a backwards collar. A terrifying prospect, needless to say. In the event, however, Rome had stepped back from the precipice at the last moment and simply issued some wholesomely anodyne statement to the effect that it is quite licit to hope for the salvation of unbaptized babies, but that we can have no absolute assurance on the matter.

"And that's a good resolution to the issue, is it?" I ask.

"Yes, of course," rasps Brennan, "because the whole point is that we can't presume on the grace of salvation. We simply don't know what happens to such souls. We only know that baptism brings us into the community of the redeemed. But . . ."

"It's not a very appetizing picture of God, though, is it?" I interrupt. "I mean, is it all that comforting to imagine a God who might exclude innocent babies from heaven on a technicality?"

I do not know why I bother to provoke him, really. I know he is a fiercely partisan and conservative Dominican who clings to his order's traditional Thomist theology of predestination with all the proud, uncompromising zeal of the most heartless Calvinist; and I also know, more to the point, that he is a vicious and saturnine old monster who delights only in what is harshest and most horrifying in his creed, and who could never love a God any less callous than himself. He has standards.

I have not angered him, however. I can tell, because he replies to me in his customary basso croak, rather than in the piercing mezzo-castrato squeal to which his voice rises when he is genuinely agitated: "First of all, an unbaptized baby is only free of personal guilt, but not of the stain of original sin . . ."

"Yes, so I gather."

"And, secondly, the limbo of infants is a state of perfect natural beatitude. Such children would be denied the supernatural grace of seeing God, that's true, but they'd never know what they'd been deprived of, and so wouldn't suffer. In fact, they'd be perfectly happy within the limits of nature. Thomas is quite clear on this: the vision of God comes through a gracious super-elevation of the creature, beyond its nature. And, since God doesn't owe salvation to anyone, there's no injustice . . ."

"And you believe all that?" I again interrupt.

He sighs and, with a more audible note of exasperation, says, "What I believe is that baptism is necessary, and how God deals with the unbaptized is beyond our knowledge — whether hell or heaven or limbo — but . . ."

"I don't just mean the whole silly mythology of it all," I continue, as if I have not heard him: "inherited sin, magic baths, all those different compartments in the afterlife, and all that. I mean, you really believe that it's all just a question of what God owes us? After all, surely it's ultimately a question of what sort of God you believe in — what sort of character you imagine he has."

"Grace is a gift," he says, with a sententious solemnity that suggests he thinks this a very powerful riposte.

I ignore him, however, and continue: "I mean, if a very wealthy man with a large estate chooses to throw a party for all the local children, but then elects to admit only a few of them into his house — say, the children of only certain favored families — where all the choice delicacies and the best sweets are laid out, as well as a great many gifts, while the rest, the common village children, have to stay outside in the garden and be content with dishes of cheap vanilla ice cream and graham crackers and perhaps a few balloons — well, I suppose you can say he didn't have to throw a party for any of them, so it's all very gracious of him to give the little urchins outside anything at all, but wouldn't you have certain doubts about the man himself . . . about the queer narrowness of his largesse? There's at least a hint of cruelty there, isn't there?"

Brennan shakes his head impatiently. "No, no . . . anthropomorphisms of that sort are just emotional . . ." And so on. Or something like that. I am not really listening to him.

After a few seconds, I interrupt again, for the last time: "Anyway, it doesn't concern me. It's not my church anymore — not for ages now — so I really don't care one way or the other. But I'm happy you're pleased with the verdict." And then, sparing him the unnatural effort of attempting some warm and patient expression of pastoral concern — *de rigueur,* I should imagine, when dealing with apostates of my particular kind — I tell him I must run, and then immediately make my way to the stairs.

I NOTICE, as I pause beside my car to survey the compact, dreary campus high up above the parking lot, that there are small, pointillistic streaks of bright green tree pollen on my windshield and hood. Quite striking against the dark red.

This is perhaps the last time I shall ever see this place. At least, I cannot imagine why I might return. Last year, there was some talk of a dinner in my honor — "distinguished poet," faithful servant of the college, popular lecturer, retired early for personal reasons, but *generously* granted the title of emeritus nonetheless — but I begged off, somewhat brusquely. Why let what modest fame I have achieved outside the college be conscripted into the order's interminable adventure of self-aggrandizement?

After all, I hate them absolutely. Oh, well.

The ornamental pear and cherry trees encircling the lot are in full blossom, and the air about them trembles and flitters and coruscates with the showers of white and pink petals shed continuously upon the breeze by their seemingly inexhaustible boughs; farther up the hill the Judas trees and dogwoods are also in bloom; and the buds on the red and white azaleas bordering the grounds are now so swollen that they are visible even from here. In the spring and early summer, this rather gruesome campus becomes almost attractive, at least in those places where ingenious gardeners have done their heroic best to atone for the sins of the architects. But nothing can ultimately make all that dull and serviceable brick and concrete and steel anything but depressing.

My encounter with Brennan seems to have left me inordinately annoyed. The man always irritates me, of course. He takes such insufferable pride in being allowed to disport himself in the epicene regalia of his sect, though I cannot imagine how anyone can really take pride in belonging to a society that strove for so many centuries to erect the edifice of a renewed Christendom upon a *fundamentum inconcussum* of charred human corpses. He once had the temerity to tell me, without any intentional drollery, that we lay scholars should count it an honor to belong to one of the only two Dominican regular colleges in the world, and to be able to aid the brethren in their "mission." A curious delusion, I must say, given the real feelings of the lay faculty towards that whole morbidly unaccomplished caste. As far as I can tell, the only mission of the brethren here is to live lives of parasitic inutility and luxuriant idleness, contributing as little to the world as possible, while demanding as much from it as they can contrive to wring from the credulity of the faithful. Even I, for all my lovingly cultivated cynicism, am still occasionally scandalized by the lavish appointments of the college priory — the televisions, the recreation lounges, the fine food, the liquors, the fleet of new cars — and by the lives of pampered indolence, furtive dissipation, and dreary extravagance nurtured within its walls.

None of that, however, accounts for the special distaste I feel for Brennan just at this moment. I suppose it is only a passing mood, but I honestly think that, if I had a slightly more developed capacity for violence, I could quite happily throttle the last dregs of life out of that wizened throat. It is not simply that he is often an inadvertent Satanist; that is his tradition, after all, and anyway, confusions are inevitable here below in the land of unlikeness, in this great emptiness we walk in. The god of this world and all that, as the Apostle says (and who can always know where his orisons go when they float upward like the smoke of incense, and as an evening sacrifice?).

Really, though, how odd it is when Brennan — or anyone in that sterile faction — talks about children. How peculiar that he should imagine he even has the right to speak of their innocence, or of their sin. What, after all, can he possibly know?

It is not a question only of moral credibility — the small matter, for instance, of that ordained child-molester that the Dominican province sheltered for nearly thirty years, and moved from parish to parish and even country to country in order to conceal his deeds, and finally assigned as a youth minister to the Dominican church and day school just across the road from the college. It is a question of moral intelligence, of emotional competence. They cannot grasp how profound the mystery of a child's innocence really is — how utterly captivating it is, how it delights and then wounds us, how charmed and then helpless it leaves us — and so how abominable its betrayal is. When the predator in their midst was exposed (quite by chance), most of them behaved as if it were a matter no graver than the discovery of yet another alcoholic in their ranks, and seemed more resentful of the parishioners who demanded explanations than horrified by the evil their institution (and some of them) had knowingly protected for so many years. Certainly none of them put off his habit in indignation and returned to the world where responsibilities force men to acquire moral characters.

Not that that surprises me. It is only to be expected. These things in white dresses are not men; they are abortive sketches of men, tragically arrested in emotional development, their consciences still unformed, their souls still unawakened . . .

But who gave them leave — was it you? — to hide themselves so, to trade the labor of morality for the ease of unearned deference, to live forever insulated against the terrors of love? Why should they suffer none of it? And what right can they have to say . . . ?

Well, of course — what right?

The flowering Judas trees, and there a yellow swallowtail . . . The dark purple hyacinths in the garden at home bloomed early and have already begun to die. The —

My hand has begun to ache, but there are still quite a few hours of daylight ahead, and I intend to go on while I can.

This bamboo sword was also, I should note, the Vorpal Blade with which Christopher, when he was barely six, repeatedly slew the Jabberwock. And then also, in the person of Badger, he often wielded it as a cudgel to drive the wicked weasels, stoats, and ferrets from Toad Hall. He learned the habit of heroism early.

No stain of blood upon his hands, though. He was innocent — perfectly innocent — more innocent by far than any vengeful god who might accuse him of anything.

It was always "Christopher," incidentally, never "Chris"; somehow the shortened form could never quite attach itself to him properly.

This quiet place — a place of recollected bliss —

Once, when he was three and a bit, I brought him here in the morning, still in his sky-blue pajamas and red slippers — I do not recall why precisely — and sat watching him slip again and again into the green depths of the bamboo culms only to emerge somewhere he thought I would not expect (though of course I heard him as he crept awkwardly about), gleefully calling out "Here I am!" each time he showed himself, with a prolonged, rising inflection of the final syllable, smiling rapturously, as if it were the cleverest joke that anyone had ever conceived. I was wholly entranced, wholly vanquished. Paradise. Paradise.

Surely a man who has never known such a moment cannot be entirely a man. He simply cannot know.

WE COULD NEVER BE certain what would suddenly cause him distress, what would alarm or dispirit him, what would become all at once too oppressive to bear. Usually it was a matter of too great an assault on his senses all at once: too much noise, too confusing a spectacle, too much . . . But then, also, if a story went astray from the path he had laid out for it in his imagination — he dwelt so entirely in any story — the path, that is, leading to a happy ending, in which no one is finally lost. I ought not to have told him of the crab that bit Morgante, or of Arthur at Camlann, or of Christopher Robin going off to school.

Or, of course — the most obvious example — of what befell between Agricane of Tartary and Count Orlando: How the paladin found the pagan in a verdant glade of the shadowy woods, separated from his defeated army, resting by a marble fountain, but still in his armor and helm, and how such chivalrous courtesies passed between them that Orlando desired that they might part in peace, if only Agricane would receive baptism from him; but the Tartar king declared that he would rather have the privilege of striving with Christendom's greatest warrior than a throne in paradise. From noon till evening, Durindana and Tranchera rang out in the clearing, and when the sun descended below the western mountains and stars glittered in the sky, the two warriors agreed to lay their arms aside and rest until dawn, when they would have light enough to resume their combat. And as they lay there in the darkness, Orlando beside the fountain and Agricane at the edge of the glade, the paladin sought to convert the infidel to the true faith, exhorting him to look upon the silver moon and golden stars, to think upon the shining sun, and to adore the God who made them all. The Tartar, however, soon changed the conversation to talk of war and love, which led each in turn to profess his inextinguishable love for Angelica; and so, spurred by jealousy, they rose again to fight in the darkness, more fiercely than before, until at last, in the pale rose-and-pearl light of breaking day, Orlando dealt Agricane a fatal blow. As he was dying, the Tartar professed faith in Christ and begged baptism of Orlando before death could carry him away to hell, and the paladin — his eyes brimming with tears — gladly consented. When Agricane died, Orlando left him upon the fountain's marble rim, his sword still in his hand, his crown upon his head . . . lying in state within the empty glade . . . surrounded only by the solemn forest, the morning mists, the ferns gently swaying and gleaming with dew. . . .

A lovely final tableau, but Christopher was oddly pensive: Why, he wished to know, why did Agricane have to be baptized to go to heaven? Because, I explained to him, that is what people believed — what many people still believe — that no one can see the kingdom of heaven who has not been born again of water and . . . But within a few seconds I could tell that the thought had disturbed him, that the frightful calculus of so strange and pitiless a doctrine had immediately become obvious to him, and that his agitation had begun to grow and would become uncontrollable if I did not quickly put his mind at ease. No, no, he insisted, already on the verge of indignant tears, that can't be right, that's all wrong, because all the people, all the children . . . And no, of course not, I assured him; it's a silly and depraved idea, a hideous picture of a monstrous god; but they knew no better, honestly, they had no concept . . . But why did they think it? Because of Adam's curse, my son, because they thought we were all bound over to condemnation, because we were born in guilt . . . But, again, seeing him shake his head violently at the notion, I tried quickly to comfort him: they were deceived, they lived within a close and confined world, they had no way of imagining . . . Please don't be so upset; don't worry; you were baptized, you know. A foolish remark, this: of all things, this was what he did not want to hear. The damage was done. He was frantic and sad until I could at last distract him with something else — an hour, perhaps.

A pall of horror hung over those stories for the next week or so, and I had to tell him tales of a different sort.

So it is: from out the mouths of babes and sucklings. The wisdom of innocence. The pure eye that sees those obvious truths somehow invisible to the eye of experience.

Poor old — dismal old — wretched old Brennan: he and his "stain of original sin." A Jesuit New Testament scholar once told me it was all a gross misreading of Paul, or perhaps a faulty translation, or both (I cannot quite recall). Not that I care; the New Testament thoroughly bores me, except for a few parts of the Synoptic Gospels. I do know how to read a story, though — I know precious little else — and I can see that the lovely fables of Genesis have nothing to do with the great cosmic, moral tragedy of Christian doctrine, all of which just spoils a delightful fairy tale, gilded with countless ingenious touches of fancy. Not that first creation account, of course, the Elohist narrative — first cousin of the *Enuma Elish* — which is beautiful and grand and full of radiant trumpet fanfares, but which is also rather too epical and hieratical for my tastes on most occasions. The second account, though, the Yahwist story, is pure and brilliant whimsy, myth at its most magically buoyant and ironic, a sparklingly droll "Just So" story ("How the Snake Lost His Feet"), as perennially appealing, and nearly as profound, as *The Wind in the Willows.* Yahweh, the king of the gods (hereinafter to be referred to, with periphrastic fear and trembling, as the LORD), plants a garden wherein grow the two magic trees that nourish the gods: the one whose fruit grants them the wisdom to discriminate good from bad — precious from worthless, gems from pebbles, splendid raiments from naked squalor, and so forth — and the one whose fruit endows them with unending life. Then he decides he needs a gardener to tend heath and tilth and orchards, so he forms a little clay automaton for the purpose — no doubt in the image and likeness of the gods (hands, feet, face, buttocks, and so on), just as in the Elohist account — and brings it to life with his own breath; he then sets his creature to work, naked and abject, but too rude of wits to feel any shame or resentment. Fearful lest the man should eat from the garden's magic trees, however, the LORD lies to him and says that their fruit is poison, and that a single taste brings death before sundown. Then, rather tardily, the LORD realizes that the man will need help in his work, and so goes about making an assistant for him — rather maladroitly at first: first he creates all the world's animals, hoping one of them might be equal to the task, and only when this fails does he decide to rock the man to sleep, pluck a rib from the poor creature's side, and fashion it into a woman. Thus Eve is born of Adam's dream, more beautiful than he, but no less ignorant. But the serpent — who is not wicked, and certainly not the devil, but only the most cunning of the beasts the LORD made during his earlier experiments in finding Adam a helpmeet — knows the truth of things and decides to share it with Eve. Who can say why he does this? For mischief's sake, perhaps, but (then again) perhaps out of compassion. Maybe he feels sorry for these silly, deluded, guileless tenants of so exploitive a landlord. Call it the birth of revolutionary consciousness. Whatever the case, he is an honest beastie, through and through. He tells Eve that the fruit of the tree in the center of the garden is not poison, but will instead open her eyes and give her the wisdom she lacks, the knowledge of the value of things, the secrets that the LORD has hidden from her and Adam, for fear they might become rivals of the gods. And so she eats, and prevails upon Adam to do the same, and their eyes are opened — and we know the sequel: the LORD's alarmed discovery that his creatures now know themselves to be naked, his recriminations at their ingratitude and contumacy, the punishment he pronounces upon the head of the noble snake for its indiscretion, his cursing of the man and the woman with perpetual toil, puerperal pain, and death, his expulsion of both of them from the garden, and the cherubim set to guard the gates of Eden and the fiery sword — and why, pray tell? Because — so the LORD quite candidly tells his fellow gods — they have eaten of the tree of wisdom, and now man is like one of us, knowing what is good and what bad; what now if he should stretch forth his hand to eat from the tree of life, and thereby become immortal? Would he perhaps eventually overthrow the gods themselves?

Ah, great Milton, to have composed so sublime an organ fantasia, with so many pedal points and so many stops pulled out, on so effervescently, frothily facetious a little tin-whistle tune.

It was ever thus with the LORD, incidentally. One sees it again in the story of the Tower of Babel — which, of course, is a story not about a tower, or about some thwarted human attempt to storm the heavens, but about the anxiety occasioned in the LORD when he discovers that humanity has devised that mighty and terrifying new technology, the brick. Seeing that men have now found a way to escape from the hovels to which they were confined in the days before kilns and mortar, and have built a great city with a high tower rising from its heart, right into the sky, such is the LORD's surprise that he immediately runs to the other gods and frets that, if left to their own devices, men will ultimately accomplish anything to which they set their hands; let us prevent this, then, he urges, by going down among them and confusing their tongues and scattering them to all the far corners of the world.

A strangely sympathetic sort of god, really, in a dreadful way — at once magnificent and inept, brilliant and dull-witted, bountiful and jealous, magnanimous and petty, kind and cruel, wise and erratic. One might almost love . . . or pity . . . but, of course . . .

What can one say? How deeply can one love one's own terror? One can, of course, crawl, creep, cringe, and grovel before him — but love him? Not a god to cross, we can all agree. Samuel hewed Agag in pieces before the LORD in Gilgal, after all. But love? The most desperate and defenseless and tender thing we have to give?

Curious, though, how those tales have been read again and again, centuries on end, and so few have noticed what they say. How have you contrived to make that happen? What enchantment have you worked upon us?

Not all of us, of course. The Gnostics of old certainly noticed. The Ophites even went so far as to adore the serpent as an enlightener, a secret emissary from a world far above the empire of the demiurge, descending from a plenitude of light . . . of mercy . . . of pity and love.

Silly old snake. Darling old snake.

I too have noticed, of course.

EVERY NIGHT, all the little figurines — the knights and damsels, chargers and palfreys, kings and courtiers, fantastical beasts — had to be arranged upon the shelves by his bed, exactly in the same positions each time, or else he could not sleep.

Nine years, ten months, seventeen days.

Why should I not hate you? Truly, I should like to know.

THE LIGHT, palely golden in the fluttering leaves, and between the slowly swaying culms . . . and, when I look up, that great eye of soft, luminous blue, fringed by the mercurial sparkle of green and silver leaves . . . that blank, quietly menacing, mysterious gaze. . . .

How delightful the breeze has been all day. It reaches me even here.

He and I, on a few occasions, caught fireflies here on summer nights — here in the emerald world, that is — and briefly held them in a jar with a perforated lid. Not, I suppose, entirely kind, but we let them all go again soon enough, once we had seven or eight or so altogether, and had had a few moments to delight in their unearthly, golden beauty, languidly flaring and fading, in constantly changing combinations, as they crawled along the concave surface of their transparent prison, or drifted from one side to the other, faintly and oddly reflected in the elliptical glass. When he was very small, Christopher would cry out in sheer ecstatic wonder. And then, when we released them, and the last of them floated free into the night, what magic fire rose from our hands — what spirits of fire . . .

A metaphor so obvious I should not allow myself to indulge in it.

That, though, was Ptolemy's greatest improvement upon Aristotle's cosmos. The exquisite silver tangle of all those epicycles and equants and deferents and eccentrics of his was lovely in its own way, but his true genius — aesthetically speaking — revealed itself in the idea of the *primum mobile.* Admittedly, there was poetry enough in Aristotle's vision of the sphere of fixed stars as the First Moved, the highest heaven whose spiritual intelligence is eternally consumed with adoration for the Unmoved Mover, and whose great changeless sidereal odyssey is only a grave, glistering, gorgeous symbol of the immutable object of its love — motion's desperate imitation of eternal stillness — highest potency forever striving to become pure act. Even so, Ptolemy showed himself the still better poet by imagining the highest heaven — the farthest circumference of the great cyclophoria of the eternal machinery of the interlocking heavens — to be a final invisible barrier, incorruptible ethereal crystal, alight with all the fluent, incandescent splendor of the empyrean beyond, but surely more impenetrable than adamant. There was some sublime intuition at work there, some knowledge that what most truly imprisons us always eludes our sight, always awaits us as a last bitter surprise, an impervious irony at the outermost circumference of things, a kind of oblivion at the end of hope, a substantial nothingness, an enveloping, sustained bass note of despair behind the music of the spheres.

The way that leads beyond, after all, is so very hard to find.

Even so, even so, the blessed spirit — the innocent spirit — the liberated spirit, encumbered by neither terrestrial body nor celestial soul — the spirit that shines from within itself, with its own uncreated light — the spirit cannot be contained even in that imperishable glass, rage though the archons might. He has overcome the world.

I WANDER ABOUT inside my house for several seconds looking for my wife, only at last to spy her through the kitchen window, still out in the garden, sitting on the near wall with her back to me, staring off towards the butterfly meadow and the sky beyond. I nod my head slightly, attempt a forlorn or sardonic smile, and set about preparing a simple lunch for myself (brie, rare roast beef, and cucumber on buttered baguette, with a glass of cold mint tea, if you care to know). As I eat, I watch her, scarcely moving as she sits there, looking away into the distance. I am aware that I am still in a state of mild agitation over my brief exchange with that withered gelding at the college. I really must put it out of my mind if I am to be in any fit condition to visit Christopher.

As I clear away my plate and glass, I find an eclectic bouquet of flowers from the garden, tied with a bow of slender scarlet ribbon and standing in water in a tall jar beside the sink: five half-opened white roses, some gold and crimson snapdragons, delicate blue bellflowers . . . a few others. . . . Not a combination I would have thought to concoct, but she has an unfailing feel for these things. The arrangement, modest thing that it is, is quite oddly beautiful. I gaze at it for several seconds, for some reason counting the blossoms, briefly lost in its quiet turmoil of colors. And then, somewhat idiotically, I realize too late that tears are filling my eyes, and the flowers are merging into one another as the world around them dissolves, like melting glass. I might have expected this. There are always these unguarded moments, tediously predictable, when my grief furtively steals up on me and overwhelms me, and I temporarily break down, and I have to wait until I am able to freeze my emotions into stability again. Perhaps if I had not been occupied with thoughts of Brennan and his noisome religion, I should have noticed it coming on. Whatever the case, I cannot go out of the house until I have brought myself back under control. Fortunately, my wife continues to stare away into the sky from her perch on the garden wall, unaware that I am even in the house. A choking sound wells up from my throat three times; I clench my fists and press them against my lips; I tremble slightly; but none of it, thankfully, reaches her. She sees only that dazzling emptiness . . . that fathomless, beautiful blue.

At last — after perhaps seven minutes or more — I am composed again. I release a thin stream of cold water from the tap into my cupped hands and wash my eyes several times; then, turning the water off, I dry my face with the pink dishtowel my wife hung out this morning. A comb run twice through my thinning hyacinthine locks, a few manly clearings of the throat, a stiffened back, a straightened shirt, and I am ready to proceed with my day.

My wife turns her head only for a moment when she hears me approaching along the flagstones, and then turns her gaze again westward.

When I place a hand on her shoulder, she simply says, "You're back, then."

"Yes."

"Were you going to have some lunch before you go?"

"I've just had some."

She nods and then looks over her shoulder at me. Her eyes linger on mine just long enough for me to realize that I am not quite as perfectly presentable as I would like to think, and that she can tell that I have been weeping. She says nothing, however, and with only the slightest hint of sympathy in her expression — a brief tautening of her lips, faintly approximating an understanding smile — turns away again. "I've left some flowers inside for you to take to Christopher."

"Yes," I say, "I've seen them." And then, after a few seconds: "They're lovely."

"Are they?"

It is not a question to which she wants any answer, so I simply bend over and kiss her gently on the cheek. She raises her hand, places it on the opposite side of my jaw, turns to kiss my cheek, lets go, and then resumes her patient surveillance of the void.

I dry the stems of the flowers with the pink dishtowel and leave the house. Christopher is only twenty-five minutes away by foot. It is, I have occasionally reflected, extraordinarily convenient for me that my entire world is now enclosed in a space so hospitably exiguous that I can walk across it in less than half an hour, and comprises almost nothing but groves and gardens and umbrageous knolls. And the way is pleasant: tree-shaded pavements along an unfrequented road, a gloriously neglected hedge of blossoming barberry, a deep, grassy bank of wildflowers in a profuse riot of bright primary colors, an elegant wrought-iron gate set between two weathered granite posts, a quaint, late seventeenth-century spire in the middle distance, just visible between two venerable yews — positively idyllic, really.

She never comes with me on these visits, though she does occasionally (albeit increasingly rarely) go on her own. Her garden is her home now, her station, her sentinel tower on the vast, dark frontier of the habitable world, and she is not disposed to abandon her post. Blue-daubed barbarians with matted hair, blue and golden hordes borne on the thunder of a hundred thousand hooves . . . the threats are innumerable. And, I suppose, she keeps watch over that border for both of us, while we wait.

There is, you see, that lingering sweetness between us, that unspoken understanding that must preserve us for as long as we must go on. If there is anything like holiness in our life, it is the reverent silence we keep here, the veil drawn before the inner sanctuary of our shared knowledge, the secret we do not allow to be profaned by the eyes or tongues of others (especially not yours).

What we *can* say, but what does not need saying — and what, in truth, we should not deign to say to a world where venomous ghouls like Brennan are always on the prowl — is what we know about our terrible and heart-wringing tenderness for our strange and delightful only child. That is another, more inward garden, which only we can enter, and from which neither of us could ever bear to depart. So many memories, so inexpressible in tone and texture, with so great a power to enrapture and to wound. Our secret world, just ours.

I recall, for instance — the memory comes unbidden — that afternoon at the playground. Christopher had just turned five the month before. He had wanted a party, of course — the idea of a party appealed to him, and he expected it — but he really had no friends at the "prekindergarten" school. Not that he knew this, of course, my gentle boy, who could not . . . connect. In a quite abstract sense, all the other children around him were "friends." So, in the event, we succeeded in coaxing six other children, through their parents, to come for cake and games. After three hours, during which our heartless little guests had paid far more attention to one another than to our son, the miserable affair had ended. Christopher had been entirely content with the experience, as it happens; he had had a party, much as he imagined a party should be. I, however, was hideously despondent for days afterwards. Now, though, as I came to collect him from the school's playground, into which all the children had been released at the end of an arduous afternoon of storybooks, or of construction paper, paste, and glitter, or whatever, I was greeted by a sight that momentarily brought me the most exquisite joy. The play of the children was wild and rapturous, astonishingly loud and blissfully shrill, a ceaselessly coursing whirl — or, rather, whirls within whirls, clockwise and counterclockwise, flowing together and apart, combining and scattering and coalescing into ever-new patterns — of twenty-five or so little ones, around and around the swings, and around and up and down the ladders and slides of the central wooden platform with its green tin roof, a tempest of laughter and cries of exultation; and there, in the middle of it all, at the heart of that glorious tourbillion, that happy, tumultuous *bacchantische Taumel,* I saw Christopher, spinning about with his arms outstretched, his eyes turned upward to the sky, smiling ecstatically, laughing, lost to the world; and, as Wordsworth might say, my heart leapt up. But then, after only a few moments more, my elation died; I became all at once aware, rather terribly, that he was not actually playing with the other children at all, nor they with him. All those other little imps were rejoicing together, on all sides of him, but he was set apart, his cavorting and cries of jubilation entirely ignored by everyone else. He was immersed in the thrilling chorus of their delight, yes; he was, as far as he could tell, part of their games; he was quite happy, unconscious of that fuller communion from which he was excluded, too small and too peculiar of temperament to notice that he was in fact alone in the midst of all that frenetic happiness. Quite utterly alone. And the realization struck me to the core of my being with one of the fiercest pains I had ever felt. As I hurriedly strode across the playground to catch Christopher in mid-gyration and gently tell him it was time to leave, I even briefly felt the most shameful detestation for all those other — those callously normal — children. Foolish, of course. He was perfectly untroubled. He did not want to leave yet, but I was insistent, anxious to escape my own suffering, to which he was quite properly insensible. He, like every pure spirit, brought his joy with him into the world.

How long, though, I found myself wondering that night, would his innocence protect him from his own loneliness?

Not long, as it happened — but that is neither here nor there.

These things are not nearly as dreadful as we imagine, perhaps. Every child . . . every child . . .

In any event, it is this that none of them can possibly know: this entrancing anguish that one's love for one's child can excite in an instant and sustain for all the years thereafter, often recurring as small, sporadic paroxysms of grief, arriving unexpectedly, in one's most defenseless moments. If they did, they could not possibly be so cavalier about the evils they harbor in their midst; they could not embrace and celebrate the diseased ideas of someone like Thomas — that plump, perfidious porpentine bristling with malice against everything holy within our nature, who believed that salvation was as rare as genius, and that the vision of the torments of the damned would increase the beatitude of the saints; they could not . . .

But why do I keep returning to this today — to them? They are only so many irritants, as insignificant as they are sterile.

As for us . . . well, as for us, my boy, let us leave now, let us go from the echoing green, from the playground, let us return to our own world, our emerald world. I have more stories to tell you. Perhaps I shall tell you tales from the *Shahnameh* today — we have neglected Persia, after all — the deeds of mighty Rostam — perhaps Rostam slaying the dragon. Not the tale of Sohrab's death, however — why trouble you with something like that? But, still, let us go apart to our hidden place, right now, and I shall tell you of the Oxus flowing down from high Pamere, till/His luminous home of waters opens, bright/And tranquil, from whose floor the new-bathed stars/Emerge, and shine upon the Aral Sea.

THAT WAS quite long ago, I know. Pardon me a moment's fantasy, though, if you will — you who sit on high and laugh. Though perhaps that is unfair, really. I may have no right to reprehend. When all is said and done, really, I cannot decide how I should feel towards you.

So perhaps a few confidences whispered between you and me, god of this world — maker of this world — all strictly *sub rosa,* as it were. Or perhaps I should say *sub foliis bambuseae.* If you are listening, that is, or can hear me.

Why did you frame the world thus? Did you, in fact, frame it at all, or do you merely preside over it in its brokenness, as a desolate inheritance? Did we perhaps all frame it, in a time before time, you and we together? And how did we come into it? And how can we flee home again?

Not that I expect answers. It does not matter, really; whatever the case may be, however it arose, you bind us to it with the fetters of desire, and imprison us within it behind walls of illusion. Not just *tanha,* though, not just the brute, impervious *conatus essendi,* not just the mindless will to power: none of that, by itself, could have enchanted spirits of light, or trapped them within the subtle crystal of the First Moved. Rather, age upon age, you dangle the lure of love before us to tempt us into life, to draw us from the shining, golden seas of being into the perilous shoals of birth and death, of hope and despair, of belief in the future and the venture of love. But there lies your folly too, because the sheer exorbitance of our love — its utter prodigality and extravagance and heedlessness — reminds us of what you want us to forget: that it comes from beyond, from far above the savage economies of this world, and so must inevitably subvert them. Love will always find the hidden light of the other world here below, in fugitive or captive form, in beauty; it wakens nameless memories in us; we glimpse our own transcendence within what imprisons us. The Good beyond being...

Certainly that is what we both saw, she and I, in Christopher: that transcendent innocence, that unworldly grace, that charm that drew us out of all our private worlds, that fragility, that angelic otherness — whatever it was that shone out from him, and that went out from us to him, surely came from beyond this world of violence and terror, transient joys and abiding sadnesses, Darwinian processes and mechanical law. That infinitely precious innocence of which you despoil us all in the end, one way or another.

But no need to quarrel. Perhaps your story is the greatest tragedy of all, a dark tale hidden in the abysmal depths of the heavenly ages. I no longer have the strength to want to judge or the energy to care. I want just to slip away, very quietly.

THERE REALLY IS so much for desire to feed upon here below, however — that much I cannot deny. The beauty of it all is no illusion.

Earlier today, a few hours ago, I was brought to a pause over these pages by the repeated, sweetly piercing song of a male oriole — that terse, amphibrachic trill, rising suddenly to one exquisite high note and immediately descending again — as I tried vainly to tell what direction it was coming from. After a minute, though, the mystery resolved itself; the oriole suddenly darted from the eastern end of the grove and through the air only three feet or so over my head, flashing bright golden orange amid the soft golden green of wavering sunlight and leafy shade; then, just as he came to the edge of the small clearing here, he turned his flight sharply upward and disappeared through the central opening in the bamboo crowns above.

Let all who have eyes to see . . . Again, I cannot deny it.

Butterflies upon the flowering thistles, at the near verge, not far from the iron gate . . . aureate fritillaries and Astyanax Purple Admirals . . . a little beyond that, monarchs and painted ladies amid the milkweed blossoms . . . two goldfinches in flight . . .

It was a bright winter day under a soft blue sky, Christopher was four, a shallow fall of snow from the previous day glistened on the ground and among the leaves of the pyracantha bush that stood under the bay window through which he and I were gazing out, and three or four bluebirds were fluttering their gemmed wings and ruffling their russet breasts among the heavy clusters of flame-red pomes and the slender, lingulate leaves and the glittering ice, when Christopher suddenly remarked, quite unexpectedly, but with a sage and emphatic nod of his head, "I like all different colors."

Now that, of course, is true eloquence: aphoristic brevity, exquisite exactitude, piercing truthfulness. The purity of the infantine eye, the overflowing wellspring of original bliss. Traherne's orient and immortal wheat —

And, yes, my only child, my beloved son, my wise innocent: This world is depth upon depth, layer upon layer, of endlessly varying color — fluid translucencies, lush opacities, alchemies of light, airy tinctures, mineral pigments, efflorescences, irisations — forever changing, forever yielding to deeper, richer, more mysterious hues. For, you see, the ethereal crystal of the *primum mobile* is also a prism, a boundless ocean of prisms, in fact, at once absolutely simple and yet also somehow, magically, an infinity of limpid facets — a geometrical *coincidentia oppositorum,* simultaneously a perfect sphere and a polyhedron of infinitely many surfaces — by whose constant revolutions the clear radiance of the world beyond is transformed into a ubiquitous, dazzling, incessant, rapturous flow of beautiful brilliancies, in which we live and move and have our being here below. How odd and delightful we always found it, in the early mornings and late afternoons of spring and summer days, when the shadows cast among the green stalks turned to that opulent maroon; how enchanted we were that time we watched the gathering evening falling across a farmer's field just before harvest time and saw the long, lateral rays of the sun, filtered through ever deeper fathoms of atmosphere, brushing the blanched gold of the wheat everywhere with a red and purple sheen, though every stem retained its own pallid luster all the while — and even the dark green blades of grass where we sat smoldered with crimson and violet light. Everywhere, nowhere . . . palpable, elusive. . . . Oh, there are such worlds of color, my child. Gulfs of green and blue, archipelagoes of peridot and ivory set amid azure seas, shining coral atolls encircling lagoons of bice and sapphire and lapis lazuli, rose anemones, magnificent mottled sea-cucumbers, blazing with the brightest cutaneous dyes — and need I mention the resplendent glamors of the glorious mandarin fish? Have you seen the Cook Islands? — Well, no, of course not — but those verdant slopes rising up from sugarwhite shores, swept up out of waters of a thousand transparent blues, those boughs heavy with glossy plums or pendant oranges or dark coconuts or delicate lychees like Chinese lanterns in their bright pink, papery skins, and those fields of flowering pineapple, and soughing groves of teak, and silvery green fields of tea, those phosphorescent seas like endless streams of stars, those ghostly, glimmering reefs . . . If you could see it — had seen it. . . . Though why linger only in sun-drenched latitudes? The palette of the North is every bit as varied. Wooded mountains, glowing peaks, softly lapping streams, ancient forests — the hazy iridescences of morning, the honey-hued light of day sifted down amid the richly tinted shade below the trees, the sleek, sumptuous green of pine needles slowly fading away at evening into the deepening indigo shadows — and fjords with their steep, brooding slopes and vitreous waters and silky skies, the slight aquamarine of the glaciated karst, plunging cascades sending up great clouds of mist, occasionally crowned by rainbows or transformed by twilight into cataracts of cold fire — and (still farther north) the boreal wastes, vast wildernesses of ice, incandescent emptinesses, white abysses haunted by ondulous auroras. . . . But then again, of course, even the arid regions of our bright porcelain bauble of a terraqueous globe shine with numberless colors: delectable desolations, parched purities, where golden sands stretch and billow beneath magenta skies; where eddies of dust rise suddenly in glittering spirals, coalescing for a moment into spectral shapes, only to disperse again just as quickly amid the trembling pillars of heat rising up continuously from the pale desert floor towards the inexpressibly deep cerulean above; or where — some lands coming into the fullness of their beauty only at night — ancient wadis, bathed in moonlight, gleam softly, like veins of marble in the dark bronze of the wastes, while the creamy crystalline glaze of broad salt flats, memorial of vanished seas, shimmers in the velvet darkness . . . everything quite still, quite dreamlike. . . . And do you recall the time we found those lovely bluish-green lichens spreading across a rust-red rock, or the first time you saw the plumage of a peacock's outspread tail . . . the scarlet blush of parting day . . . swelling green limes among delicate white lime blossoms . . . ?

Well, enough of that. It goes on forever, of course. Whole worlds of color that — if they could just be purged of their omnipresent alloy of unbearable suffering — would bespeak only an artisan of incomparable taste, invention, benignity, and resource. But it is impossible. And so we say, my beloved son — must say — that it is all only a stolen beauty, secreted hither, made captive in the glass of time, immersed in the ocean of prime matter, a dim reflection of a fuller — ineffably fuller — beauty. Now we see as in a glass darkly, as in a darkened mirror, scored with countless fractures . . . now we see —

I cannot go on much longer. My hand aches abominably. And it will soon be too dark to continue writing.

SUCH A small fellow — and all alone.

As I approach the place, I find myself again summoning up the memory of that day on the playground. Why? Absurd how we contrive to torment ourselves in this fashion, return continuously to the sources of our pain, compulsively reiterate the trauma. Perhaps Freud was on to something after all.

It is not that I am so foolish as to rank it among the most tragic moments in Christopher's life. The sadnesses of childhood lie before us all, and lie behind us all; they are inevitable. And so much else can happen — could have happened — immeasurably worse. So many evil fates your world contains, so many horrors lying in wait for all the hapless children who wander through its dark and empty places, as carelessly as if they were merely strolling through a garden, never suspecting that the idyll is an illusion, concealing perils and terrors that adults cannot bring themselves to name, till some kindly serpent at last wakes the children from their dreams, pouring the poisoned nectar of his wisdom in their ears. He could have been killed by mischance, or maimed in an accident on the road; he could have lost both of his parents when he was very small; he could have been kidnapped by a child murderer, or abused by a predatory pedophile in a white cassock; he could have died in a burning house; he could have been killed by a rapidly metastasizing cancer . . .

Ah, did you catch that? Did you note the ironic insouciance with which I slipped that last item onto the list? Because, if you recall — do you?

Well, I cannot tell it now, with the daylight waning, with the memory of it so intolerably clear. He feared physical pain so extraordinarily; the idea of it seemed to disturb him more than the reality; with the reality he bore, I suppose, no worse — nor any better — than other children, at least after the first few moments of alarm. And the pain, and the weakness, came strangely late. The darkness spread through his small body for some time without his even being aware of anything wrong — such is the insidious subtlety of that deep malevolence that resides in matter . . . in the intractable substrate (absolute evil, as Plotinus said).

It was I, in fact, who first discovered it, one cool afternoon little more than a month after his ninth birthday, as we wandered along the edge of the bed of black bamboo, the leaves stirring in the constant breeze, murmuring and sighing and chattering, sunlight and shadows splashing and dancing all around us, the air sweet with the scents of autumn, when I placed my hand on his back as I laughed at something he said and felt an unusual, hard protuberance through the cotton of his shirt, no larger than a small coin, just below the right shoulder blade, and an uncanny thrill of terror passed through me, even before I knew what I was afraid of, even before I had looked to see what it was my fingertips had felt. All at once, scarcely consciously, I sensed the ordered world collapsing, the foundation of things shifting suddenly, violently. Somehow I knew before I knew, as if it were something long expected . . .

Why was that?

Well, no need to rehearse it all again. Either you recall or you do not: the diagnosis, the unbelievable extent of the affected tissue, his mother's constant weeping, his fear; the therapies that seemed to be killing him more rapidly than the cancer, the terrifying, bleak sterility of the hospital room, the withering away of that small body; the rapid decline near the end, all those needles that he hated so desperately, the unavailing tenderness of nurses, his inability quite to grasp . . . the lonely expression he often had . . .

I must not . . .

There was not room for all his figurines by his hospital bedside in the last weeks, though he had some with him — the one with the sword raised up above his head in both hands, for instance, whom he had long ago chosen to play the part of Orlando. A constant companion in the dreadful night.

He had talked about making a dragon costume for Halloween, before we knew of his illness. We were planning to get him a pet dog that year also, come to think of it. I believe he would have enjoyed that a great deal.

One afternoon, three weeks or so before the end, he reminded me of the tale of Orlando and Agricane, his pained perplexity over baptism and hell, and I knew I must not allow him to work himself into a turmoil again — though, in fact, he was too weak for that in any event — but I reminded him once again of his own baptism, and once again that gave him no comfort, in fact missed the point altogether, and then I recovered myself by assuring him that there is no such place as hell — only the infernal pains we visit on ourselves — and certainly no hell for children. And then I realized that I had just, without intending it, without actually saying it, adverted to his death, however indirectly, as something inevitable and imminent. I had never done that before.

Curious. When one allows one's mind to drift forward on the tides of expectation and dread, one can always encompass the thought of one's own death — exit, ideally stage right, in the ovine ranks; but the idea of the death of one's child is impossible to contemplate rationally, even as the remotest of possibilities. There had been instances in the past when even the thought that he might die in advanced old age, long after my own departure from this life, had struck me as much too sad to bear.

No, there is no hell. We have all our prisons and our penances right here. Pain enough here — so very much pain — so much pain, really, my son, my small friend, my deepest joy. My boy, my boy, my boy. My little boy.

Do not be afraid. Please do not. Please know that we are only wandering gods, lost for a time in a dream, under a dark enchantment. We will awake.

I remember, I noticed on the day he died that the jessamine was still in full, bright yellow blossom. Today I noticed that there were not yet any signs of flowers on its branches.

THESE EPISCOPALIANS are a fastidious breed. Everything is immaculate, everything is perfectly tended. The grass is always mown, no weeds are ever in sight, the areas around the headstones are always cleared of any drifting debris; and yet I have never seen any gardener or groundskeeper at work.

Among all the other graves, Christopher's is one of the humbler affairs: a plain marble marker with a smooth crescent top, all still quite clean and bright after nearly a decade, with only his name, the legend "Our Beloved Child," and his dates — bracketing all nine years, ten months, and seventeen days of his life with us — recorded in sharp, shadowy intaglio. Neither my wife nor I wanted more than that.

I place the flowers right up against the stone and remain there for some time, on my knees, sitting back on my heels, staring at the words but thinking nothing. Now, so all my calculations tell me — confirmed a hundred times or more as the days on the calendar have drained away — it is nine years, ten months, and eighteen days since then. Gone now one day longer than he was alive with us. I suppose I could extend my reckoning for another nine months or so, to encompass the period of his gestation, but I could never be quite as precise then. And I need an exact date from which to measure . . . something. All the pitiless immensity of space and time, perhaps, the endless before and after, the uncrossable beyond — the cruel absurdity and stony indifference of it all. Everything of your contrivance, everything that holds us fast below the waters of the firmament, the roof of crystal, everything . . .

As I have said, I know the secret — we know it. Love comes from beyond the whole of things here below. This world has no claim on it, and never had any claim upon my son. He was the plunder of heaven, the spark that must fly upward again. And we —

Well, for us there is only now the waiting, the time that must be accomplished, and nothing else.

The air is so fresh today that it is almost intoxicating. The fragrance of honeysuckle is floating all about me, issuing, I think, from the tree line on the far side of the iron fence.

I have to stop. I cannot write about that place.

MY WIFE IS still in the garden. Or rather, I suppose, in the garden again. But I have seen her nowhere else today. Again she is seated on the garden wall, beneath which the ink-blue shadows are just beginning to lengthen in the grass; again she is staring away quietly westward, and again I am watching her through the kitchen window.

As it should be, I suppose. Look to the lands of evening, my love, the Western Lands, far past the desert places. There our rest awaits us.

And, oh, I love her so, with this terrific, sad tenderness, which can heal nothing, and for which no words suffice, and of which none can be spoken. So we wait — for another world, another age, over there, on the other side of the dark waters.

With my pen in my shirt pocket, the books in one hand, the bottle in the other, I approach her along the flagstones, and as before she turns her head to me when I draw near. I tell her in a few words of my visit to Christopher, that I left the flowers she had prepared for me, and she nods. Then I tell her I want to go sit among the bamboo for a while, perhaps the rest of the afternoon, and she nods again: "All right." I kiss her on the cheek, for a moment she leans her head back against my chest, and then I detach myself from her, pass through the opening in the wall, cross the garden, pass through the opening in the opposite wall, cross the meadow, towards the passage between the stands of golden bamboo, and enter into the heart of the emerald world.

IT REALLY IS too late to continue. I am writing in moonlight now, though the moon is so fiercely bright beyond the fringe of leaves above that I can still make out the words. But the sky is no longer the deep blue of evening. I can see the stars beginning to emerge from the darkness above. And how my hand aches — I doubt I can straighten my fingers now.

Anyway, I am exhausted. I can think only in fragments. And I am all but out of words. I needed — I *need* — to put an end to words now — to write nothing more, ever.

Soon the stars will have filled the sky . . . like those phosphorescent southern seas. Oceans of stars.

To which the fireflies rise up when freed from their glassy prison.

The true stars lie still higher up, perhaps, in a truer heaven, to which the souls that have passed even beyond the *primum mobile* aspire —

A very pretty conceit, my lad.

Do not be afraid.

And you — I can still hide from you, or conceal what is inmost within me, what is most secret and most precious. Here, in this sheltered place, how can you find me if I do not answer when you call?

I have come to understand many things these past several years, you see.

Again, do not be afraid. The Red King dreamed it all. Paris still stands, impregnable among the pools of shadow and golden-green sunlight; its brightly colored stones are all in place.

And, please, ignore the cherubim, the fiery sword. Do not be afraid.

And — and . . .

Oh, please — release your grip on me. Please please please, just let me go. I understand, I forgive everything, so just let me depart in peace.

How long must we wait? Imprisoned by memory? Please . . .

And yet —

Those lustral waters, that radiant dawn —

Leapt from its sheath, bright Durandal —

Up there, higher up, in the true and peaceful heavens, in the empyrean, all is purity, all is light. Here below, all things flow, from nothing to nothing, under the turning and returning and always dismally returning spheres. But, even through the moonlight, I can just discern the Milky Way now, dimly glimmering in the deeps above, a distant reflection of another place, a glimpse of the true, the endlessly coursing stream of stars, where souls are afloat in the oceans of the infinite. There — above — lies the glittering path across the vast abyss. There.

The path that leads beyond.

2009

The Ivory Gate

My friend had grown quite old, it seemed, in the three years since our last dinner together. In the rich golden light that shone through the restaurant's French doors onto the garden terrace — to which we had retreated after our meal to enjoy the night's unseasonable coolness and the *bel canto* of the crickets — his skin looked almost like parchment, stained with a faint patina of decay. In his eyes, as he stared at or through the amber cognac in the glass on the table before him, I fancied I could almost see where thin white webs of blindness had begun to collect. And the light here, frankly, was comparatively kind to him. He had looked far worse five hours earlier, when the taxi had left him at my porch and I had seen for the first time the ravages of his recent ill health. Then he had seemed almost wraithlike to me, with his fragile gait and his tremulous hands and the floating gaze of his failing sight. My alarm at his appearance had been so obvious to him from the excessive gentleness with which I addressed him that within only a few moments he was offering me reassurances. "Really," he said, "I'm not quite so near the brink as you seem to think I am. I'll be all right. I just need to rest a bit before dinner. It's been a long trip."

An hour later, claiming to be fully refreshed, he had resolutely refused to let me drive him to the restaurant, insisting that we walk the four-fifths of a mile along the paved bicycle path behind my house, past "my" fields and woods. "It's such a lovely stroll," he said, "and this may be the last time I'll have a chance to see any of it. Anyway, this coastal terrain of yours is as flat as parquet. I won't have any trouble." Then he had risen, only a little unsteadily, before I could help him from his armchair. "We'd better go now, though. I'm slower than I used to be, and I like walking slowly anyway. You don't mind. After all," — he smiled a slight, wistful smile as he looked uncertainly at me, trying to discern the expression on my face — "it will be only the two of us tonight."

The sun had not entirely sunk below the horizon when we started out, and there had been enough of the day left to allow him, despite his poor vision, to take in my trees and flower beds. He had paused for a few minutes by the ornamental maple at the eastern end of my property, briefly holding one of its samaras close to his eyes and inspecting the vinous purple staining the lower halves of its wings. "It's as if they'd all been dipped in blood," he murmured. "The pagan in me is strangely stirred. Nature mourning for Adonis or Osiris . . . or Attis, or Christ, or Dionysus, or one of that crowd. I don't suppose there are any sacred groves of maples on Mount Ida. But you know" — he let go of the samara and turned to me — "nature really is just a system of intelligible symbols, inviting us to read its secrets . . . and always keeping them concealed. The veil of Isis, you know."

"Of course," I had replied; "what could be more obvious?"

The rain that had fallen throughout most of the day had left the air exquisitely fresh and almost chilly, as though it were early spring or early fall. Hovering a few inches over the yellow wildflowers in the meadow beyond my garden was a glistening gray mist, which under the darkening sky created an impression rather like smoke rising above distant fires. The long, shallow ditch between garden and meadow, with its tall, languidly swaying reeds of pallid green and brittle ochre, was full of standing water, rippling at its edges in a slight breeze, but otherwise quite still, reflecting only the sky, so that the banks seemed to be brimming over with a soft, silvery light. And, as we left my yard and for many minutes thereafter, I found myself quietly absorbed in one of those lovely optical tricks by which the outer twilight between day and night makes one aware of an inner twilight between active and passive consciousness: the glossy, bituminous surface of the path farther ahead, shimmering off and away among long grasses and scattered sprays of lavender, seemed as if it were constantly melting before me into both a pinkish violet and a pearly indigo, not simultaneously, but alternately — now one, now the other — entirely as I chose to see it; but, while I could induce the transition from one color to the other at will, not even for a moment could I make myself see the path as both at once. The mirage persisted for only a short time, though. It was fully evening when we came to the narrow spur of forest still separating us from our dinner, and the path ahead was now just an indistinct gray, and we walked through the trees in deepening darkness. Fireflies drifted and gleamed and faded among the dim boles and fallen limbs, while overhead the clamor of the insects in the upper branches rose and fell in an almost perfect choral syncope of strophe and anti-strophe, rising to its peak in one part of the wood just as it had fully descended in another. My friend rebuked me, though, when I called the noise "stridulations." "Don't be imprecise," he said. "Surely those are mostly cicadas, and they don't actually stridulate, you know. They make that sound by flexing their timbals. Timbals and timbrels . . . harps and tambourines. . . . No violins, though."

As we had walked, it had occurred to me more than once that all the clear, individual lines and colors surrounding us were for him, if not invisible, at least resolved into a kind of gossamer haze at the remoter edges of his range of vision, and this had struck me as a particularly sad thought. But by the time we had arrived at the restaurant it had been night, and the world outside was equally dark for both of us, and he had taken such evident delight in his meal and in the exorbitantly priced Bourgogne he had ordered that I was able to put melancholy reflections aside. If nothing else, his appetite had seemed to attest to as yet unexhausted reserves of life hidden somewhere in that frail body.

But now, as we sat on the terrace, I sensed that he was beginning to tire, and would want to remain a while and talk rather than attempt the return journey; and I was certain that, even when he was prepared to leave, he would have to let me call for a car.

2

"*Un ange est passé,*" he said at one point, just after several moments of silence had elapsed between us. "I've always loved that phrase. For a godless race, the French have a great aptitude for stained-glass idioms." He ran a finger around the rim of his glass, with only a few slight quivers of his hand. "You're worried about me. Don't be. I know I look terrible, but I'll let you know if I come over all faint. It's true I'm going blind and, well, of course, I am dying. But I'm not terribly bothered by either of those things, and I think I've gotten used to the rhythms of my sickness. I'm not in any great pain, believe me, and I don't feel any great fear. It's more like a kind of tacit surprise, as if I can't quite believe I'm dying, because dying is simply one of those things one doesn't quite know how to do. The only thing I'm really afraid of these days is boredom. That — that, I have to say — does have the power to make this prolonged attenuation of things seem unbearable. Just visiting with you is a great antidote, believe me — though I'm not sure what shape you'll be in after a week of my conversation."

"Oh, goodness," I replied, "you're one of the world's last great conversationalists. You know everything, and you speak off the cuff better than most of us write. You can stay on indefinitely as far as I'm concerned."

"That's kind of you," he said, "and I would if I could, but there are other people I absolutely must see while I still can. Anyway, I haven't all that much 'indefinitely' left in me, and I doubt you'd want to bother with a corpse in your kitchen or garden. And, of course, I carry my best defense against the monotony with me."

"What's that?"

"My great singular talent, my gift for dreaming, of course."

"Oh," I said, snapping my fingers, "yes, that. Well, yes, I'm sure you can dream up better interlocutors than me."

"That's not what I meant." He laughed and tilted his head to one side. "It's just very good to have that refuge to retreat to when the day gets too long and unendurable. And, anyway, I'm so disenchanted with the world around me, as it is now at least, that I can't help but prefer the worlds I find within. I know I've said it all before" — he waved a hand vaguely in the air by his head, to let me know that he was presuming on my patience — "but I still doubt you can grasp just how vivid and coherent my dreams are, and how fully I live inside them when I'm asleep. I don't know why I have this faculty, or what peculiarity in the structure of my nerves or brain causes it . . . or what little fairy blessed me with it. I simply know that I've never met or heard of anyone whose dream worlds are remotely as real as mine. It's a useless capacity, probably, but right now it's really my best support. The days do get long — not from the sickness, but just from the remoteness of all the old interests and employments, you know, the damnable boredom — and I find real solace in the knowledge, every day, that there's that other, brilliantly visible world waiting for me, or so many worlds, full of strange and beautiful and frightening and touchingly familiar things . . . where what's infinitely precious . . . to me . . ." He closed his eyes for a moment and lightly rubbed his temples. "Someone . . ." And then another pause.

"Should we go back?"

"Oh, no," he said, opening his eyes again and peering at me through their veils, "I'm not worn out yet; I'm just thinking. The brandy's good, and I like it here. No, it's just that I know that, no matter how often I tell you, I can't quite communicate how it is for me. I was in my teens before I really understood what dreams are for everybody else — those shadowy deliria that creep through men's brains in the night . . . fragmentary, shifting, dissolving away into incoherence. It actually shocked me. It still seems ghastly to me when I try to imagine it, to be honest, like something between life and death, or between sanity and madness."

"It's not really as bad as that," I said. "It can be very pleasantly unreal sometimes."

"Maybe. I suppose I wouldn't know, though I've had some pretty formless dreams of my own, usually after long insomnia. And I do have several recurring dreams that seem like little more than moving vignettes, or needlessly elaborate motifs. Just a series of enigmatic images, and a few aimless motions, repeated in the same sequence as on previous nights, and then just ending, always at the same point, inconclusively. But even those feel very real. I simply need palpable things, I think. And connections too — and those connections appear to be unique to me. I mean, I think that what makes my dreams so powerfully odd isn't just their concreteness or their detail, but their endlessly receding corridors of inner chambers. It's like wandering through a labyrinth, with some great blessing or horror waiting for me at its center, if I can ever find it. . . . Though it's a fairly well-lit labyrinth, I have to say . . . like an inner Versailles — mirrored walls and flambeaux in gold sconces and crystal chandeliers — a great, shining maze of metaphors and haunting fables, none of which I can quite interpret, but all of which . . . summon me."

I sensed, simply from a slight quickening in the cadence of his voice and an almost imperceptible shifting of his body into a more upright posture, that he was beginning to sail out of harbor into the open waters of his own eloquence.

"You know, of course," he continued, "since I've said it so often, that I'm able to have dreams within dreams. No one I've ever asked has been able to report anything comparable. I can dream that I'm dreaming, and then again dream that I'm dreaming, descending from one dream into another, and into another, so that the more outward dream always now has the aspect of the 'real' world I'm escaping. It's as if I were moving between different levels of the sea, since I always rise again into the same earlier dream, and from that into the still earlier . . . and so on. And sometimes, when I've ascended again to the original threshold of the dream, I find myself rising into a still higher level of dreaming, as if the sea has risen above me while I swam in its depths, so that the outer context of my dream is suddenly enfolded in a still wider context. There's no clear limit to the vertical layerings of my dreams, downward or upward, and yet the continuity is never lost, which is surely a remarkable thing — well, unless I'm suddenly awakened from all my dreams at once. And then there are all the lovely and infuriating and spectral interconnections between the dreams, the interpenetrations of their distinct stories, the symbolic resonances and shared figures . . ." He coughed, drank some of his cognac, and continued. "It draws me on, constantly, and I never really feel the desire to return. The farther in I go, the more enchanting — but vivid — it all feels, and the more I forget this reality. The feeling is fairly wondrous, really. It's as if I'm pressing on through deepening emerald shadows of forest foliage towards a hidden city, or descending amid coral spires and grottoes and deeper down along fabulous reefs towards some fairy kingdom in the canyons of the ocean. In a dream I sleep and another dream takes me, and it echoes and varies the outer dream in more vibrant and more elliptical symbols, so that that outer dream seems like a plainer reality in need of mythic enrichment — and this simple charm makes illusion seem like truth. And then symbols of symbols ramify endlessly through my . . . *oneiric* worlds. Nice word, that — 'oneiric.' And I really never recall, as I descend and ascend, which is the truly true world — assuming there is one."

"Well, I hope there is," I said. "Otherwise I'd have a hard time accounting for my sense that I'm part of this conversation."

He nodded. "Unless you're only dreaming me."

I shrugged and tapped the table with my index finger. "My imagination isn't that interesting."

"Every man is a great artist in his sleep," he replied with a soft laugh. "Anyway, I don't think I'm really anyone's masterpiece." He stared away, above my head, into emptiness. "I don't mean to repeat myself. I suppose you've heard all this before. I think I can say this much, though: my gift helps me understand the mechanism of dreams. I certainly don't believe in any purely psychological or neurobiological explanation of them, especially not the latter. I know that dreams really might be just the machinery of the brain continuing to run on after we've stopped consciously directing it for a while, in which case they're just a diverting alternative to death. But philosophically I'm unable to take that idea very seriously. I mean, I tend to think of all materialism as an arid superstition and materialists as savages huddling in caves — in Plato's cave, I suppose I might say — and I definitely reject any notion that the order of causality in dreams proceeds entirely from this world into that one. I'm not just talking about Freudianism or anything else of that sort, either. Even Coleridge thought dreams were just the effects of certain emotional states, tricked out in gaudy apparel. But I think it's clear that the causality is actually reciprocal. Dreams are independent realities, even if we don't understand their nature, with their own internal logic and their own purposes; as much as they draw on the daylight world, they also intrude upon it and alter it, and in terms native to themselves, out of realms of reality that they've generated within themselves."

The tenor of his voice had become surprisingly emphatic, and serious enough that I did not allow my lips the faintest crispation of a smile (not that he would have been able to see if I had). He, however, did smile, having himself evidently noticed the same change in his tone; and, after a moment, turning his eyes back towards me, he continued in a gentler key.

"I sometimes wonder if the dream world doesn't have designs on this one, and whether we're not all vehicles — of varying quality — by which it's trying to break through, in order to widen its empire. Maybe I'm just the battlefield where its greatest victory to date has been won. There was a time when I liked to flatter myself that I might have represented some evolutionary next step, the prototype of . . . oh, I don't know . . . *homo somnians,* rational creatures able to walk with equal ease in this world and the dream world. After all, for me the partition between the two realities often seems so very thin and transparent . . . a thin, trembling — another nice word for you — a pellicle. Of course, seen that way, the whole thing might seem a little sinister. I mean, I'm quite sure, as I say, that there's a reality to that other world, but perhaps I can't assume it's beneficent in its designs on us. Perhaps by absorbing us into its symbolic and emotional world — into its whole spiritual sensorium, so to speak — it acquires greater substance. Perhaps it wants to feed on us. I certainly feel at times as if it doesn't want to let me go. And the prospect isn't entirely unpleasant to me, I have to tell you. Sometimes I wonder if I might just slip quietly and permanently over the border one night, leaving only a babbling shell of myself behind. Then all of you out here would simply think I'd succumbed to old age, and that I was conversing with my inner ghosts in the queer glossolalia of deep senility; but I'd actually be living on elsewhere, among more radiant and tenderer visions. I'd . . . but you think I'm joking."

The remark sounded good-humored enough, but also perhaps as if it contained a note of genuine reproach. "On the contrary," I protested. "I take you entirely at your word. I'm not at all . . ."

"Well," he immediately interrupted, "you'll have to excuse me. Anyway, I'm being facetious. I don't really think there's anything dark or terrible lurking out there in the night with designs on us. But I don't think dreams are just secondary realities, either. And they do really . . . as I've said, mine *summon* me. There's something like an invitation in them, or a promise, or a foretaste of something on the other side of this life that doesn't threaten, but that's . . . hospitable. Certainly those little recurring dreams I mentioned to you all have the same quality about them — anticipation, tantalization . . . something more. They're all about *going* somewhere, moving *towards* something, being *enticed*. For instance," — he paused for another sip from his glass — "there's one that comes particularly often. I can't quite capture its feeling in words, but it's positively haunting. It takes place in the mountains — I don't know where. Maybe Switzerland — it looks somewhat Alpine — but it doesn't really look like any place I've actually been. As it begins, it's very early morning, only just dawn, in fact, and I'm ascending a path — not too steep, but clearly on a broad mountain shelf. To my left, a few dozen yards away, there's a ledge, beyond which are thin air and the distant prospect of another mountain and, nearer to hand and lower down, a forested valley of inexpressibly deep green, submerged in shadows of even deeper blue. To my right, a steep slope of gray granite rises upward, and small, sinewy trees in full leaf cling to its craggy face. There's mist everywhere, nearly a fine rain, and the path is carpeted with a thick moss of dark beryl green, which yields pleasantly beneath my feet as I walk. The air is intoxicatingly fresh and cool. And, as I round the flank of the mountain, I come upon an old, disused wooden gate, hanging listlessly on rusted hinges, with wooden rails running from its posts, as far as the ledge on my left and as far as the sloping granite to my right — I can't imagine what its purpose would be — and bending over the right gatepost is a great mass of . . . well, I suppose it's something like eglantine, in full blossom, and wet with the morning mist. As I pass through the gate, having to lift its free end from the ground because the hinges are so loose, I inadvertently shake the white flowers, and they shed drops of water on the back of my hand, and the chill is almost icy. Their fragrance hangs about me for a few seconds as I continue on. Then at last, after just a few more minutes, I reach the end of the path. It leads to a small plateau or open ledge, a sort of scalloped bay in the mountainside — I suppose that explains the gate, now that I think of it: it was originally meant to prevent people wandering up in the dark and falling off the edge. But the ledge is in fact quite broad and safe. The moss is even thicker on the ground here, and there are clusters of white clover and ferns and small blue flowers, and all of it is drenched and silvered over with dew and mist, and when I lean down to look more closely — as I can't resist doing — the silver sheen dissolves into an endless crystal profusion of clear, glassy beads of water. And there's a great tree there, about five feet from the edge, with massive twisted roots plunging deep into the rock, with thick moss among them, and thickly clustered dark leaves above — I don't know what kind of tree it is, for some reason — and I can't quite get out from under it as I come forward, as that would take me over the edge. But what stuns you — stuns me, rather — into rapt contemplation is the vista that opens up before me. I'm looking over an immense mountain gorge, set between two great granite massifs that rise high above my level and stretch away towards a pass far off at the horizon. The sun is still too low to illuminate the mountain walls fully, and the oblique slant of its light through the gorge leaves the escarpment to my right entirely dark while painting only a slender band of sullen gold along the crenellated ridge of the one to the left — though a bit lower down some jutting outcroppings catch a few rays of the sun, where it runs athwart the rock face, so that the dark granite is here and there cresseted with points of startling red and gold. And clouds are rising from both ridges, like smoke, or great ghostly pennons in a slow breeze, into the colorless radiance of the morning sky. And enough of the pale morning light spills into the gorge that I can see the gleaming silver thread of a river wending its way through darkly glistening rocks far below. There are clouds and falling mists in the gorge too, hundreds of feet below me, sometimes hiding the river from view. And then, far away at the end of the pass, there lies . . . something. I can't tell exactly what it is I'm seeing, but I can make out colors: a fiery green, a luminous, sparkling yellow, a wavering, trembling blue — whether the blue of the sky or of water I can't tell. It's like the blue of morning glories, but the branches of the tree overhanging me strangely curtail my view of the top of the pass there, and I can't tell if I'm seeing a clear sky breaking over a sunlit green valley full of golden flowers, or the blue of the sky mirrored in some mountain tarn or gulf of motionless water, or something else altogether. I don't know. . . . But I feel a kind of sweet elation, as if, despite the distance, I'm very near something utterly beautiful, and I have this great desire to find a way down into that gorge, so that I can then find some long, easy path to that valley, or whatever it is. The desire is almost overwhelming, actually, and has a kind of serene happiness in it, as if I've finally found something I've been searching for; it has a quality of anticipation and . . . joy about it." My friend fell silent for several seconds.

"And then what?" I asked.

"Nothing, I'm afraid. The dream simply ends, leaving me suspended up there on that plateau. It never goes any further than that. I wish it did. I just wake up or start dreaming another dream altogether. But what I have to emphasize is that, however slight the structure of the dream is, the whole thing is absolutely sensuously solid to me. I feel everything, I taste the morning air, I sense the cold, I see it all, and it's all *real* to me. Every bit as real as those horrid hydrangeas in front of the restaurant here — absurd, pompous flowers. And when it's passed, the sense of something happily portentous and yet still achingly inaccessible lingers with me for a long time afterwards, whether I go on to dream another dream or just wake up."

"But," I said, "when you're awake, you know you're awake. There is that difference."

"And when I'm dreaming, I also often know I'm dreaming," he replied; "that's all true. But even then it's often only a matter of degree. This world definitely has an advantage over its rivals, in sheer persistence and regularity and deadening predictability. But sometimes it seems fairly unreal as well, as if it too is something from which I still have to wake up, into something even more real. And sometimes, when I'm very deep in my dream worlds, everything is more palpable, more vivid, more lucid . . . more *visible* than life out here generally is for me, especially now. So, who's to say? I've always loved the story about Chuang-Tzu dreaming he was a butterfly and then, on waking, not being able to decide whether he was really Chuang-Tzu having dreamed about being a butterfly or a butterfly even now dreaming he was Chuang-Tzu. Sometimes it almost feels like that."

"I'm quite real, I assure you."

"Oh, I'm not questioning that. I'm simply unsure that they — the persons and things I dream about — aren't just as real, in their ways. You know, an idealist like me can't make himself feel the reality of something more just because he can cut his hand on it, or break his jaw. Oh," — he shook a finger at me, as if something of some significance had just occurred to him — "there's another dream I have over and over again that you'd probably approve of, since it has a library and a forest and a beautiful woman in it: three of your favorite things."

"Oh, by all means, tell me."

"Yes, well — here's the part that should really delight you — it takes place in a library that's also a forest, or at a place where a library more or less seamlessly becomes a forest. And the woman is Asian, and wearing a beautifully brocaded Chinese silk dress of brilliant blue . . ."

"I'm captivated," I said.

"Well, don't get overly excited. There's not much more to tell than I already have. It's all very beautiful, though, in a strange way. It simply starts with me walking through one rather lovely — if mostly empty — room in a house I don't know but in which I seem to be perfectly at home, a room with white walls vertically framed at regular intervals by slender oblongs of polished cherry wood — at least, I'd guess it's cherry — set into the wall like pilasters but without ornaments, and with similar beams running across the white ceiling at the same intervals, and a crimson carpet underfoot patterned with immense blue and ivory and green Chinese dragons and flowers and . . . well, a Chinese carpet. I don't want to get lost in the details. The room seems rather Japanese, though, despite the Chinese décor. There's not much else in it, actually, except off to the left a small table whose base is a filigreed cylinder, elaborately carved from what looks like teak, also with the dragon motifs, on which a bowl of etched brass sits, filled with blue and white flowers. But, as I say, I'm passing through — and this room seems to be just an antechamber — and to get where I'm going I have to walk around a black wooden screen, in four folding sections, and inlaid with tinted mother-of-pearl arranged into scenes of Chinese villages and bridges and waterfalls and butterflies . . . everything you'd expect, in a wonderfully kaleidoscopic Chinese tangle of soft pinks and milky white and pale blues and lime greens and so on . . . and then I have to pass through a dark green wooden door of a particularly ornate Asian design. Dragons again, that is. Anyway, the next room's the library, immaculately kept, not enormous but quite capacious, paneled and wainscoted in what I take to be walnut, though again with pilasters — properly speaking now, with bases and capitals, and each with four regular vertical grooves — and ceiling beams, and there are bookshelves set into the walls to my right and four or five long, free-standing, double-sided bookcases extending from the wall to my left; and all the shelves are full of volumes bound in the most exquisitely attractive leather, tooled and spangled and dyed in reds and browns and blues and dark greens. In short, it's every bibliophile's fantasy of a perfect private library. I don't stop here, though. I'm on my way towards something literally just around the corner. The room is almost a rectangle, but there's an alcove off to the left at the far end and, as I come around that corner, the library more or less melts away at the alcove's far end — or, then again, it doesn't, because everything remains in place, but the end of the alcove isn't a wall, but an opening out onto a narrow path, strewn with brown leaves and white petals, winding out of sight into a deep forest. And I don't mean the wall has fallen away or is missing; I mean that, right there, the library and the forest meet in a natural continuity, one simply merging into the other with fluid simplicity, so that the library is in the forest and the forest is in the library. I even notice that, near at hand, one of the pilasters on the left is also — as my eyes move from left to right — the trunk of a tree whose top I can't see for the ceiling above me; but there's no discrete fissure in the wood at which it ceases to be a pilaster and becomes a tree, though I can see where the capital meets a ceiling beam on one side while the trunk continues on out of sight. And then I note that the path into the forest is also — again, without visible juncture — the hardwood of the floor in the alcove. And the forest itself overflows into the room with its verdure, much of which is broad-leafed and tropical, but much of which is also of a more northerly deciduous kind. I suppose, if it's a real forest, it's in one of those liminal zones of Eurasia, or maybe some part of New Zealand where a transplanted English woodland collides with an indigenous jungle. Anyway, vines with great scarlet blossoms with yellow coronas wind up along the trunks of the nearest trees and reach out into the library, clinging to the beams in the ceiling for several feet and extending small, tender tendrils along the blue Persian carpet on the floor. And all at once I can hear the gorgeous, chaotic polyphony of countless birds, from low booming squawks to high liquid trills and everything in between. There's one great rock near the path in the middle distance, looking like limestone that's been deeply scored by years of erosion, above which a veritable curtain of those same flowering vines hangs from the branch of a tree otherwise hidden from my view by other trees. There are ferns along the edge of the path and among the roots of the trees, some bending into the room, dripping with what is obviously recent rain, but at this moment there's sunlight falling from above in golden sprays, down through the green shade; and, in addition to that, as I look down the path I see a still brighter — or at least a warmer, a more concentrated — golden glow, seeming to emanate not from above but

from deep within the forest itself, small and distant, but shining from behind the dark shapes of the trees and through the spaces between them. I
can feel and taste a fresh, somewhat humid, but still cool breeze coming
from the forest, and there's a mingled fragrance of living vegetation and
flowers and decaying leaves. Once again, I feel that sweet sense of urgency, that desire to press ahead, to follow the path deeper in, towards
that light. I even take a step forward before I'm arrested by the sudden realization of the girl there — or young woman, I suppose I should say,
maybe in her early twenties — simply standing silently to the right of the
scene, more or less exactly at that elusive boundary between forest and library, at once next to an inset bookcase, filled with a large collection of
volumes in bright red, uniform bindings, and also under the shade of a
tree with an enormous branchless trunk, like some great leafy palm —
though I again can't see its crown. She's beautiful — that strikes me immediately — East Asian, Chinese, I suppose, with a lovely figure and dark
eyes and long, straight hair parted in the middle and pouring over one
shoulder. Her hands are folded together at her waist, dressed, as I say, in a
close-fitting silk dress of brilliant cerulean blue, adorned with all those
exorbitantly polychromatic embroideries that Chinese design seems so
adept at making work — our Western wariness of ungoverned color
would generally prevent our attempting anything so luxuriant. And she
doesn't move; she's simply looking at me with a gentle smile, one that has
a certain quality of intelligence about it, as well perhaps as a touch of in-
dulgence, as if she's been waiting for me and knows what's supposed to
happen next. I stare at her for several seconds, hoping perhaps that she'll
move or speak, but perhaps also fearing that she will, as it might break
the spell. But she remains still, apart from the occasional blinking of her
eyes, and perhaps the slightest widening of her smile, perhaps the slightest inclination of her head towards me. . . . I really could look at her indefinitely, I think, as much as I want to venture out onto that forest trail, but
I'm distracted by something out of the corner of my eye, a sudden flash of
iridescent blue as a brightly plumed bird — a bird of paradise — suddenly
flutters into view and alights on a branch just below the level of the ceiling; and so I turn my eyes again towards the forest, and immediately find
myself fascinated again by its sheer lushness and by its utterly undeniable
. . . thereness. And the longer I look into the forest, the greater the wealth
of details I note, the more inviting its aurous depths seem to me, and the
more peaceful and complete my desire to follow the path becomes. I
know the beautiful woman is still there; I see her from the corner of my

eye still standing at the threshold, perhaps somehow silently urging me to go over it; but I don't look at her directly again. I believe that, while I'm dreaming this dream, I'm conscious that it's a dream, but at the same time I'm absolutely convinced that she's someone I truly know — out here, that is, in this world — and this doesn't even seem open to doubt. But she isn't, curiously enough; I've really never met her; and even in my dream I don't think I could put a name to her, or call up any memories of her. . . . Perhaps in some other world . . ."

My friend fell silent, staring away distractedly into the night.

"Is there more?" I asked.

"No," he replied, turning his gaze towards me, "nothing. It just fades. It's just another fixed tableau hanging on one of the walls of my dream palace, appearing at irregular intervals as I wander the halls. It's frustrating, to be honest, but I've grown used to it. Still, I would so like to take that path through the trees. Who knows, though? It might just lead into another dream after all. And, anyway, these little recurring dreams are so rare and so lacking in the complexity of my other, more episodic dreams that their repetitiousness and their brevity make them seem like mere fillers, wedged in between the more developed fantasies that fill my nights — like the notes of some sort of *basso continuo*, occasionally sounding out in the intervals between the primary musical phrases. But, I have to say, they do haunt me."

"Well," — I paused, expecting him to interrupt me, but he did not — "well, what do you make of them, then?"

"Oh, nothing really — just that quality of invitation I was talking about before, that feeling that something, some intelligence — perhaps my own intelligence — wants me for itself, wants me to enter in so deeply I can never leave again . . . because I'd have forgotten the way, maybe, or forgotten this reality altogether. You know, I . . ." — he turned his head at the sound of a footfall behind him — "Is that the waiter coming?"

It was, carrying a bottle, and when we had accepted his offer of more cognac and he had refilled our glasses and left again, my friend resumed speaking.

"I was only going to say that over the years I've frequently found myself trying to tease some sort of metaphysical or mystical meaning out of my gift. It doesn't come to very much, but it's entertaining. Sometimes it takes on positively Gnostic or hermetic or kabbalistic hues. For a long time, for instance, I tried to make a working metaphor out of the dream of Adam — of Eve rising out of his sleep. It was something about how deep within the soul of each of us sleeps the unfallen Adam, from whose dreams all the possibilities of our existence issue forth; and how perhaps the spirit's one great labor in this life is to waken the sleeper within, and to return to the self in its first innocence, before all illusions, before this world . . ."

"This world?" I prompted when he had, once again, paused for several seconds. And then, after several more seconds and a sip from my glass, "I'm not quite following you."

He drank as well, breathed deeply, then coughed drily and somewhat violently, and then drank again. "Sometimes I see what Novalis meant when he talked about the moral vocation to see this life as a dream. It's not a matter of fleeing reality at all, but rather of realizing that, at some preconscious level of our being, we know that there's a greater reality out there from which we're always shielding the eyes of our spirits with the veils of illusion we weave every day. Perhaps we're always asleep, and perhaps all our quotidian experiences are nothing but distant reflections and mirror inversions, and something is seeking to rouse us, and calling us to pass through the mirror of our dreams into . . . the real as such. Anyway, we all know perfectly well that we dream this world too. Any competent philosopher of the transcendental conditions of thought — any boring Kantian — can tell you that the world comes to us as it's fashioned by the mind's apparatus of perception, and by the supreme fiction of the synthetic *a priori.* So, really . . ." He waved the back of his right hand limply at the darkness, as if casually dismissing it.

"Yes," I said after a moment, "quite. But that only means that some degree of illusion is necessary for us to see anything at all."

"Maybe . . . but let's not assume it's a permanent condition. Perhaps we're only fallen from ourselves for a time, only temporarily estranged from the one who sleeps within — or maybe, I should say, from the one within who is always more awake than we, but from whom we've all parted for a time, to wander in the realm of illusions. Anyway, he must be there. Since we have to supply that illusion that lets us see the world — or, rather, some transcendental I within each empirical I has to supply it — we must already know something of the truth behind it — surely. I mean, if there's a prior act of consciousness within each conscious act, one that prepares the world for us, and prepares our minds for the world, then surely at that level we already know what we're dissimulating with our play of dreams. Of course, I'm an older sort of idealist; I think the fit between mind and world has to do with the reality of the forms. But, in either case, the old enigma of the circle of love and knowledge remains, doesn't it? That we have to intend the world to know it — we have to desire and love it, in some sense — but then again we can't love it or desire it until we know it. We're simply born into that circle, at least at the level of normal consciousness. And so, in whom — by whom — is the circle sustained? Not by the empirical consciousness, certainly. So who's that inmost I that sleeps within . . . and who is it that lies at the ground of that I? There are so many ways of thinking of it, you know."

I said nothing and, after a few moments, he continued.

"After all, even that hidden creator within me who crafts this world you and I share — this intelligible language of living symbols — and who's nearer to me than I am to myself, always dreaming all my worlds into being and dreaming them all away again — well, even he must rest upon some deeper foundation of love and knowledge, some . . . infinite source. I'm thinking, I suppose, of that wonderful image of Vishnu asleep upon the infinite ocean of being — and from Vishnu's sleep Brahma arises and creates, and from Brahma, Indra comes forth to rule the world, and this sequence is repeated an infinite number of times. And, well, here I am, a little Indra ruling over a tiny cosmos, unknown to myself in my inmost depths . . . always secretly borne up upon the dreams of God . . ."

"Have you become a Vedantist now?" I asked.

He smiled and shrugged. "I always have been. Or a Platonist. The same thing at the end of the day, you know. Or maybe I should just say I'm a 'perennial philosophy' sort of man. But don't be distracted by the mythological illuminations at the margins of the text. I'm just trying to say that my peculiar talent leads me almost inevitably towards certain reflections on the nature of consciousness. There simply is this — well, there's no other proper word for it — this god within me, or within and beyond me, beyond my little diurnal self, who sleeps when I'm awake, but who, when I sleep, stirs within me and begins to pour forth worlds. And maybe he's more awake when I'm more asleep, and so those dream worlds are nearer the original truth of things than the common dream world we all share, and that we experience as more concrete the more active our little selves are. That's a bit of a convoluted way of saying it. Sorry."

"No," I replied, "I follow you."

He nodded. "All right. It does make me ask, though, who am I, exactly? What is this fleeting, mutable, composite ego, with its chaotic assemblage of impulses and impressions? Is it just a poor, distant reflection or fragment or echo of that maker and destroyer of worlds . . . on whom it depends . . . in whom it subsists? And where am I most truly *I* in that order?"

"I couldn't say."

"And of course, naturally, when one thinks in that way, one begins toying with ideas of the soul's pre-existence."

"I suppose one must, really." I found myself staring upward, into the dizzying abyss of the cloudless night, at the delicate glitter of the stars, and at the slim, limpidly brilliant crescent of the moon that had risen over the trees. "Up there, above the heavens, we saw the eternal forms . . . right? Where's the doorway in and out, then?"

"You mean, how did we get here?"

I looked at him again and nodded; and then, recalling that the gesture might not be perfectly visible to him, I said, "Yes, that's what I mean. Unless you mean pre-existence as just a metaphor, and I'm taking you too literally."

"Oh, no, not at all. I mean it quite literally. I take very seriously all that Platonic imagery of the infant soul, newly washed in streams of forgetfulness, gently ushered into this world to begin anew the great dance of repentance and return . . . down from opalescent altitudes, high up above the world's golden meridians, between the ivy-twined trellises at eternity's gate . . . Porphyry's cave of the nymphs, and so forth. I can't take the idea of endless cycles of reincarnation very seriously, of course — you know, of the sort some of the Platonists believed in — because it turns the drama of personality into a kind of recurrent climatic effect that ends up being too static to be credible. But I really do think that there's something in experience that make it at least imaginatively plausible to think that this life comes afterwards, as a moment of contraction or withdrawal from a fuller life. . . . You know — and, of course, you *do* know — I have very little use for the orthodoxies I was fed in childhood: inherited guilt — which is about as logical an idea as a 'square circle' — the soul's special creation at the moment of conception, babes born already under sentence of final perdition — what an utterly barbaric notion — eternal suffering imposed by a loving God, and all of that twaddle. There are heavens and hells, within and without, I have no doubt, but only as changing states of the pilgrim soul. And, of course, I couldn't flee the embrace of mother church swiftly enough once I'd reached the age of reason, and sloughed off the clammy pall of morbidity that that tribe of petticoated eunuchs had wrapped about my childhood, with their asinine pomp, and their spiritual terrorism, and their cheap will to power, and their obscene sterility . . ."

"Ah," I said, "we seem to be stroking the mystic chords of memory again."

He laughed. "Yes, well . . ." He breathed deeply, this time without coughing, and then shook his head. "I suppose the resentments of childhood are the ones that remain with us to the last. All I meant to say was that, if there's any part of the Christian mythos I could still comfortably inhabit, it would be a version of Christianity like Origen's. That makes moral and imaginative sense to me. I can believe in that story of our fall from the 'there above' into the 'here below' — from the land of vision to the land of unlikeness — and of our eventual ascent again to vision out of the shadows of illusion and cruelty. Sleep and waking — nothing more. Though the way the Origenists tended to describe the pre-cosmic pleroma, as far as I can tell, made it sound a little barren. I like to imagine something more on the order of a living community of spiritual intelligences, in spiritual bodies, acting and interacting, a whole polity and ecology of the unfallen world, full of mysteries and delights and stories — not just a congress of immutable and anonymous essences arranged around a central, anonymous essence. And I simply can't imagine a universal fall. Rather, I imagine the occasional vagrant soul, wandering away from home, lured by some sprite or *ignis fatuus* into forests of oblivion, falling into a stupor, getting lost along winding paths . . . leaving others behind. That's the little thought that really haunts me, I think. Could we who've come this way have departed from the company of others to whom we belonged . . . luminous beings who didn't follow us, but who wait for us? What if for each of us, or at least very many of us, there's at least one of those souls awaiting our return, who can communicate to us only in cryptic symbols in our dreams, calling to us in the dark, across the chasm of time . . . someone we can't quite recall, but for whose face, without knowing it, we always secretly long? As I said," — here his gaze did momentarily succeed in meeting mine directly — "something seems to invite me, or someone. But" — and again his eyes wandered away from me — "it may just be the proximity of death that makes me talk this way. I've always tended towards those kinds of fantasies, in an inconstant way, but these days it may be getting a bit obsessive."

"That's understandable," I remarked.

Again, as the French would have it, an angel passed; each of us was pursuing thoughts of his own along some divergent path; the crickets chirped on drowsily; the moon continued to rise by imperceptible degrees in its shining mandorla of transparent blue; and there was now an unanticipated sadness between us, for which I had no proper words.

At last, though, just before the silence became awkward, my friend spoke again. "I don't want to bore you, but could I tell you about one of my long, many-layered dreams? I had it some years ago, maybe nine or ten, but I know it's not one I've told you about before. I know I've bored you with plenty of others over the years, but if you'd indulge me, I'd be grateful. I think it would illustrate my point. If you don't mind."

"Of course," I said. "Please."

3

"It was a dream about Sonia — and, yes, before you say anything, I know that all the dreams I tell you about are about Sonia. I can't help it if they're the ones that affect me most deeply. I suppose I'm just a doting husband, at the end of the day. But this one wasn't at all pleasant. It began in Madrid — that much I knew as soon as I sank down into the first stratum of the dream — and it was morning, bright and hot, and I was standing on the balcony of an obviously rather luxurious second-story hotel room, looking out over the Calle de Alcalá towards the Plaza de Cibeles, which was near enough that I could see the tall plumes of water rising in the square from the fountains around the goddess in her chariot. The immense quasi-Gothic stalagmites of the Palacio de Comunicaciones were so dazzlingly white that they didn't seem to be quite standing still; it was almost as if the whole edifice were gently floating side to side in the clear sapphire of the summer sky. The pristine Spanish sunlight fell full across my balcony, and gave an almost unearthly vibrancy to a cluster of African violets that stood by themselves in a small, red-clay planter on the broad rail of the ornate iron balustrade. I had already bathed and dressed, I knew, and was awaiting my coffee, but Sonia was still in bed, sleeping, as lovely as when I had first known her, though I was somehow aware that — at the moment in our personal chronology in which the dream had placed me — we had been married nearly twenty years. In any event, I had no desire just now to wake her, as I wanted the moment to myself. It should have been an extremely pleasant scene. I like Madrid, even amid the monstrous clamor of the morning traffic. But I was conscious from the very first moments of the dream that in fact I was suffering from some sort of inner turmoil, the precise cause of which I couldn't identify. Something at the borders of my mind was troubling me. Or more than that, really: an almost vertiginous feeling of impending misery; but I wasn't able to put a name to it. I turned my eyes to the violets — to the deep, vivid purple of their petals, and to the ghostly red shadows tangled amid their dark, lustrous leaves — trying to subdue the invisible violence of my changing thoughts, so that I could isolate the source of my distress. And then all at once it came to me that I was losing my wife. Now, here really is proof of the sheer ingenuity of the hidden artificer behind my dreams, because this sudden little apocalypse broke into my consciousness with all its details instantaneously arranged into a perfectly plausible and convincing order. In one sense, the effect was extremely subtle — I didn't notice how perfectly precise the alignment of elements was, or how deftly woven the fabric of supposedly remembered events — but in another sense it was shattering. As I stood there, I seemed to recall several strangely melancholy moments that had passed between us, quite incomprehensible at the time, little more than transient pangs of troubling possibility: oddly enigmatic exchanges, lugubrious silences, pensive glances — in short, a thousand tiny signs of a growing remoteness, each in itself trivial, perhaps; but suddenly, now, I felt a host of embryonic doubts coalesce into the emotional certainty that something in our marriage had gone terribly amiss. I'm not given, as you know, to fits of neurotic anxiety; but I felt such a sense of foreboding that it was like nothing I had ever known, in that world or this, a premonition of something I couldn't avert but that I was certain would crush me. Of course, looking back now it all seems a touch absurd, but at that point in my dream I had already, in a matter of seconds, been carried beyond the reach of waking logic. Everything was so intensely real. And it's useless to observe that all my previous experience of Sonia apart from this dream should have precluded any panic on my part that she might leave me. Just then, as I stood on that balcony in Madrid, I was utterly convinced that she and I had drifted apart, and that we would drift farther apart in the days ahead, and that until this moment I'd been too obtuse to notice. My heart began beating more quickly, as if I was actually terrified — which in fact I was — and I felt myself tremble, and that odd, chilly, tingling feeling passed over my skin that I get when I find something particularly ominous or when I'm suffering from an incipient fever. And yet I didn't know what to say, to myself or to her — because, I suppose, she'd said nothing to me. And so I continued to try to control my emotions. . . . And the violets were very lovely, in their wholly unassuming way.

"A moment later we were in Venice. This wasn't another dream or another level within the dream; it was simply what happened next at the level where I'd begun. That's the most cinematic aspect of my dreams: that these transitions are instantaneous. The most agreeable aspect of the oneiric realm, I suppose, is that it will allow only the most significant episodes to occur within its borders. But the effect is not, as you might expect, to call my attention to the fictive nature of the experience. In one sense I was, on this occasion, spared several days of fretting and uncertainty; in another sense, though, because I was insensible to the essential artificiality of the narrative elisions, I was worse off for thinking that I remembered quite clearly — even if, in reality, it was all an atmosphere rather than an actual inventory of details — all the torments of those pretermitted hours. And now here we were, Sonia and I, next to one another on the Rialto, at the apex on one side, behind the shops that sell all that horrendous crystal jewelry. I was just finishing the last morsel of a slice of fresh coconut I'd bought at the foot of the bridge. The sun here was even brighter than it had been in Madrid, and higher in the sky — just past noon, I imagine. At least, I was certain we'd already had a light lunch. We were standing at the rail, looking over the canal. Or, rather, she was looking over; I was gazing at her profile. She was only nineteen when we married, and so, at this point, was still not yet forty, and she looked far younger — that lovely fair complexion, that glorious raven hair, all under the broad brim of a particularly flattering Italian hat, light gray, and those limpidly blue eyes. . . . There, though, was the problem: her eyes. That's what stirred another little spasm of dread in me. Even at this angle, something in the way she was looking off across the water, without turning to me at all, worried me; I had an intimation of some deep unhappiness in her; I thought I could see alien distances in her eyes, something remote, searching, dissatisfied . . . perhaps resigned. Idiotic, I suppose, but . . . there you have it. And then it occurred to me, quite suddenly and irrationally, that she was not so much lost in thought as distracted by the crowds on either side of the canal, as if she were actually looking for something in particular, some particular face, and was somewhat lost for having missed it, like someone hopelessly trying to find one tree in a forest. For a moment I thought she looked almost bewildered. Now, again, this may seem absurd, because it was, but it was remarkable how convincingly I tortured myself with this abrupt but elaborate fantasy. Perhaps, I thought to myself, when we'd last visited Venice, two years earlier, she'd met someone who, in the intervening time, had acquired a certain romantic grandeur in her memories, and her eyes were scanning the banks of the canal now in that straying but intent fashion because she was hoping — without really hoping, of course — to glimpse him in the crowds. It's not that I imagined she'd had an affair or anything of that sort. If that were even conceivable to me, it would have made my state of mind less ludicrous. But, as it was, I couldn't suspect her of any but the most subliminal, the most internal and unintentional infidelity — and that's not even the right word. But I also knew that she was no different from anyone else in her capacity to live the life within far more profoundly than the life without — the life imagined, that is, the mind's essential . . . what is it? Futurity, I suppose, for want of a better term. Whereas, I reflected, she might have easily forgotten a mere lover, or at least tired of the memory, she would have had a far more difficult time uprooting an entirely fantastic infatuation from her thoughts. Anyway, I don't suppose I believed any of that. It was more as if I was looking for some sort of concrete analogy of what was going wrong with our marriage, some sort of narrative trope to make it seem intelligible to me, and this phantom paramour was something on the order of an allegorical figure. In a moment the fancy faded. I turned my gaze from her down towards the canal, to those impenetrable, obsidian depths and the continuous riot of fluctuating turquoise and flashing gold dancing over them, and at that moment the tapered prow and shell-like hull of a gondola passed beneath us, emerging from under the Rialto, almost a silhouette amid the innumerable eruptions of light rising from the surface of the water. This seemed to waken Sonia from her reveries, and she turned to me, and I turned to her, and after a moment, with unmistakable effort, she spoke to me, very quietly, and suggested we get away from the press of people on the bridge. Her expression was still distant, distracted, and obviously somewhat melancholy, despite a rather feeble and touchingly tender smile. Everything felt wrong. Throughout our married life, there had always been a kind of quiet . . . I suppose I'd say sympathy between us, some common understanding, a common feeling that couldn't be uttered, and that didn't need to be. But now, for the moment, it had vanished — at least, it felt as if it had.

"We went. I won't bore you with our itinerary, and really — in the economy of my dream — the rest of the day passed quite quickly, in a succession of vivid but brief images. I felt a kind of silent frenzy through it all, but nothing I said or did would have betrayed the fact to Sonia. At least, I don't think so. What man quite understands the emotional perceptiveness of women? We did move somewhat restlessly among sites both of us had known and loved for years, at my urging. I suppose my manner might have been somewhat frenetic. I think, though, I managed to cover it under an appearance of mere cheerful energy, however distraught I was. And it did help to immerse myself again in Venice. It's pointless to try to sing the city's marvels; and so many poets and artists have poured out so much glory on it that one could never really add anything of significance. In fact, it's hard not to see the city through the art. I mean, Turner's radiant picture of the great canal, with its impossibly broad stretch of water, is so true, in an ideal way, that the actual, much narrower canal seems like its shadow. And, in a sense, Venice is haunted by itself: by all those other Venices, layer upon translucent layer of time — the Gothic, the Byzantine, the Baroque — through which the eternal idea of Venice variously and imperfectly shines. Venice is already a materialized dream — infested with rats. But there's the intractability of prime matter for you, alas. In any event, I thought that just seeing it all again, together, might help revive any dormant part of her feelings for me. And, by the time we stopped, for a second time, before the magnificently anfractuous façade of Santa Maria Zobenigo — Admiral Barbaro, brash and bewigged in his architrave, amid Corinthian columns and cherubs and personified virtues, entablatured atop those stylized, three-quarter Ionic pillars, and all the rest of that glorious petrified froth — it was late in the day, and I'd begun to feel that perhaps I'd had some success. At least, her smile seemed somewhat more unforced, and her words had begun to flow more easily. We returned to our *pensione* — a rather nice one, in fact — to rest. But then we were at dinner at a pleasant but nondescript restaurant near our room. Again, my dreaming mind had edited the transition with perfect fluidity. And again that feeling of remoteness seemed to settle between us, that sense of emptiness or aimlessness. Her expression was often distracted, her conversation halting and parsimonious, and my every attempt to enliven the evening evinced only the most dutiful, transient, and utterly uncomforting of smiles from her. By the time we returned to our room, I was in a worse state than I had been on the Rialto.

"After what I recalled as being a sleepless night — though, again, all of that was left on the cutting-room floor — we spent the next day behaving like a pair of excitable tourists, flitting constantly from one place to another as if we were afraid we might have to have a proper conversation if we stopped. Perhaps we were. We went to the Accademia, gliding past *objets d'art* we'd seen half a hundred times, took the launch to Murano and were back before noon, then went to the Doge's Palace by way of the Ponte dei Sospiri, wafting along amid the Titians and Tintorettos, and then to San Marco. Again and again — here's my obsessive side, I imagine — I became almost morbidly sensitive to anything I took as a sign of emotional space between us, and started imagining vast implications behind the most minuscule deviations from what I thought her normal behavior. God, it's embarrassing to recount it, even if it was a dream. And, strange to say, she was actually somewhat more cheerful than she'd been the day before — not giddy or ebullient, mind you, but able to smile for several moments at a time, even laughing now and then — but such was the perversity of my anxiety that I took this as cause for greater worry: perhaps she was concealing her true mood, or perhaps she had become comfortable with the idea of a growing estrangement between us. I don't know what I was thinking, frankly. And, really, I wasn't thinking at all. Somehow it all struck me most forcibly as we walked through San Marco. Is there any place on earth more astonishing, or unworldlier in its very solidity? It's such an amazing marriage of Byzantium and . . . well, and Venice, I suppose, but the effect is more than that, too. It's like an emanation of some fabulous Orient of the mind — a touch Persian, perhaps, with those sinuously apiculating arches and those weird, orbicular domes and cupolas rising above it; or maybe something of Prester John's palace in far Cathay or Abyssinia; and inside, a mineral paradise, awash in gold and shining gems and tessellated marble. I'm fairly immune to the allure of Byzantine iconography, I have to admit, and tend to find most of it depressingly hideous — dense, dark, static, sublimely dead — but on those rare occasions when a touch of genius has been applied, I'm as susceptible as anyone else to its special pathos: that fusion of this world and the glory of another, just breaking through. No matter how often I visit the basilica, at any rate, I feel the same sense of transport. Another of my dream worlds, I suppose. But here, now, especially as Sonia and I stood together before the great, massy glitter of the Pala d'Oro, all I could feel was my fear. I sensed that her thoughts were in fact standing several paces off and wouldn't allow me to approach. But, again, I had nothing to say, nothing to point to, nothing to ask that would sound intelligible. As we left the basilica, passing beneath the shadows of the gold mosaics into the clear radiance of the late Italian afternoon, I merely smiled at my wife.

"We ate a very late lunch or a very early dinner at one of the open cafés on the piazza, while a lady pianist seated at a baby grand far too unwieldy ever really to appear there — but my dreaming self was unaware of the implausibility, it seems — played Scarlatti, but in that overwrought Romantic style of the fifties that I usually intensely dislike, because it spoils the elegant sparkle of those flowing clavier lines; it almost always has a jarring effect for me, one of gaudy incongruity and vulgarity. But in this instance I found the music oddly comforting; the emotional fulsomeness of those storm-wracked Romantic ruins of the Baroque were, just then, quite affecting. Moreover, my dreaming mind, with its customary gallantry, had endowed the pianist with a technique like Landowska's but a face and figure like Ava Gardner's. Sometimes I wonder if my subconscious doesn't occasionally insert these little heterogeneities of texture into my dreams to remind me I'm dreaming; if so, it doesn't work. Anyway, I became calmer, though certainly no happier. And the light had a lovely glassy quality about it as the day began to decline and the shadows began to swell across the square, and the upper portions of the walls across from us were soaked in that faintly cymophanous glow that the descending sun throws out on things — those phantom hints of purple and red that the eye sees but can't quite locate. From where I was sitting, I had a direct view of the Torre dell'Orologio rising over the square, with its Moors and winged lion and Christian *magna mater* and that golden zodiac encircling its starry, blue-enamel heaven. Had this been literature rather than a dream, I expect I would have immediately recognized how obvious the symbolism was, how potent an image of inexorable change was that great, antique, ingeniously intricate clock wrapped in the first flush of the crepuscular light; but not then. Our conversation was nothing at all — mostly threadbare observations on the Renaissance masters. I recall uttering some stilted banality about 'Sassoferrato's saturated hues' or some such rot, as if we hadn't exhausted all those pompous apostrophes back in our courting days, when we were young and clever. Even so, the talk had a sedative quality about it that gradually began to lessen my misery. I might even have begun to think I'd been worrying about nothing if it hadn't been for an entirely unexpected moment of . . . well, not exactly crisis, but still very sudden, very piercing pain. We arrived at a pause in our conversation, as I had just been holding forth on something neither of us needed to hear again, when I saw that she was staring directly at me, so candidly, with such a melancholy look of deep scrutiny, that I thought she was about to say something drastic and irrevocable; there was even the slightest suggestion of a smile on her lips, which made it worse. It's a terrible thing, you know, to look into the eyes of someone you think you know so well that a glance could conceal nothing, only to find a mystery. At least, I found it terrible. Was she looking at the ghost she'd finally found the strength to exorcise, I wondered melodramatically — though only a little later, after my initial surprise had subsided. And her expression, in fact, evaporated after only a few seconds, and she looked away, towards the clock tower. From that point on, I succumbed to something very near despair, without of course saying anything about it. But my behavior, I imagine, was eloquent enough. Just as we were about to leave, I asked if she would mind if I had a bit more of the excellent Chianti we'd been drinking first. She had no objection, of course, though was clearly a little surprised at the suddenness with which I asked, and more surprised at the two glasses I then drank with rather unusual rapidity. And when I did something I would generally never do in Italy in the summer — order brandy — she was obviously somewhat perplexed. All she said, however, was 'That's a bit more than usual, isn't it?', to which I replied only that I was in an unusual mood. She asked nothing more. It was all enough to induce a mild delirium, or at least light-headedness, accompanied by a very slight numbness in my legs — an effect wine has on me, not hard liquor — which made our walk back to the *pensione* a little unsteady on my part. And I stopped on the way at a small bar only a few minutes from our room and had another drink, which met with no protest from her; in fact, she hardly looked at me, again seeming lost in thought, which only further fired my imaginings. We did finally reach our rooms, and it seemed fairly obvious we were not going to go out to dine later; so I bathed, gradually drifting back in the direction of sobriety without quite making shore, donned a bathrobe, and lay down on the bed to rest. Within a few moments I'd fallen asleep, and some time thereafter had begun to dream — one of my oneiric pleonasms, a descent down to the next stratum of consciousness, the inner folding of an inner folding.

"In this more inward dream, Sonia and I were not in Venice but in Vienna — maybe a setting chosen by my dreaming consciousness purely on grounds of homophony — in a well-appointed room, which I seemed to recall was being paid for by someone else, out of concern for us, though who I don't know. We were more or less the same age we'd been in the more outward dream, I imagine. The only light on in the room was a small lamp with a topaz-colored crystal base and a yellow silk shade, not particularly bright. The wallpaper was patterned with rosy arabesques against a background of creamy white. Beyond the large window, pallidly visible between the inward curves of two great indigo curtains, a silver snow fell continuously against the azure dusk. On the glass of the lower panes, the upper semicircle of a streetlamp's radiance shone light mauve through the falling snow. And I was sitting silently, with my head bowed, on a small armless chair borrowed from the writing desk, beside the bed, where Sonia lay dying beneath a counterpane of red satin. Again, you see, in an instant all was presumed; I again seemed all at once to remember everything, though I doubt now I could have said what her actual illness was. All the feelings you would expect weighed down on me: grief, terror, unbearable loss, impotence, a sense of her utter isolation in the intensely personal act of dying. There's no need to describe any of that, though. I knew after a moment that we'd been in Austria over Christmas when we'd learned of her condition, and that once everything had been done that could be done, and to no avail, we'd retreated to this hotel, in rooms provided for us by a wealthy friend — maybe the proprietor — where nurses visited at regular intervals, but where no one else would disturb us. Sonia has always hated hospitals, and always dreaded dying in the cold embrace of some clinic, among strangers, ensnared in a web of bandages and adhesive tape and plastic tubes; so this arrangement made perfect sense for us. Not that I can say whether it actually accorded with Austrian law, or with any plausible diagnosis in this world; but in the dream within the dream it all made perfect sense. And I was too preoccupied by my sorrow to notice any implausibility in the situation. And here's a perfect example, by the way, of what I mean when I talk about the autonomy of dreams. The feeling of sadness was both instantaneous and utterly devastating; and even if you remark that my misery in this dream was the effect of my suffering in Venice, where I lay dreaming of Vienna, that doesn't change the fact that Venice itself was a dream. And even if that dream had been prompted by some nameless anguish or anxiety out here in the material order — at that point, immeasurably remote from me — clearly my dreaming self had so transformed that original impulse as to create a set of emotions far in excess of anything my experiences of the waking world could have caused.

"Anyway, this dream had soon established its own narrative structure and its own logic, and I was entirely lost in it. I suppose it was because the setting was Vienna that my mind had arranged for there to be distant music, seeming to rise through the floor from the room directly beneath our own. I even recall the piece that was playing as the dream began: the andante of Schubert's fourteenth quartet — you know, 'Death and the Maiden,' which I suppose was another little jest on my mind's part. Sonia lay very still, with her eyes closed, but clearly awake, her hands spread rather limply at her sides, outside her covers, her face visibly drawn from pain and weakness, her skin as pale as alabaster, lightly tinted by the sallow glow of the lamp. Though, just at this moment, neither of us was speaking, I knew that we'd been exchanging quiet, sporadic talk throughout the day; and I knew that the strange, constant tremors I felt passing through me were sheer terror at the rapid approach of that moment when she would cease to hear me altogether, once and forever. It had been a struggle all day, I knew, to contain myself well enough to reply calmly to her when she spoke to me, and to speak soothingly to her whenever I saw a spasm of discomfort or a look of deep fatigue cross her face. She did not want to sleep — she'd been quite adamant about that — and medications had reduced her pain to endurable proportions. I remembered now — the narrative backdrop having had some more of its details daubed in by this point, apparently — that the first intimations of her long death had come to her in a series of sudden, painful paroxysms, several weeks before, just after we'd walked back to our hotel suite from a concert — a typical Viennese confection of Mozart and early Beethoven. Earlier on that day we had had a very pleasant time strolling among shops and drinking coffee and taking in the bright winter light; and after lunch we'd sat in our hotel reading to one another from the *Duino Elegies.* This was a very odd detail, since both of us have always cordially disliked Rilke, especially the overrated *Elegies,* only some of which are as good as one's supposed to think they are. I mean, I grant — we would both grant — the power of his language, at its best, all that flowing, thunderous lyricism, but the later poetry, with its insufferable vatic pretenses, is so tiresomely sententious and portentous at times; and it really does somewhat spoil the poetry when you know just how disappointingly stupid and incoherent and falsely profound Rilke's personal philosophy was: all that cretinous, vapid twaddle about raising things up into the invisible, and that ghastly idealization of the deaths of young people. But this was all part of the story my dream was weaving for me, obviously. Now, as I sat by Sonia's bed, certain lines came back to me with an almost unbearable poignancy: 'Freilich ist es seltsam, die Erde nicht mehr zu bewohnen'; and then 'Und jene, die schön sind,/O wer hält sie zurück?' And I knew she was slipping away from me. The strange stirrings of the little life left in her were becoming fainter and fainter; her soul was fading away behind the veil of her flesh — I could see it — and I knew she was now slowly but continuously disengaging her perceptions from the world around her, even now from her own body. Mostly, though, I was conscious of my own weakness, my exhaustion, and the abysmal depths of sorrow into which I was sinking. I took her hand in mine — very cold and so very frail — and held to it gently as the night continued to darken beyond the window; and all the time I could sense the . . . I almost want to say the *majesty* of the great wave of total emotional desolation that was continuously rearing itself up above me, preparing to fall on me and carry me down into gulfs of black despair. At one point, when she was not yet dead but I could tell that what remained of her life was at a great distance from me, withdrawn into a minute flickering of awareness on the edge of the darkness, I knew she wouldn't last beyond the hour, and I began to shake silently, uncontrollably, and my eyes filled with tears.

"Mercifully, however, I was spared the final moments. This level of my dream relinquished its hold on me as easily as it had initially pulled me down into itself, after not very long, relatively speaking. My unconscious self seems to have decided not to be too cruel to me on this occasion. For the first time that night I awoke, rising up back again into my dream of Venice. I sat up in bed, breathed deeply, somewhat tremulously, after several seconds remembered where I was and that Sonia was quite well, and turned to her where she was sleeping beside me, quite visible in the strong moonlight coming through the window standing open across the room; I could see that her hair was tied back and that, given the warmth of the night, she was uncovered and wearing only a very short, fleecy, fairly diaphanous pink chemise I'd bought her in Paris the year before — the sort of lacy little thing a man buys a woman only so that he can have the opportunity of coaxing her out of it. It was not what I'd expected to see her wearing, actually, and I wondered whether she'd put it on solely for comfort's sake or so that I'd find her like that in the morning. This latter was a hopeful thought. But I was still too perturbed by the dream from which I'd just awoken to think about it long. Either because of that, or because of the anxiety that had been tormenting me for so many days now, I was too agitated to stay in bed, so I rose quickly to walk to the window. The sky was the deep, clear, dark blue that often comes a few hours before dawn in the Italian summer, and beyond the shadowy confusion of the city's roofs and domes and avenues and canals, with its countless caverns and dells of fulvous light, the Venetian Lagoon glistened like smooth lead and polished pewter, and the low, brilliant, gibbous moon spread its train, sparkling like diamonds, in a narrow fan from the horizon to the shore. 'Christ,' I murmured, scarcely loudly enough to be audible to myself; but Sonia, being such a light sleeper, had, it seems, been roused when I got up, and her voice almost immediately followed on mine, quietly: 'What's wrong?' I turned to see that she was now sitting upright in her gauzy mist of pink, gathering her lustrous hair over her left shoulder and smoothing it . . . such a beautiful woman . . . almost ridiculously too beautiful for me . . . though now with an expression of quizzical concern on her face. 'You've been acting very odd all day,' she added, without any hint of rebuke in her voice. I said nothing for several seconds, and she continued to stare at me with such a look of earnest worry that I began to feel slightly foolish. All at once I realized I was seeing nothing in her eyes but a very familiar look of affection, and I found myself entirely at a loss to know what to say, or even what to feel. Finally, fearing that I was beginning to look like a man in a trance, I left the window and sat at the foot of her side of the bed, and then reached out to take her hand.

"I don't want to recount the conversation in any detail — though, as is often the case in my dreams, it went on for a while. Simply enough, I told her — plainly, clearly, already somewhat abashedly — what had been preying on my mind, all the suspicions I'd called from the vast deep of my dementia, only occasionally looking to see the expression of surprise and fitful bemusement on her face. When I admitted, hesitatingly, that I'd even begun to think there might be some other man in her thoughts and that this had been driving us apart, she actually gasped. At that point I fell silent and turned what I hoped was a fairly hopeless gaze in her direction. After several intolerable moments of her staring at me as though she thought I'd gone mad, she at last lowered her eyes, shook her head, and said — quite fondly, actually — 'You really can be a fool sometimes.' Then, after a few more seconds, she gathered her legs under her and drew close to me, resting her head on my chest so that I had to put my arms around her. I cautiously mentioned that she had, after all, been strangely preoccupied and melancholy for some time now — I wasn't imagining that — to which she replied, simply, 'Yes, I have. But it's nothing to do with you — or, at least, nothing like what you've imagined.' For a while, neither of us said anything; it occurred to me, at one point, that this was the first time I had held her like this for weeks, and it was really quite delightful. At last, she began speaking again: 'If it's any comfort, I can't quite say what's bothering me myself. I think it's age, mostly. I seem to be going through a period . . . when it's hard not to think about the time that's slipping away. You know' — she pressed her head a bit more insistently into my chest — 'I'm not a girl anymore, and . . .' She stopped, but I urged her to go on. 'It's simply one of those times in life, honestly. When we married, we were young, and everything seemed possible, and . . . and now I feel as if the future . . . my sense of the future is fading away. I'm almost forty . . . and we, you know, we never had the children we wanted. And I did so want children.' I began to say something — no doubt I was going to assure her there was still time — but she shook her head and squeezed my arm, almost fiercely. 'It's not something I want to talk about now. Please. And, anyway, it's not just that. It's all of a piece. You know, you shouldn't always be so quick to interpret my moods.' I agreed with her, but then asked what was all of a piece. She continued to rest her head against me, but stared now at the window and the limpid, deep blue of the early morning. 'I love you very much,' she said, 'and I'm very happy with our life. It's just a passing spell of fear, I think. It's really all so silly. I just — I've lately been more aware than usual of how transient our life together . . . how fragile and limited . . . no matter how we cling to it, how I cling to it, our happiness can't be sustained. Something wants to part us, something inevitable . . . just time, I suppose. I think everyone must have these episodes, you know, when you're suddenly conscious of mortality in a new way, of the fleetingness of things . . . everything vanishing. I just know that, right now, I want to hold on to something that . . . can't be held on to. It's like trying not to wake up from a dream. But, for goodness' sake, my problem's not with you.'

"She said more, of course. I said various comforting things, as they occurred to me, all quite sincere. The sky beyond our window grew gradually lighter. Everything resolved into an exquisitely kindly tenderness between us. We both felt somewhat idiotic, I imagine, but we clung to one another, and that revived — in me, at least — a trace of an old accustomed bliss, belonging just to us. I'd rarely ever seen Sonia in a somber mood, and in the past her sadness had always been occasioned by something not so . . . nameless. But it was a deep, deep relief — something verging on joy, something unexpectedly enlivening and somehow refreshing — to know that my wife was still my wife, and that we'd perhaps both been suffering from nothing more exotic than the goads of incipient middle age. Moreover, an obvious if maybe temporary solution to our twin anxieties was slowly beginning to recommend itself to me. Somewhere within me, a deep, resonant chord of happiness was rising up. And there was something else that rose up alongside it, accompanying that sense of release — or renewal — something sweetly urgent stirring in me . . . at the root of things, so to speak. Well, I'm a man, after all, and there she was, pressed against me, soft and warm and overflowing with affec-

153

tion, and clad in nothing but that tiny, delectably filmy chemise, which didn't conceal anything at all, but only lent her skin a sort of rosy glow. There were a few tears on her cheeks as I began to kiss her, and as my hands began to declare my intentions; and then, of course, after a few moments, there was the predictable dramatic entrance onstage through the parting curtains of my robe — not with the sudden, nimble, gallant flourish of old, admittedly, but still with a certain panache. . . . Anyway, far from being alarmed by my change of mood, she was altogether amenable to the direction in which I was tending, and I soon had her out of that chemise, and everything was going very, very well. The golden honey was swelling heavily in the comb, the morning blossom was opening languidly to the sun, the ice was dissolving into whirling, glittering shards on the surface of the stream — and so on.

"But, if my inner poet had chosen to be merciful to me earlier in the night, now he chose to be miserly; he'd spared me the anguish of her death, but now denied me the pleasure of her body. Well . . . a sanitary precaution, I suppose. I woke again, for the second time that night, and within only a few seconds realized where I was. It was the wholly familiar bedroom of the house we'd rented in Copenhagen for my year at the university, giving my lectures on Murasaki Shikabu and *The Tale of Genji*, and on Shei Shonagon's *Pillow Book*, and on Heian literature and art in general, and Sonia was in bed beside me, quite asleep under several covers, no doubt dressed in a sensible nightgown, her hair — still dark, but with a sheen of iron gray — tied back. Here too there was moonlight, but also some rain gently running down the glass of the room's window. We were not, of course, the ages we'd been in my dreams of Madrid and Venice and Vienna — she in her late thirties, I in my early forties — but nearly twenty years older. And, as soon as I'd completed my ascent to this next level of consciousness and had gotten my bearings, two thoughts occurred to me. One was that my interrupted dream had left me with a powerful urge that I could satisfy only if I were inconsiderate enough to rouse Sonia from her sleep — which I wouldn't have hesitated to do if we'd actually been twenty or forty years younger, but which was now out of the question. The other thought, though, was how completely deceived I'd been by my dreams, how absolutely convincingly they'd drawn me into their narratives. I don't know what accounts for the terrific subtlety of the dreaming mind. It's something we've all experienced — in this, at least, I'm not unique — this spell it casts over us, this illusion of deep background, by which so much that isn't seen is simply presumed in the very fabric of the dream, so that it somehow feels true, like something truly remembered, so that even if one can recall that one's dreaming, one still can't help but believe in the deeper illusion on whose surface the dream floats. That's the source of the real torment our dreams can visit on us — the indubitability of all those prevenient falsehoods: someone dead is there alive again, someone living is dead, something lost is found, or the reverse, or one thinks one feels — which is to say, one feels — an ineffable tenderness for a girl one doesn't really know, or one thinks one remembers a face one's never really seen. Embarrassments, terrors, desires, memories, presuppositions, prejudices . . . a whole other life, lived outside us or within us. And, while we dream, we're at its mercy; our emotions are prompted and shaped and provoked by God knows what. I suppose it's a rather elegant sort of subterfuge, really, the mind distracting us with one, fairly obvious fiction while simultaneously convincing us of the truth of another — and more elaborate — fiction, till even the most shattering or delightful lie can assume the character of plain, undeniable fact. And when one wakes, and it all vanishes, one feels as if one's played the part of a marionette. Which only goes to reinforce my point: Dreams aren't simply the residue of the day's emotional states; they generate whole worlds of sensibility and feeling out of themselves. Here I was in Copenhagen; everything was in place; all the remembered and half-remembered things that had been so appallingly unbearable to me as I stood on that balcony in Madrid, and that had sent me spiraling ever deeper into forlorn fantasy, weren't real at all. Their memory had in fact been their genesis. My relief, of course, was immense. It was no great boon, I suppose, to recall that I was a far older man than I had thought a few moments earlier, but I couldn't help but feel as if I'd been delivered from a prison by the knowledge that all the suffering of the night, all the fears and quite genuine anguish, had rested on nothing, on melting shadows, ashes, phantom lights . . . mists . . . nothing. It had all been just a nightmare, even if it had grown rather sweet at the end. I looked at Sonia, sleeping, not a young woman any longer, but still so very lovely, there with the light of another moon pouring over her through another window, to be caught glimmeringly in her hair, and cast across her shoulder and cheek, and seeming to dissolve continuously in the molten shadows of the droplets trickling down the panes. . . . Everything was at peace; everything was as it should be. A profound contentment grew in me, a sort of thrill of confident pleasure, or serene delight: to know, despite all the strange machinations of my dreaming mind, that Sonia had never given me any cause to doubt her love for me, and that she was still very much mine, and had been for all these years, provided me with one of those brief, precious, incommunicable moments of utterly unalloyed joy that are so oddly rare in life. Honestly, when all's said and done, I really don't think I've ever known a more purely *happy* moment than that in the entire course of my existence."

4

My friend said nothing for several moments. Then, with a meditative deliberateness, he picked up his glass and drank the last of his cognac. After a few moments more, staring away from me into the night beyond the terrace, he set the glass aside and sighed. "Well, there's not much more to tell, apart from the obvious." He shook his head slightly, at some thought of his own. "I know you love Sir Thomas Browne as much as I do," he continued. "I have a special love for that wonderful short essay on dreams, with those magnificent opening and closing sentences — both of which are indelibly inscribed on some wall in my brain, especially the latter: 'unto mee mere sick mens dreames, dreames out of the Ivorie Gate, and visions before midnight.' Of course, midnight doesn't seem to make a difference one way or the other." He laughed, rather humorlessly. "Perhaps I should just dismiss all those fabulous ecstasies and torments in the darkness as just that. You know — *falsa ad caelum mittunt insomnia manes.* Perhaps I'd be saner. And, I mean, if you can't believe an oracle from Cumae . . ." He smiled, but not with enough conviction to chase the melancholy from his eyes. "I don't really think of them that way, though. I can't. I'd go mad with despair."

I waited for him to say more, but when several more moments had passed, I leaned towards him and said, "Let me order a taxi now. I don't know about you, but I don't want to go feeling my way back through the darkness."

"No, of course not," he said. "I'm ready to leave."

I summoned our waiter, who happened just then to be peering at us from the French doors, and asked him whether the front desk would make the call for me. He assured me it would be no difficulty and went off to see to it.

"Do you like the name 'Sonia' as much as I do?" my friend suddenly asked.

"Oh, yes, definitely," I replied. "It's a lovely name."

"And a mysterious one," he added. "Diminutive of Sophia, you know — well, of course you know that. Maybe I was enchanted as much by her name as by her beauty when she appeared in my life. Another name might have been a disappointment. It has a kind of metaphysical glamor to it for me. I always liked that Silver Age Russian mysticism about Lady Wisdom, the divine feminine, the bride of God, in whom all things are woven together . . . whom all men love . . . who dwells in all women. And of course it's a name that works wonderfully for me with my infernal gift; it suits the paronomasiac logic of dream language — Sonia, *sogno* . . . if you see what I mean. Two intertwining riddles, perhaps."

"It's a lovely name in any case," I said. "I expect the taxi will come in about twenty minutes."

He nodded, though in a way that suggested he was not really listening. "You see what I mean, probably. If I were to trace the emotions of that night back to their most original source, I'd find only dreams within dreams; I carried all those feelings *into* this world, not out of it. And that's really been the whole story of my life. It's been my peculiar fate to take up a kind of permanent station by the ivory gate, believing, or desperately hoping, that it's really the gate of horn, and that there's really no difference between them, and that the figures that issue from between its posts are genuine visitants from a world beyond this one, all the time patiently waiting for that word that will grant me leave to pass through the gate myself, finally, to find a world more real than this . . . I'll remember . . . find who waits for me. . . . I must sound a bit demented to you."

"No," I said.

"Senile, then, and self-pitying."

"Absolutely not."

"I have no choice, in any event. More and more, these days, as I go on vanishing away into myself, I feel as if I'm praying without meaning to . . . sending my hesitant but very sincere entreaties upward . . . to the God who's both hiding at the center of my soul's labyrinth and dwelling far beyond the horizons of my self, begging his permission to come to him, to wake him from his sleep in me . . . I mean, to wake him from my sleep, or awaken myself from my sleep to his eternal wakefulness. The metaphors get a bit confused here, I know. But, it's so tantalizingly near now . . . and I have to believe I'll at last find what I desire more than I desire myself. I really have come to believe — maybe it's a childish fantasy, but there's nothing I can do to change it — that we come here to die . . . that we owe a death, and that everything external waits upon an inward death that we all have to accomplish, one way or another." He shrugged listlessly. "Now I'm certain I'm sounding deranged, or incoherent at least. I'm in perfect possession of my wits, though."

"I wouldn't doubt it," I answered.

"You may understand this one day, if you enjoy the luxury of watching your own death gradually approach from a good distance, as I've done. There comes a point — at least, there has for me — when all fear simply gives way to anticipation. Of course, I've been living that out all my life, perhaps. But, more keenly than ever before, I can feel that . . . that invitation, ceaselessly bidding me onward through that distant mountain pass, or into the smoldering gold of that forest's heart. . . . The way will grow suddenly clear, and I'll see it all at once. . . . Well, anyway, I'm dying, whether I like it or not, so it's just as well I feel that way. What could the prospect of death be for me, anyway, in my endless round of waking from one world to another? For that matter, what should death be for any of us? We're all lying on our deathbeds every day, enclosed within that room in Vienna; but it's pleasant to think the heavy curtains will be drawn back, the night will recede, even the walls — however solid they appear — will simply melt away like a tenuous mist, and reveal sunlit fields, full of shining . . . goldenrod." He laughed now, somewhat more easily. "Well, I'm getting too tired to keep struggling for new images."

"I like goldenrod," I said. "The image works perfectly well for me. One man's Elysian fields are another's catarrh, I suppose, but . . ."

"I wanted something bright . . . golden."

"Yes," I said.

My friend closed his eyes, as if trying to recall something, then looked at me, or at what he could see of me. "Anyway, take it as good news that you don't have to worry about my state of mind. I'm almost giddy with excitement, really. Or, at least, I'm not afraid. I see it as just the final, truest dream. Till I die, I'll go on every night as I have all my life. I'll descend ravenously into that other reality . . . to hear its soft rain falling upon its green leaves. There's everything there — men and women, bitter partings, sweet concourse, nobility and terror, joy, tenderness, mercy, loss and restoration . . . rest . . . effortless intimacies, vast labors. . . . And I'll continue, every morning, to take only the most reluctant leave of all of them. This world's more a dream to me . . . more a prison. After all, what loyalty do I owe it? I mean, you know how the story ends each time — how it ended that night, when I woke up for the third time, rising out of the dream of Copenhagen, where I hadn't been a lecturer for years, emerging from the ocean of my sleep like a fish vainly struggling on a hook, drawn up out of the sheltering water, and remembered — even more shatteringly than usual — what waited for me out here. That whole night was such a wild oscillation between misery and joy. In agony, I'd watched her dying, and then had felt the absolute rapture of finding her alive again, and then there had come the quieter and deeper happiness of simply returning to the secure contentment of our marriage, and then, finally, the cruelly inevitable dénouement. You can imagine how it felt, surely." He briefly raised his hands before him, with his palms turned away from himself, in a gesture that suggested simultaneously both surrender and contempt. "What could possibly ever bind me to this world, or make me fear leaving it, when, according to its pitiless logic, Sonia is no more than an imaginary figure who's inexplicably recurred in my dreams since I was a very young man, while I've lived alone all these years, incapable of any other deep or lasting attachment, enduring the same piercing moment of pain over and over again, year after year, for the sake of a passionate devotion to and a deep, intricate, immeasurably rich love for a woman who does not really exist?"

I did not reply for several moments, and my friend's gaze drifted downwards, away from me and towards his own chest. Then, at last, I said simply, "Yes," and then, after a few more moments, "quite."

1985

The Other

The rather tall, rather handsome American, apparently in his late forties and wearing an obviously very expensive dark gray suit and blue silk tie, was not really called Mr. Ambrose; that was merely the name in which he had made his dinner reservation.

The extremely lovely girl with dark hair and green eyes who tended the book on its mahogany podium watched him enter the restaurant's outer door from Myslikova Street with the rose and lavender light of evening at his back; as he passed through the narrow vestibule, the mirrored walls briefly multiplied his figure into an infinity of reflections receding to either side, while the beveled edges of the twelve large glass panes in the inner door made it seem as if he were rapidly dissolving in iridescent waves and immediately coalescing again. She had seen the effect countless times before, but on this occasion was somewhat more fascinated by it than usual because she found the man so immediately appealing, and when he emerged into the restaurant proper and resumed a single, stable form, she greeted him with her most enchanting smile. He paused for a moment, a look of mildly captivated surprise appearing on his face, and then smiled in return, gazing directly into her eyes with the frankness of a man long practiced in charming women. He began to make an observation on the delightful weather outside but all at once, and with exquisite ease, changed it into a compliment upon her beauty instead, and then mentioned his reservation before she could quite think of a reply. She hesitated for a few seconds, still smiling and staring back at him with what she hoped was a knowing expression, and then looked down towards her book. "It says it's a reservation for two," she said after a moment; "and you're the first to arrive." She raised her eyes again. "Would you care to go into the bar to wait?"

"No," the man replied, "my friend may not even be in the city yet, and may not come at all. We're to meet here if possible, but otherwise I'll just dine alone."

"Oh." The girl tapped her lips with her red pen. "Is your friend a man or a woman?"

He raised an eyebrow, seemed to be considering the matter for a moment, and then leaned slightly forward. "Which would you prefer me to be waiting for?"

She tilted her head to one side, also seemed to be considering her reply, and then said, "A man. Definitely."

"Would you be desolate if it were a woman?"

She laughed. "Well . . ."

"Because I certainly hope you'd be desolate. As it happens, though," — his manner became a little less playful, and he took half a step back — "it's a man. And I'll just wait at my table for him, if I may. I promised I wouldn't delay my own dinner if I didn't see him here."

She led him to his table herself. As he followed, far enough behind to admire her in full, he thought to himself how attractive he found her slight ineptitude at flirtation. Maybe all of twenty-one, he mused; twenty-five at the oldest — and such a splendid shape.

Everything within the restaurant swam in a soft golden light. There were no candles on the tables, but the lights ensconced in the walls shone through cream-yellow shades, and the flocked velvet of the arabesque wallpaper was a dark gold, as were the frames of the various paintings of Prague's skyline that hung all along the walls. The white linen tablecloths seemed to have a gentle yellow luster about them, and even the dark red patterned carpet of the room seemed faintly glazed with a golden sheen. His table was set for two and stood somewhat apart in a corner, as he had requested when he had phoned the day before. He hardly need have bothered with any reservation at all, he reflected to himself, since more than half the other tables were unoccupied — a Wednesday night, after all — but at least he had been able to specify in advance how he should like to be situated. He had to hasten his last two steps to prevent the girl from holding out his chair for him, gently laying his hand on hers as he did so. Then, when he had seated himself, she leaned down to him and remarked that all of the usual waiters who spoke English were out tonight, but that the proprietor would be happy to take his order if he wished.

"I thought everyone in Prague spoke English," he replied.

"Not everyone. Certainly not everyone working here."

"Yours is quite good, though. Flawless, really."

"Thank you. I went to university in England."

"So did I. Where did you go?"

"Cambridge."

"So did I. What college?"

"St John's."

"I was at King's. Practically neighbors, then — well, apart from the quarter-century between us. What mark did you take, and in what?"

"Only a 2:1," she said, "in history."

"A 2:1 is a very good mark," he replied, "and history is an excellent subject." He tapped the table twice with all his fingers and sighed. "Those were good days for me. But I'm keeping you from the front, aren't I? Listen, I'll take you up on your offer and give the owner my order. That'll be better than struggling to make myself understood."

THE PROPRIETOR WAS a man of not-quite-average height, broad through the chest and shoulders, with thickly massed black hair above his ears and only a few wisps atop his head, a heavy mustache, and eyes that suggested a gentle, genial weariness. His English was nearly as good as the girl's, he apologized twice for having no waiters on the floor that spoke anything other than Czech or Slovak, and he tried to persuade the man to have a drink or two before bothering with the menu, just in case his friend might only have been delayed. But the man shook his head: "No, he's unlikely to arrive if he hasn't already, and if he does, I don't mind keeping him company while he eats. It's a very informal appointment."

"Right, right," the proprietor replied. "Just as you like, certainly." He recited the day's menu, and the man, with little deliberation, chose the mussel and saffron soup, no fish course at all, and the saddle of venison with port and currant sauce, accompanied by white asparagus with pine nuts and new potatoes roasted with shallots and rosemary. Then the man asked whether the proprietor might bring the sommelier over in person, in case there should be any need for translation. There was not, however; only a few moments after the small sommelier with the wire-rimmed spectacles handed over the list, the man returned it, pointing to the bottle he wanted. "Here we are: the Château Cos d'Estournel Saint-Estèphe '96. That will be perfect."

Before leaving, the proprietor apologized for the third time for the linguistic limitations of his staff, but the man shook his head. "No, please,

I travel all over the world — really, just about anywhere you could imagine — and I have only English and French. I'm used to making myself understood one way or another."

"What's your business, if I can ask?"

"Traveling all over the world." The man laughed, almost as if embarrassed. "You see, I was born with an abundance of curiosity and of money, but without much spirit of enterprise. So I just . . ." He walked his right hand across several inches of tablecloth on two fingers. "Not really a very useful vocation, of course."

"But that's wonderful," said the proprietor with what seemed like real feeling. "That's what I would do if I could. It's better than sitting at home with your money. I'm glad to know that someone's able to do it. Have you been to India?"

"Many times — though there English is rarely a problem. You know," — he pointed away vaguely towards the restaurant's doors — "that girl up front, the very pretty one, speaks excellent English."

"You think so?"

"Yes indeed."

A look of amusement came into the proprietor's face. "I know. She's my daughter, actually. She's just come back from three years in England. She was at the University of Cambridge. You know it?"

"Oh, yes, I know Cambridge. That's very impressive. You must be exceedingly proud." He glanced away towards the front, though the girl was not visible from where he sat, and then looked back to the proprietor. "She's very intelligent — very lovely too. You must have to fight off all the young swains."

"Pardon me?"

"The young men, I mean. I'm sure the young men hover around her like moths around a flame."

"Oh, that." The proprietor briefly glanced upward, in an attitude of mock supplication. "Yes, ever since she was young. Too pretty. But she's engaged now, so they . . ." — he faltered for a moment, trying to recall the proper idiom — ". . . well, there's no luck."

"Well, good for her," said the man. "It's the best age for marriage, if you've found the right person. Nice fellow?"

At this, the look of cheerfulness quietly deserted the proprietor's face, his eyes seemed to become a little wearier, and he shrugged. "She could do better."

"Ah."

THE SOMMELIER RETURNED a few minutes later and ceremoniously presented the bottle for inspection. "Yes, yes?" he said, with a hopeful urgency that suggested he had thus exhausted his supply of English.

"Yes," the man said with an encouraging nod, "very good."

When the sommelier had opened the bottle, the man declined to taste the wine first, but simply gestured for the glass to be filled. He breathed in deeply as the sharp, tannic fragrance rose up to him and then stared into the wine's deep ruby hue almost affectionately. Then he pointed to the glass across from him at the other place setting. "That one too, please." At first the sommelier was uncertain he had understood, but the man continued to encourage him with a number of smiles and nods of the head, still pointing to the empty glass. When the sommelier at last complied, the man thanked him and then added, "Sympathetic magic, you see." But this only brought a look of confusion to the sommelier's face, so the man thanked him again and allowed him to leave.

He waited before drinking. It should really be decanted first, he thought to himself, but one ought not to be too precious about such things. When he did take his first sip, he let the wine lie on his tongue for a moment, his lips slightly parted, and then closed his eyes before swallowing. It was even better than he had hoped: a dozen years along, the acidity had mellowed and a richer depth and fuller range of flavors — fruits and flowers and golden saps — had emerged, along with a mildly citric finish. A wine just coming of age, he mused — and one still yet to grow in wisdom. Then he set it down and stared intently and expressionlessly at the other glass until the food began to arrive.

When the waiter brought the soup, the proprietor came along as well and, on seeing wine poured for two, asked whether the man's friend had arrived after all. "No," said the man, "it's just a bit of sympathetic magic. I'm trying to conjure him up, so to speak."

The proprietor nodded thoughtfully. "Do you think that will work?"

"Well, after all, it's a very good wine."

The proprietor laughed quietly and withdrew again.

As he ate the soup and then in turn the venison, the man continued to gaze at the glass of wine across the table from him. From his own glass he drank only very slowly, not emptying it till he was finished with his main course and the plate had been cleared away. The proprietor returned when the waiter brought the salad and was just about to replace the man's empty glass with the full glass from the other setting when the man stopped him. "No, please, just leave it for now."

"You still think he'll come?" the proprietor asked, mildly surprised.

"I'm still trying to summon him up," the man replied, with no obvious sign of whimsy, and filled his own glass again.

After the salad, the proprietor and waiter returned again with the cheese board, from which the man chose some of the hermelín and a few oat biscuits; in the course of eating these he finished his second glass of wine and poured a third, emptying the bottle in doing so; drinking much more quickly now, he emptied the glass before the proprietor returned with the waiter yet again. The man declared himself to be ravenous tonight and ordered a crème brûlée. And still he would not allow the other glass to be moved. The proprietor surreptitiously exchanged glances with the waiter, momentarily widening his eyes as if to suggest he was beginning to doubt the man's sanity, but said only, "Good, good, yes." The waiter brought the crème brûlée, and the man ate it in silence, his eyes still fixed on the glass across the table. A little later, the proprietor brought coffee in a small pink and white porcelain carafe, served it in a cup and saucer of the same design, and with the man's consent topped it with fresh cream, which he poured expertly over the back of a small soup spoon. This time the proprietor did not even look at the untouched glass of wine before departing. The man drank and stared, slowly, moving as little as possible, and with no discernible expression on his face. Then, after a time, the proprietor returned and suggested a final cognac. At first, for a few seconds, the man made no reply at all; then he turned his eyes upward, away from the glass, and the proprietor saw at once that they had a look of alarmingly deep sadness in them. All the man said, however, was "I'd prefer a calvados Pays-d'Auge, if possible."

"Certainly it's possible."

"Do you have a Père Magloire or a Daron?"

"Yes, of course, both, of course — every kind."

"Well . . . some Daron XO then. Oh, and just leave that." The man pointed to the other setting.

"Yes, I know."

"Could you just bring the bill along as well? And a pen and a piece of blank paper if you can. There's something I want to make a note of before I forget."

The proprietor brought everything the man had requested, asked whether there was anything else he might do, smiled cordially when he was told there was not, wished the man a good night, and left.

The man allowed himself to linger over the brandy, holding the small snifter up before him with the bowl cradled upon his fingertips and admiring the clear, reddish gold tint of the liquor, breathing in its autumnal fragrance of apples and pears, then sipping it almost reverently, luxuriating in the sweet apple flavor, with all its elusive traces of vanilla, cinnamon, honey, wood smoke, and roasted almonds. "God bless the French," he murmured. At last, though, he was done. He set the snifter aside, took up the pen and small pad of yellow paper the proprietor had brought him, wrote out his true name and the name of his suite at the Hotel Élite on Ostrovni Street, tore off the sheet, folded it in half, and set it aside. Then he drew out his wallet from within his jacket, laid out more than twice the sum recorded on the bill, put his wallet away, picked up the piece of paper, took one last wistful look at the untouched glass of wine, and rose. As he walked towards the front of the restaurant, he realized that the alcohol was having a slightly greater effect upon him than he had anticipated: a mild, somewhat delectable dizziness, a faint, hebetant warmth in his limbs, a slight sense of detachment from his own body — all of which, he knew, would fade in less than half an hour.

The girl was still at the front, as he had hoped, looking somewhat tired now, resting obliquely on the edge of the high stool behind the podium, her legs stretched out and her feet still upon the floor. She turned as he drew near and stood up, smiling much as she had done when he first arrived. "Was the meal up to your expectations?" she asked.

"And better," he said. "It was a very happy choice, this place. I must come again if I get a chance — though I'm not going to be in Prague very long."

"Oh? How much longer?"

"Only another three days, I think. Which reminds me . . ." He smiled at her, not quite as before, but almost a little bashfully, and set the folded piece of paper down upon the open book. "This may seem a bit forward of me, but I don't mean anything by it, and feel free just to ignore it. It's just that I have only a short time in Prague and would like to see some more of it before leaving, and someone who speaks English would be a wonderful guide, and . . . well . . ." — he pointed to the piece of paper — "I've written my name and hotel address down there. My name's not Ambrose, you'll see. That's my friend's name. But if you're free at all tomorrow, and you'd be willing to show me some of the city, I could promise you a very good lunch. I'd even pay for your time, if you liked."

She looked down at the piece of paper, not yet picking it up, and then looked again at him, still smiling, but now with a hint of cautious curiosity in her eyes. "Why me, exactly?"

"Well," he said, beginning to assume his charming manner again, "as I say, you speak excellent English, and you're very bright, obviously, and very lovely too, which is always quite pleasant, and . . . well, you seem like good company, and I've no one to talk to here. It's only a thought."

"I don't . . ."

"But don't answer now," he interrupted her. "As I say, it's only a thought. Just think about it. I'd be grateful, but I'd understand if you had misgivings. Let's just say that if you don't call my room before ten tomorrow, I'll assume you had other things to do, and I'll wander off into the city on my own. I'm sure I'll be quite safe."

"Yes, I think you will be." She placed a forefinger on the piece of paper and stared at it as she considered the idea. "Really, I'm not sure . . ."

"Tomorrow," he said. "You really don't have to decide now. All right?"

She sighed, looked at him with an expression somewhere between amusement and doubt, and then nodded. "All right. I'll phone whether I'm coming or not and let you know."

"Wonderful, lovely, thank you. I'll wait to hear from you, then." And with a final inveigling sparkle in his eyes (she would not have known how else to describe it), he turned and left, and she saw his wavering form caught again in the crystal reticulation of the inner door's scintillating window panes, and refracted again into innumerable bright ghosts by the vestibule's mirrored walls, until he disappeared into the darkness beyond the outer door.

THE MAN STOOD for a time on the pavement outside the restaurant, enjoying the mild warmth of the night and the sight of the bell tower of the New Town Hall in the distance under the cloudless sky. The city lights made it difficult to see much of the stars apart from a delicate silvery haze floating in the darkness far overhead, but he was gazing up at them nonetheless when he heard two voices conversing in English — with distinctly Scottish inflections — drawing near. He turned to see an elderly couple approaching along the pavement, almost certainly on their way to the restaurant; the gentleman had a thick white mustache with neatly upturned ends, the lady on his arm — obviously his wife — had a bright pink British complexion and merry eyes, and both were formally dressed. Perhaps coming from the theater, the man thought. When they were about five feet from him and clearly turning towards the restaurant's door, he suddenly bade them a good evening, and they stopped to return the greeting. "If you haven't dined here before," he added, "I can tell you it's marvelous. I've just had a very fine dinner myself."

"Oh, we know," said the lady. "This is our third visit."

"What part of the States do you come from?" the gentleman asked.

"Virginia — by way of New York. And where in Scotland do you come from?"

"Edinburgh," said the gentleman. "Well, I'm from Aberdeen, really, and my wife's from near Perth, but Edinburgh now."

"Wonderful city," remarked the man; "not unlike Prague, really. I mean, you know, the same sort of beautiful, spiky skyline."

"I suppose so," said the lady. "I hadn't thought of that, but I see what you mean. Prague seems just a little bit more exotic, though. Edinburgh can be a bit gray and grim."

"Maybe so," said the man, looking about him. "It is rather stunning, isn't it?" His gaze wandered up and down the street for a moment. "A pity it can't last much longer."

"I'm sorry," said the gentleman with an uncertain laugh. "What's that? What can't last?"

The man looked at them morosely. "All of it," he said. "You know: the whole thing." He waved his hand casually before him, taking in the entire horizon. "All of it will pass away — fairly soon, I imagine. Like wax in the fire." He looked away again, into the sky above the city. "The whole of it."

"Oh," said the gentleman. "Yes, I see. Well . . ." He and his wife briefly looked at one another with slightly worried expressions. "Yes, well," — the gentleman affected a pleasant smile — "I suppose we'd best be getting inside."

"Yes," said the lady, "we're already late for our reservation."

"A good night to you," said the gentleman, placing his arm around his wife's shoulder and turning towards the door.

"Yes," said the lady, "very good to have met you." And she looked at the man one last time, her eyes somewhat less merry now, before turning away altogether.

The man smiled as he watched them enter the restaurant. A lovely couple, he thought to himself; probably been married for fifty years. After a few moments more, he decided to take a walk before returning to his hotel and began strolling east towards the Vltava. When he reached the Masarykovo nábřeží and its coursing streams of cars, he crossed over to the riparian side and turned north, merging into the leisurely flow of the nighttime crowd, occasionally running his fingertips along the top of the parapet's iron railing, passing the Slavonic Island with its domed granite tower to his left and the row of immense, soaring white and gold baroque façades and steep red roofs to his right, till he reached the National Theater in all its massive and lustrous splendor, and then continued on, past the Legions Bridge, up the Smetanovo nábřeží, towards the Charles Bridge. As he walked, he stared continuously out over the Vltava's black and quicksilver waters, to the west and the north, at the spire of Our Lady Victorious, and the dome and turret of the Church of St. Nicholas, and the soaring, wedged roofs of the great tower gates, and farther beyond that, surmounting the barbed riot of the skyline and rising from a cloud of gold and blue and purple lights, the castle and Cathedral of St. Vitus; and the reflections of the whole gorgeously luminous tumult undulated on the surface of the river all along the opposite shore. "Like wax in the fire," he whispered to himself now and then. He turned back just past the Charles Bridge, before reaching the Alšovo nábřeží, keeping to the river walk until he passed the theater again; then he crossed over to Ostrovni Street.

On returning to his suite, he switched on all the lights and lay down upon the bed for half an hour, staring up at the extravagant molded plaster ceiling and the large, circular oil painting of Apollo and Cupid at its center, his mind all but entirely devoid of thoughts. Then he rose, undressed, showered, and donned his blue silk pajamas and red satin dressing gown. When he felt entirely refreshed, he removed his fountain pen and diary (a compact, thick, and rather handsome volume, bound in green Moroccan leather) from the top drawer of the bedside table, seated himself on the pale yellow sofa in the corner near the wardrobe, adjusted the cushions behind him, opened the diary on his lap, found the first blank page, removed the cap from his pen, paused for a moment with the nib hovering just above the paper, and then — breathing a resolute sigh — wrote the day's date in the upper right corner, in the American style. Then, after another pause of several seconds, he began writing, in a peculiarly graceful and fluid cursive hand:

> I waited again today, as I wait every day. I looked for you in crowded streets and in empty places, now here, now there, sought your face, listened for the sound of your voice, hoped that I might hear some word of you. I was, as ever, disappointed, but — for

what it may be worth — I still haven't faltered in my fidelity to our agreement.

I even played that little game of which I'm so fond, making a reservation for the two of us and leaving a glass of wine for you. Tiresome, perhaps, but diverting, and I have to confess that on such occasions I often feel as if you might arrive after all, might deign to show yourself — sometimes it's almost as if I know I'll see you, as if I can almost feel your approach, just at the edge of my thoughts — though that was not the case tonight.

There was an exquisitely lovely girl there at the restaurant, though, and I invited her to come along tomorrow, which she certainly will do, as that's what she wants — some sort of adventure, something new and a little daring. She's clearly bored and not at all confident about her future. She seems extremely sweet, and she's certainly very young, and is engaged to someone whom I suspect to be a fairly worthless fellow, as otherwise she would have refused my invitation immediately. So I expect I'll take her to bed with little need for further seduction, probably early in the afternoon: that much was more or less implicitly agreed between us, even though we talked probably no more than five minutes altogether. It should be quite wonderful. I liked her father, and for his sake I'll endeavor to say something to her that might encourage her to reconsider her marriage plans — to think better of her own prospects and abilities. It seems the least I can do.

That was all a happy accident, however. But for her, and for the truly excellent meal, I would have come away from the restaurant with nothing but that dismal sense of emptiness that descends on me at night, each night. After almost thirty years, that much hasn't changed — every day, the same strange, melancholy, quite irrational hope that you'll at last keep your promise — a hope that isn't really hope, of course, and yet one that always yields the same pain, the same intolerable disappointment. It becomes quite unbearable at times, to be honest. I wish you knew. I know I shouldn't repeat myself, of course; but the complaint remains the same because the same old pain persists.

Really, I wish it would just end sometimes, all of it, so that the curtain might at last be torn away.

Oh, I told the girl tonight that you're a man. For all I know you are. That was the point at which she and I tacitly made our assignation, and silently agreed to become lovers. She really is a beautiful creature. I wish that I were younger, or that that sort of life were still a possibility for me.

There might have been that sort of love for me, of course, if I hadn't received your summons when I did, or consented to it where I did — lying there on that fragrant bed of brown pine needles, near the dry stream bed and the bank of red thorns, where I had been with her in the morning, under the swaying trees — there where the light was soft but not dim and everything glowed in the tender sunshine and the shadows shook and quivered and flowed about me and the birds were singing — there was such a magic hanging about that place, and I heard you and almost saw you — almost. Something of your form seemed to steal through the light, as part of it, or behind it — I don't know.

That was long ago, however. I ought not to keep bringing it up. I'm not sure why I did.

Anyway, I'll be waiting again tomorrow. Please try to remember me.

The man stopped writing, having filled his allotted three pages. He waited for the ink of the last few words to dry and then closed the book and replaced the cap on his pen. For fully twenty minutes he sat there, scarcely moving, scarcely thinking, his eyes fixed upon an empty space high up upon the opposite wall, near the base of the sweeping concave barrel vaulting of the ceiling. Then at last he rose, crossed the room, replaced the diary and pen in the bedside table, went about the room turning the lights off, removed his robe, laid it across the foot of the bed, and got under the covers. He knew that insensibility would come fairly easily — it always did for him — but he was not certain it would come soon enough to spare him that sudden convulsion of despair that always overwhelmed him whenever he lingered even a short time at the border of sleep. He still felt slightly restless, but he strove to make his mind quiet. The room was very dark; the sounds from the streets were all but entirely inaudible up here. The evening had been a pleasant one. In the morning the girl would certainly call, and the day would be delightful. There was no need . . . But then, all at once, it came, and he was defenseless against it. The tears filled his eyes and ran down his temples and cheeks, a groan welled up from his chest, he turned his face into the pillow, clutching it with both hands as he shook throughout his body, and said, over and over, half-choking, "I can't, I can't, I can't . . ." And he continued to weep — as he had done on most of the past ten thousand nights — for thirty minutes or so, until the mood began to subside of its own accord, and the effort of trying to control his grief had left him spent, and he drifted at last into sleep.

His dreams, when they came, would be peaceful, painless. He would wake before dawn, as the first pale light of morning slipped in around the edges of the room's heavy curtains, and would once again begin to wait.

2010